He's always near, yet never in sight.

He came first in a dream, and, finding
a way in, returned again and again.

Now he doesn't need to wait for sleep to come.

He's coming closer to me every day.

Soon I'll be him and he'll be me.

at will we do?

gs will we do?

THE RUNESTONE

BOOK 1

SAGA

THE FETCH

CHRIS HUMPHREYS

ALFRED A. KNOPF
NEW YORK

SCOTLAND

Newcastle

York

Shropshire

The Wenlock
Edge

Derby

Stretton
Eaton-under-Heywood

Ludlow

WALES

London

ENGLAND

Dover

NORWAY

ENGLAND

Ålesund
Hareid Island

Trondheim

The Jotunheim Mountains

Galdhøpiggen
Lom

gen

Oslo

Non Omnis Moriar

CHAPTER ONE

DEAD OF NIGHT

"Who's there?" he asked. Softly but out loud, he was sure. Almost sure.

No reply. Sky gave them five seconds. It was a reasonable question. If he'd woken up because someone had spoken, it was only fair that they speak again. Said who they were. Stated their business.

"Did you say something?" His tone was less polite now.

Silence still. He couldn't hear breathing, but anyone could hold their breath. He could hold his for two minutes and twenty-two seconds.

"Look . . . ," he started, quite angrily, then stopped. If someone was going to speak, they'd have spoken by now. Unless they had a reason not to. But there were other possibilities to consider. Number one . . . was he even awake? The fact that he was standing up didn't prove it either way. Not when you were King of the Sleepwalkers.

He reached his hand forward and it almost disappeared, the room was so dark. Reached slowly, because if there *was* someone still holding their breath there, you really, really, didn't want to be touching them. . . .

Nothing . . . nothing . . . nothing . . . uh! . . . hardness . . . *wall!* Two walls and inside, too, he could tell by the slight give of the wallpaper. One there, one . . . there. Joined. So, a corner. He was in the corner of a room. Probably his bedroom, but he couldn't be certain of that yet. He'd woken up in lots of other rooms. He'd woken up in no rooms at all.

Still, a corner. A good place to get your bearings. You weren't close to a light switch . . . but at least no one could creep up on you from behind.

He wedged his back into the join of walls, narrowed his eyes, tried to see anything in the blackness . . . Aha! Light. *Red* light. His clock radio: 4:17.

Now that was strange. He'd woken up at 4:17 the previous three mornings. But he'd definitely *woken up* those mornings; so the odds were good that he was awake now. He'd also been alone; so he was almost certainly alone now.

This was better. Still, to be on the safe side, he needed to get his bearings.

With the clock there, his bed was beneath it and the window over . . . there! Yeah, there it was, a rectangle of slightly lighter gloom. Hadn't one of his teachers, three schools back, said, "It's always darkest before the dawn"? His parents hadn't gotten round to putting curtains up yet, so the darkness wasn't blocked by any-thing except itself. It had been raining quite heavily when he went to bed, and the clouds must still have been thick out there. Yet even as he looked, something silver shot through the intense dark. It came, went, as if someone had shone a flashlight, then snapped it off.

That needed checking out. Perhaps that was what had woken him.

He pushed himself away from the wall, took a step toward the window. A floorboard creaked, loudly. It was full of creaks, this old house they'd rented. With the wind blowing, as it was that night, it had taken him ages to fall asleep because of all the shiftings and set-tlings. They sounded like voices; and this creak had a definite cry to it, the word "Don't!" So he didn't. Didn't take another step, just stopped, waited. The wind picked up outside, something moved against the window, a thump followed by a scratch, like a finger placed then dragged away. That was . . . not good. He almost turned, ran to where the door had to be. Then he remembered his father's words from a few weeks back.

"That needs trimming or it'll break the glass in a storm," he'd said. They'd been standing in the little orchard-garden of their new house, and he was point-ing at an oak whose branches pressed against the wall. "And you'd probably use it as a fire escape!" Henry had grabbed Sky around the shoulders, twisting him in a wrestling move. "Too tempting for you, my lad."

Of course, Sky thought, that's all it is!

3

Confident now, he stepped forward, the movements in the floor just creaks, the thump and scratch just a tree. Then, as he reached the window, the clouds shifted, allowing moonlight through again . . . which explained the on-off light. The garden, previously dark, was instantly full of contrasts, the sides of the trees facing the moon silvered by it, their backs streaming away in shadows. He pressed his cheek against a pane, sought the moon to the right of the house. It was low down, just above the treetops, nearly full.

And it was red. It looked like it was covered in blood.

He knew what that was. The sun had risen enough over the curved surface of the planet to bounce its rays off the departing moon. He knew this for a scientific fact; but it didn't stop the shivering that came.

And that's just the cold, he thought. *So I'll go back to bed, pull the duvet over my head, doze till the alarm goes off and the music starts or until sunlight—yellow, not red—moves into the room.*

He took one step toward that sanctuary. Just the one before a sudden movement below halted him. Something had slid swiftly from moonbeams to shadow. It failed to blend there because it was wider than the tree it moved behind, and Sky saw a long cloak settle onto grass, saw bleached, white fingers wrap around the trunk, saw another hand reaching toward the house, a finger uncurl. Saw a black hood tipping back, up.

He shut his eyes so he would not have to see any more. But he could not shut his ears.

4

"They are here." The words wheezed up from the darkness. "Bring them. *Bring them to me!*"

More than anything now, he wanted to believe he was still asleep. That this was one of his nightmares. However horrible, at least they were familiar. They ended when you woke up. You could be comforted after a nightmare.

This wasn't a nightmare. He was awake. So this . . . *thing* was real; the skeleton hand, the black cloak, real. The empty hood that should contain a face, a face that should even now be reddened by moonlight, real.

His scream, though, when it finally came, *could* have come from a nightmare—squeezed out, dead slow, stuck for the longest time in his throat. While whisper slowly grew to wail, the hood stayed motionless, lifted up at him, that beckoning finger raised. At last, he heard his parents scrambling for dressing gowns; corridor light etched his doorframe, feet thumped toward his room. But only at the very moment that his door burst open did the finger lower, the hood drop. Only then did the shape move away, slipping out of the rectangle of sudden bedroom light, dissolving into shadow, vanishing down an alley of apple trees.

5

CHAPTER TWO

THE SEA CHEST

It stood smack in the center of the kitchen, as out of place in that scrubbed-tile whiteness as a horse in an art gallery. And as soon as Sky saw it, he had a weird sensation, as if his life had just . . . changed. It wasn't like a bolt of lightning suddenly stabbing the darkness; nothing was made clear, nothing explained. He just knew that the waiting was over. The strangest thing being that, until that moment, he hadn't known he'd been waiting at all.

It was a sea chest, as big as two suitcases squashed together, a faded blue where it wasn't stained brown and red, tattered with age. Peeling, yellowed stickers showed the ports it had passed through—Genoa, Penang, Murmansk—just three of the more legible. Two thick leather straps had once bound the box together, but one was severed, its clasp missing, the other barely clinging on. The lock looked stout, though, if rusted;

when his mother put the large, old-fashioned key in, it gave a protesting, almost animal shriek. And animals were the first things revealed when she lifted the curved lid. Their furs, anyway, for within were a beaver cape, a coat of silver fox, a mink wrap with the creature's head and feet still attached. Though that one immediately fascinated Sky, it caused his mother to burst into tears.

Embarrassed, Sky stroked the silky skin, surprised when it gave off a heady waft of old perfume. He sniffed again, wrinkled his nose. Under the sweetness was something sour, unpleasant. As his mother dabbed at her eyes, Sky said, gesturing to the stickers, "I didn't know Momo had been to so many places."

Sonja glanced at them, glanced away. "What's inside was hers, Sky. But the chest itself belonged to my father."

7

Now, that was interesting! He'd known his grandmother a little, knew some of the stories of her life, had been sad when he heard she'd died two months before. But his grandfather, Sigurd . . . well, Sky's mum had barely known him herself. He'd abandoned the family when Sonja was six years old, gone to command a ship at sea. A year later that ship had caught fire in some port in Asia. All the crew died, including its captain. About the only thing his mum had ever said about her dead father was that Sky was, apparently, very like him. He was never certain if this was meant as a compliment. But it had made him very curious about his grandfather.

And now his old sea chest had arrived. There were bound to be clues within it. Sky delved deeper, to disappointment. There were a few books beneath the furs, tattered photograph albums, an old pen set. No masks, native statues . . . weapons! His grandfather had been a traveler, a seafarer. Hadn't he collected any good stuff on his voyages?

Sky was about to open one of the albums when his mother wiped her eyes and said, briskly, "No, Sky. Not now. You'll be late for school. That is"—she hesitated—"if you're going?"

"Why wouldn't I be going?"

"Last night . . . this morning. You were a bit upset."

He looked away. "It was nothing. I . . ." He met her eyes. "It was a just another . . . dream." He'd nearly convinced himself, so he thought he could convince her. Touching her arm, he continued, "Really, I'm fine. Anyway, it's the last day of term. We get all our summer holiday assignments."

"If you're sure"—she smiled—"then you better hurry."

She was right, the clock on the stove read 7:52. If he shifted, he might just catch the bus.

His mother dropped the furs and books back into the trunk, shut the lid. "I'll get your dad to put this in the attic," she said, staring above it, her eyes still misty. "We'll look at the photographs later." She tried a smile. "It'll be fun."

8

⁂

He missed the bus. It was just disappearing over the hill when he ran up to the stop, and no amount of waving would bring it back.

This was really annoying. There was only one school bus, and the local transport was useless. He could go home . . . or he could hitchhike. Hitchhiking was, of course, strictly forbidden, which made it the obvious choice. Scrunching down into his blazer, hands thrust into pockets—summer had not yet made up its mind whether to stay, and it was cold and raining again—he glanced up the road and tried out all the new curse words he'd learned at his new school. He didn't have the accent yet—Shropshire seemed to have a peculiar mix of Birmingham and West Country quite different from the London borough where they'd lived lately—but he'd mastered some of the slang. It was one of his survival techniques, necessary because his engineer father's job kept taking them around the country—and out of it. Wherever there were pipes, Henry would be there to design and install the systems.

"Bloody bollocks, eh?" he said, trying to get the inflection right. But he was the one bloody bollocksed. The key to fitting in at a new school was not to stand out. Not too cocky, not too shy. Stand up for himself if necessary, back off if possible. Shine when he could—he'd always been good at sports, and they'd been short a decent center forward in the Under-Sixteens' soccer. Above all, don't talk too much. His London accent—the latest he'd acquired—was just too easy to imitate.

9

And now he was going to be late. He'd have to walk into class, be reprimanded, and explain himself . . . in that accent. Maybe he should just bunk off altogether. They could send him the assignments. Then he could spend the day in the countryside. There was a nice forest nearby which he'd only just started to explore, the Wenlock Edge.

Sighing, he knew he couldn't. It would just lead to a load of other problems, phone calls, parental panics. Miss the last day of term and he'd be even more noticeable the first day of the next, after the fuss.

Noticeable! Suddenly he remembered and reached up to stroke between his eyes. Turning, the smudged and graffitied glass of the bus shelter gave him only a faint reflection and no clue. He'd forgotten, in the excitement of the sea chest's arrival, to shave. Between his eyebrows. In the last year, they'd developed the annoying habit of growing into one long one. In the nerves of his first day at the new school, he'd forgotten and someone, of course, had noticed. Though he'd been scrupulous in checking every morning since, the name he'd been saddled with then had stuck.

"You've got a Single Eye Brow, mate. We'll have to call you S-E-B. Seb, eh? Geddit?"

Sky muttered at the memory and rubbed. There was a trace there, for sure. Oh well, he'd been called worse things than SEB at a new school. Far worse.

Three cars passed, their drivers ignoring his raised thumb and brilliant smile. Between cars, he thought about that strange feeling that had come when he'd first seen his grandfather's sea chest, a sensation that the waiting was over. What waiting? What was *that* all about? Well, he'd have to *wait* now, at least till he got home. He'd never seen a picture of this grandfather he was supposedly so like. There were bound to be a few in those old albums.

"Bloody bollocks, eh?"

In his fairly limited experience of hitchhiking, there were three kinds of people who gave rides: drug addicts, psychos, and talkers. With the first, Sky would judge how badly they were driving, buckle up, and watch for drooping eyes. But he always thought that since God was bound to take the driver soon anyway, why wait till Sky had got in the car? With potential ax murderers, he'd keep his seat belt off and a hand on the door handle; any pulling into dark country lanes and he'd be out the door, paratrooper roll on the blacktop, hop a hedge. Then there were those who picked people up for a chat. These were the worst.

The van driver who stopped for him had long greasy hair over a very small forehead and he just grunted when Sky said where he was going. He drove well, if really slowly, so he was probably sober. The way he gripped the wheel was a little maniacal, though, in contrast to the plodding pace, so Sky kept his belt off just to be on the safe side. But since the man didn't seem to want to talk, Sky could do what he really wanted to do: stare at the rain crashing down, count the gap between lightning and thunder . . . and think about the previous night.

It had obviously been a dream; perhaps he'd been reading too many horror stories lately, and there was that zombie film he'd watched last week when his parents were out. The headless hood? The skeletal finger? Pure Hollywood!

The sleepwalking was another thing. He hadn't done that for years, five at least. His parents had taken him to a doctor then, a specialist, and he'd learned various techniques to use before he went to sleep or if he woke up and didn't know where—or even who!—he was. Trouble was, even if he was still asleep, it *felt* like he was awake and everything that happened, no matter how weird, felt right in that . . . other world. He'd done some strange things. Moved his dresser out into the hallway once; when his parents found him, he told them it was a doghouse and he couldn't sleep because the hound inside kept barking at him. Or the time when they caught him staring into the hall mirror and he said, quite proudly, "I take big strides—that's why they call me Longshanks!"

He chuckled at the memory.

"Something funny?"

Sky looked at the driver, who stared back. They were stuck at some roadwork in a narrow lane; a man in a yellow jacket up ahead held a red sign that read Stop. Sky moved his fingers to the door handle. Now that he looked into them, the man's eyes were set very close together.

"Oh yeah, nothing much. School, you know."

"I went to your school," the man said, that strange local accent thick. "Used to hitch rides mesself."

Ah, a talker, thought Sky. One of those who had hitched around in his youth and now was going to tell him all his traveler tales. He gave a silent sigh. Ah well. Might as well pay the fare.

"Oh yes? Have some interesting rides, did you?"

"Not really. Mostly they was on tractors," the man muttered as the sign ahead spun to green and Go. He crawled up through the gears. "Not from round here, are you?"

"Nope."

"Thought not. Thought I detected a *foreign* accent." He gave a mirthless laugh. "London, is it?"

"Well." Sky turned away, looked out the window. "That was the last place they hid us, yeah."

He didn't know why he said it. Maybe to make time go a little quicker. If they went much slower, pedestrians would pass them!

"Hid? Wotchermean?"

Sky shook his head. "I can't tell you."

"Gawn, 'course you can."

"No, I really, really can't."

"But you started now."

Sky gave another sigh, audible this time. "Witness Protection Program. They keep relocating us."

"You mean"—the man's forehead wrinkled in concentration—"you mean you saw a crime, like?"

Sky nodded, trying to recall the details of the show he'd seen on TV. "Gangland slaying. A hit. My testimony sent a crime lord to prison." Sky turned in his seat, scanned the road behind them. "He, uh, wasn't very happy."

The man looked in the mirror, changed gears. The speedometer actually went above twenty-five. After a moment he said, "Should you . . . should you be telling people that? I mean, if they's still after you, like?"

Sky turned to the driver. "You know, you're right. That was very stupid of me." He lowered his voice. "Pull over."

"Why? It's another mile to the school."

"I can't go to school now. At least, not yet. You know too much. Pull over." He smiled. "I am going to have to kill you."

No sense of humor, some people, Sky thought as he watched the back of the van disappear over the hill, the driver having found fourth gear remarkably fast. If he knew a London accent, couldn't he tell a Mexican bandito one when he heard it? Still, Sky had learned half a dozen new, and presumably local, swearwords. Might prove useful at school.

The rain had gotten even heavier, huge drops thudding onto his blazer. The storm was moving closer, the gaps between flash and bang shortening. He'd been ejected a mile from his destination, and the choice was walk and get soaked or run and get soaked.

He ran. He had missed assembly and his first class would be halfway through. Bloody math, taught by one of those teachers you did not want to get noticed by, a chalk-chucker named Riddley. Taking the front steps three at a time, he nearly didn't push in the glass front doors, nearly turned back. Then, down the corridor, he noticed the door to the auditorium swinging shut, caught a glimpse of a shape entering. Another boy? Perhaps someone else was late too. Perhaps he could split the attention and so the blame.

The next door would not open easily, the handle slightly slick, his fingers slipping off at first grasp. When it did, he stepped into an auditorium held in the shadows of the heavy clouds above, rain hammering on the glass roof. Some teacher on a cost-saving binge had switched off all the lights.

Sky blinked into the gloom. It was very dark—dark enough so that when he marched forward he struck his knee on a chair he hadn't seen, struck it hard. As he yelped, bent down to rub, the big room brightened suddenly, lightning arcing its course across the sky above, the thunder clapping instantly and directly overhead, no counting required, its force radiating through the chair he leaned on. He looked up, and something of that flash still etched each object before him in light—the raised podium, the lectern on it, the piano and music stands grouped about it, and, on the far side of the room, a boy throwing open the door to the corridor beyond. He stood there silhouetted, held like the negative of a photograph. Sky blinked, trying to make him out. Why did he seem familiar? Sky was sure he had never seen him before. He wore his tie like they all did, the thicker end short, the thinner long. He noticed a similar secondhand blazer to the one he himself wore, leather patches on the elbows, which was strange; he'd thought he was the only one in the school whose mother could embarrass him in that way. He saw spiked blond hair not unlike his own.

"Hey!" he called out. "Hey you! Wait for me."

The other boy paused, half turned. Then lightning again lit the world, the thunder came tight on it, and the door slammed fast, faster than seemed possible, the smash booming in the empty auditorium.

When Sky reached it, the long corridor beyond was bright. And empty.

"I don't know how they manage these things in London, March. But at decent schools, we ask permission before we leave the classroom."

Riddley was glaring at him from the blackboard, chalk poised threateningly in hand. "I presume nausea was the reason for the haste and rudeness, hmm?"

"Yes, sir." Sky sat down quickly, wondering what the hell the teacher was going on about. But he wasn't about to question him. He was in his seat, and Riddley, reluctantly, was turning back to the equation on the board. And he hadn't even mentioned Sky's lateness. No reprimand, no detention. He'd gotten away with it!

Sky looked down at the table. His textbook was open to the correct page. The numbers on the blackboard were written in his notebook. Odd! They hadn't been working on this equation yesterday, had they? His pen lay beside the book, ball point exposed. Riddley was talking again, so Sky picked up the pen.

The pen was warm. He dropped it.

"Awright, Seb?" Beckwith, a table over, leaned in to whisper.

"Not really," Sky muttered, staring down at the pen.

"You can't just get up and go, just 'cause Riddley's got his back to ya."

"What?" Sky looked at the other boy, suspecting some tease. "What are you talking about?"

He never found out. The chalk piece, whizzing between their faces, put an end to the conversation.

He couldn't get away fast enough. It wasn't that the clouds had cleared and the sun was out again. They could have shone spotlights on the whole school and it would still have had too many shadows.

He had given up trying to understand. He hadn't spent a lot of time asking Beckwith and some of the others about it for fear of seeming crazy. But from what he could make out, they said he'd been at his desk from the beginning of the class, while he knew he'd been in the car at that time. And as for the boy with the similarly patched blazer? Not a trace in the playground at either of the breaks.

"Patches?" jeered Beckwith when questioned. "You're the only fashion victim here, mate."

It was some sort of mass hallucination, obviously. He'd read about such things. Maybe they put something in the water in Shropshire.

He caught a local bus back. On it, he just stared out the window, seeing himself walking into the house, going straight up to the attic, opening the sea chest, searching it for . . . he didn't know what. He was excited for a while. Yet the closer he got to home, the more that feeling faded. In the end, a stop before his, he leapt up, just as the doors were closing. "One more," he shouted, and the driver reluctantly opened them again.

There was a path, a wooden post with a walker's figure cut into the arrow. It pointed away from his home, up onto the Wenlock Edge. He took it.

He'd been told that the Edge was actually an old coral reef, flung up millions of years before. That under his feet were the shells of thousands of sea creatures where the receding seas had left them. But to him, as he climbed, it seemed like any other old English wood, leaves thickening into a canopy. He recognized oak and ash, a copse of beech. He may have been a city boy, but he'd always liked trees. Especially climbing them.

The slope was steep, tiring. He reached a crest,

18

took another path along it. Soon he was into a thicker stand, mainly ash, and when these ended in a little clearing he returned to the last tree, dropped his backpack at its base, looked for handgrips and toeholds. Soon he had shimmied up to a wide branch about a dozen feet off the ground. Taking his blazer off, he wedged it into the junction. Then, putting his back against the trunk, he closed his eyes. He thought he'd immediately see the hooded figure from what he'd finally convinced himself was a nightmare, its bony hands beckoning him, wanting him to bring . . . whatever! Thought he'd see a boy who looked like him etched in lightning. Instead . . .

He woke with a start, a sensation of falling. He wasn't, though one leg had slipped down around the branch. Righting himself completely, he closed his eyes again, drowsily listened to the birdsong. There was a wood pigeon nearby, and Sky counted the order of its calls. It seemed that even the birds had a different accent in Shropshire, for this one's final, single note went up like a question mark. The London birds had all seemed to end their call with a statement.

Another noise intruded. Opening an eye, he tracked it. A fox had come into the clearing, was sniffing and scratching in the mulch of the forest floor. Unlike the shabby urban creatures that had nosed around the dustbins in Islington, this one was big, with a full red coat, a magnificent white-tipped tail. Both eyes open now, scarcely breathing, Sky watched it snuffle its way closer. Two trees away. One.

19

The fox circled Sky's tree, cocking its leg, spraying its scent against the base. A nasty whiff, like rotten eggs, made him wrinkle his nose.

The fox was moving into the clearing, paralleling the branch Sky sat on. When it was under the tip, it stopped, turned, looked up. Straight at Sky, straight into his eyes. Then its snout opened.

"He is coming," the fox said. "Prepare."

Sky didn't see the fox run off. He was falling out of the tree at the time.

CHAPTER THREE

THE ATTIC

Dinner was endless. Partly because the thigh he'd bruised in the fall stiffened and ached as he sat; partly because every time there was a pause in the conversation, he was sure his mother would say, "Well, shall we go and take a look at that old chest?"

And that was the last thing he wanted to do.

He was desperate to see into it. Just not with his mother. It wasn't so much that there were bound to be tears; it was more that each item would no doubt come with a story, each photograph and every person in it would be discussed. And his mother's Norwegian family was so extended . . . it did his head in, trying to keep up with all the unpronounceable names. He didn't know what he expected from the chest, but he knew he wanted to discover whatever it was for himself.

Fortunately, Sonja and his dad, Henry, were more concerned with the details of their recent move, his new job, her search for local work. So when he excused himself to go read, he'd made it to the door before his mum said, "Grandfather's chest, Sky?"

He paused, mouth dry, gave a casual shrug. "Oh yeah?"

"We'll save it for the weekend, yes?"

Sky tried to keep his expression blank. "Sure," he said.

His parents were tired, went to bed early. He waited till all their sounds had ceased before he opened his door a crack. The house itself was far from quiet, especially in the wind that had sprung up in the wake of the day's storms. His parents would not be able to distinguish his footfalls on the stairs from every other creak. Though he'd already taken note of the stairs' noises so that on quieter nights he could creep up unnoticed. If any house they moved to had an attic, his parents always left it to him to make his own . . . and he always enjoyed his kingdom best at night, when his parents thought him safely asleep in his bedroom.

Safely asleep? What a joke! He never *had* liked bedrooms much—probably why he kept trying to walk out of them! Attics, though . . . what was it about them? The lack of light causing the deep shadows under the eaves? All that fluffy insulation between the beams? Like looking down on the tops of clouds from an airplane. Also, former tenants nearly always forgot something up there. He'd scavenged some great—and bizarre!— stuff over the years.

This attic had a retractable stair, which his dad had left down, so he was spared those noises. He climbed up. The light switch didn't work—a blown bulb, probably—so he found his old camping lantern, flicked it on. It cast just a small glow in the central area near the trap-door; but since that was the only area that had floor-boards, he'd keep within its spill anyway. He'd have to bring up a flashlight to edge along the beams, explore the farther recesses. For the moment what concerned him was right in front of him. His father had just tipped the chest over the edge, so Sky heaved it farther in. It was heavy; he was always amazed at how strong Henry was, getting it up those steep steps by himself. He turned it so the interior would be facing the dim bulb. He reached for the lock, the key still in it. . . .

With his hand upon it, he was suddenly reluctant. Hadn't there been enough weirdness today already? OK, he was sure the fox had just "talked" in a dream; clearly he'd dozed off on the branch. There was no one "com-ing," nothing to "prepare." But school . . . well, that was harder to explain. He hadn't really settled there yet, partly because they'd moved right in the middle of the school term. There'd been talk about homeschooling him, starting him at the new school at the beginning of the new year, but he'd insisted he begin straightaway. His parents were all right, but he couldn't be with them 24/7! Besides, no matter how tough it was fitting in at a new school, there were things he liked, things he was good at—especially soccer. Didn't matter that he had a funny accent when he scored the winning goal against the local rivals, did it?

Sky shook his head. No, school he could handle. It was the new home that was always the hardest to adjust to. There'd be broken nights, bad dreams, sleep-walking. Previously it had lasted only a couple of weeks. But they'd been in this house six now.

What he needed to do was make the attic fully his own. Colonize it! He hadn't had time, what with catching up on schoolwork.

He'd begin tonight. First thing to do—explore the sea chest. That "waiting-was-over" feeling? Was that just another symptom of a bad night, like the sleepwalking?

"Of course." He smacked himself in the forehead with the palm of one hand. "I sleepwalked to school. Explains everything."

He laughed. Out loud, just to reassure himself. Because the attic suddenly seemed very quiet. As if it were doing the waiting.

The fingers of his other hand still rested on the key. He became aware again of the wind, something scratching on the skylight. He looked up, saw a branch of ivy move across it, saw one broken pane, a hole the size of a fist in it. Beyond, that half-full moon was being teased by scattered clouds. Now you see me, now you don't.

At least it isn't red! He shivered. This was ridiculous! He couldn't sit there all night holding a key! He was going to turn it. He was . . .

24

It scraped the way it had the first time, with that animal cry. The lid had hinged metal props that locked to hold it up. As he struggled to fix them in position—they were orange with rust, and stiff—he breathed in again that heavy musk scent, tinged with that eggy something, that rose from the furs. It reminded him of the fox, and the memory and the smell made him slightly dizzy.

Lifting the furs out, he laid them carefully on the propped-up lid. The mink, the wrap that still had the creature's head attached, now looked as if it were lying over a branch, its black bead eyes shimmering in the meager light. Shuddering, he put it to the side, over the bookcase he carted from house to house, its shelves filled with all the things his parents disapproved of—war comics, horror books, a pencil case filled with pellets for the air rifle they didn't know he had, which itself was wrapped in sacking and strapped to the back of the shelves.

25

He delved into the chest, lifting each book out, laying it down. The interior was lined in paper with Chinese characters embossed upon it. It had torn away in places, revealing newsprint underneath. He recognized Norwegian even if he couldn't speak the language.

Aside from books and furs, the trunk was empty. He reached for an album. It was filled with a mix of photos both black and white and color that had faded so much it looked fake. They were mainly family shots with a few bare landscapes. He recognized Norway

from the holidays he'd had there visiting his grandmother. He recognized her, much younger; so the two
very blond little girls who played around and posed before fjords, houses, and trees had to be his mother and
his aunt.

The more he flicked the pages, the more disappointed he became. In none of the three albums was
there even one photo of this grandfather he was supposedly so like. There were gaps where photos had
been. Perhaps, after his grandfather left them, his grandmother had torn photos out so as to forget him?

It was in the very last photo in the final album that
he noticed something. It was a standard shot, black
and white, a group gathered at the water's edge of a
beautiful fjord, his grandmother, mother, and aunt. All
three had their hands raised against the glare. And flowing toward them along the ground was a dark outline—
the shadow of the person taking the photograph. Sky
could see the elbows thrust out to the side as the camera was raised to the eye.

"Is that you?" Sky ran his finger up the shadow,
tracing what he assumed was his grandfather's form. It
felt slightly hot, which was strange because the attic
itself was cool. And when he tried to lift his finger, it
came slowly, as if stuck. Yet when he touched the photo
again there was no heat, no stickiness.

Weird! Laying the album down, he peered into
the empty space of the chest. Even in the dim glow he
could see the Chinese figures on the lining paper, the

26

same scene repeated over and over—a woman carrying some sort of jug on her shoulder past a tree. It was
tatty, faded with age.

Was that it? The feeling he'd had from the moment
he saw it, of the wait being over, this was all there was?
A shadow on the ground in a photo taken forty years
before?

Suddenly angry, he thumped the top of the chest
with the flat of his hand. He'd intended to slam it shut,
but the rusted props were stronger than they looked;
they held, resisted his force, and . . . *Tok!* The lid gave
out a hollow note, like a drum.

He peered. The top of the lid was curved. Tapping
its length and width, back and forth, up and down, all
he got was the same dull sound of thick matter. *Thud,
thud, thud.* Except in one area, the one where he'd first
hit. Drumming with his fingertips, he traced the section of lid that made that different, echoey sound. *Tok!
Tok! Tok!* It was about the width of his spread hands.

He looked inside, tapped the matching curved sur-
face there, found that same, roughly rectangular, space.
It looked no different from the rest of the chest's lin-
ing. The Chinese woman continued on her journeys.
But it gave out that same, different sound when struck.
Tok!

Sky sat back, rubbed between his eyes. It was
probably—almost certainly—nothing. A part of the
chest's construction, that was all; and yet . . .

He reached behind him, pushing the mink's head

27

aside. On the shelf was his Swiss Army knife. He picked it up. He knew he shouldn't do it, but . . . he could always claim it was like that already and his mum had just not noticed.

Opening the main blade, he tapped again until he found the spot where dull and hollow met. Then he slipped the sharp point in.

It sank nearly its full length, about two inches. He couldn't hesitate now, so he began to drag it along the hollow, parallel to the front of the lid, the blade flush to some edge in there, until he reached an end. Then he turned the blade, pushed it away from him, toward the back of the lid. When it stopped, about half the length of the first cut, he returned to the other side, carved a parallel line down till the knife was again halted. He'd cut three sides of a rectangular flap, but the stiff, glued paper held it in place. He withdrew the blade, wondering if he should cut that last side . . . and then, with a loud rip, the flap suddenly fell like a trapdoor on a gallows and two objects tumbled out, landing with a thump and a clink on the sea chest's floor.

Sky gasped, fell back, the knife raised before him; stayed like that for at least a minute. Then he replaced the knife on the shelf, took up the lantern, leaned forward.

A book and a bag lay there. He pulled out the book first. It was old, with tattered black card covers and frayed leather corners and spine. A drawstring sealed it, and the knot, stiff with age, was hard to undo. When he did, the pages parted with a crackle. He was staring at tightly scrawled Norwegian words. They were written in a variety of inks as if over a long period of time. Many passages were dated.

He put the journal down but open, on its spine, and the pages, as if free now, began to flutter in the draft from the skylight's broken pane. He reached for the bag and it clinked as he lifted it, as it had when it had first fallen. The bag was soft, of dark green tight-knitted wool, a leather cord drawing its neck closed. Sky's fumbling fingers finally got the string loose. There was a cloth just inside and he pulled it out, shook it. It was a square of red silk, about the size of one of his dad's handkerchiefs. Spreading it out beside him, he opened the bag over it.

29

Stones cascaded down, striking the floor like hail hitting a windshield, each the size and shape of the top joint of Sky's thumb. The blackest things by far in that ill-lit attic, it was as if they'd breathed in night. Yet somehow they glowed, too, casting a light that had nothing to do with any lantern; for this light was crimson, as red as the moon at four a.m., as red as fresh blood, red shining in lines that had been slashed or scored into each stone's dark surface.

"Runes!" he whispered, surprised to see his breath before him, surprised by how cold the attic had grown.

He shivered, one hand raised above the stones, hovering there, spoiled for choice. Yet he suddenly didn't want to touch them because he had the strangest sensation that they . . . wanted to be touched.

He let his hand fall, breathed deep to calm his heart.

He'd done a project on the Vikings at his last school. He knew runes were an ancient alphabet, used by the Norse for documents, poems on parchment, epitaphs on tombs, threats on sword or ax-blade. He knew they were also magical, symbols representing something else, some object or force in nature. Looking down, he could even remember some names: There was an "S"-shaped Sun; here, a "Y" for a yew tree; over there, the point of a spear. And he also knew that when these symbols were chosen and arranged, those gifted with "special sight" could tell a story from the combination, answer questions about the past, the present, the future. Some people read the palms of hands, others tea leaves or tarot cards. The Norse read runes.

And Sigurd, his Norwegian grandfather, had placed his runestones in his sea chest before he died, hidden them there for someone to discover. No, not someone. Hidden them for the grandson he never knew he had to discover.

Sky now understood that feeling of a wait ended. He'd been waiting for Sigurd's runestones.

He was ready now. But just as his hand stretched out, just as he reached for the first stone, he noticed that the breeze through the broken skylight had ceased blowing, that the journal pages, which had been riffled back and forth by it, had now settled. A page was open that had no words on it, only a diagram. Five runes spread out like a cross.

He looked back to the stones before him, then began spreading them out, turning them all faceup. He picked out the runes from the diagram one by one, laying them down in the same pattern. Four were easy to find, but the last, the one that would slot into the left-hand side, the one to complete the . . . *runecast,* he suddenly remembered it was called . . . that last runestone couldn't be found.

"Oh no," he muttered, sweat coming to his forehead despite the chill, "one can't be missing!"

He ran his fingers over the stones again, searching ever more desperately. Then a thought came. He picked up the cloth bag. . . .

There was weight in it. He felt through the material. One runestone was still inside. He tipped the bag, shook it. The stone would not fall. He tried to squeeze it out, like toothpaste. It wouldn't shift.

"Come on, you!" he said, his fingers questing inside. When he touched it, it was like he'd grasped hot metal. He cried out, jerked his fingers away, pulled them from the bag. The stone, stuck to them, came, too, burning him.

The last rune was like a diamond with two legs extending out. He tried to lay it in place, tried . . . and couldn't! It smoldered there between his thumb and forefinger, held as if by superglue. He pulled with the other hand, shook it, tried to part them. They wouldn't give.

Then he heard something moving beside him.

The mink wrap, draped across his bookcase, was slowly raising its head. Dead eyes glowed with life; its sewn mouth opened. Words came out on a hiss.

"*Othala*. Rune of ancestors. You have called him. Now will he come."

The runestone dropped free, almost sprang from between his fingers, fell exactly into its position, completing the cast. At the same time, Sky fell also, backward, away, down, his head thumping onto the floorboards of the dark, frosty-cold attic.

32

CHAPTER FOUR
COUSINS

He'd visited the graveyard once before with his mum and dad. It was a nice walk from their house, a pleasant Sunday stroll to the hamlet of Eaton-under-Heywood. The church was old, a board inside saying that the first vicar had been there in 1289—more than seven hundred years ago. By day it was pretty, a little ragged and overgrown, a little sad perhaps when reading the gravestones of children who had died when they were a year old, three, nine. But that day the sadness had passed swiftly because it had all been so pretty in the early-summer sun, and they'd walked through the cemetery and up onto the Wenlock Edge that loomed above the churchyard to head home a different way.

He had never been there at night. And this night the moon and the stars were buried in clouds. The only way he could see along the avenue of thick sheltering yew trees near the churchyard's entrance was by the faint spill of light from the nearest houses.

He didn't know why he'd come. Maybe it was just to get away from the house and the attic and all it contained. From the prophecy spoken by animals. Since waking there and swiftly sealing the runes and journal back into the chest's lid with duct tape—he'd only been back to it once that day, to snatch his air rifle from its hiding place so he could shoot at the apples in the orchard when his parents were out. He wasn't sure he'd go back to it again. Talking minks? Burning stones? It was all too creepy.

The old gate was hard to push open, harder to shut, its metal latch not wanting to drop over the post. Finally he succeeded, groped forward in the light spill, through the darkness beneath the yews to a deeper darkness where the houses were hidden by the bulk of the church. Still, he pressed forward, reaching out with a walking stick he'd snatched for the journey. Though he knew he should be scared, he wasn't, not really. He'd crept out many times at night in his life, pretending to be a commando engaged on a daring night raid. He was a little old for that now, perhaps; but some of the old buzz still remained.

The stick struck something and he stopped, reached more cautiously forward with questing fingers. Cold stone greeted them and he traced its edge, felt its front surface, the letters cut there; tried to read them using just his fingertips. He had a book of matches in his pocket, but he didn't want to strike one. If he could see, others could see him. He was still enough of a commando to know you never lit a match until you were under cover. They had snipers trained to watch for just such a thing!

But the lettering on the stone was odd. He couldn't get it to make any sense and he suddenly wanted to, as if deciphering the inscription on this tomb was why he was there.

He rested the stick against the stone, reached into a pocket. A slight breeze had sprung up since he'd entered the churchyard, but he had a technique for dealing with that. The end of the match was placed between his first and second fingers, the book's striker pressed against it with his thumb, within the cup of his hands; he flicked. It caught first try and he tipped it till the bright yellow had deepened and crept up the shaft. Only then did he raise it to the stone.

That's why he couldn't read them by touch! They weren't letters . . . well, not English letters anyway. For runes *were* letters as well as symbols, and the rune he lit—he didn't know its name, but it was a jagged "R" shape—was just one of a series that he ran the match along.

Runes! The ones back in the attic had frightened him, but these intrigued. He reached the match forward, admired the way its blue-yellow flame mixed with the red the runes had been stained. And when he felt that first hint of pain, he dropped the match, let it plunge down to the turf in a last flash.

35

Another! This was cool, reading runes by match light. Eagerly, he fumbled a second one out, placed it in the fingers, drove the striker along. It flickered, caught . . .

A breath, harsh and loud, came from right beside him. He felt it pass over his hand, the coldness of it like liquid oxygen, burning him, snuffing the match in an instant. With a yelp, Sky staggered up from his crouch, away from that breath. He fell on his backside, did not try to rise, just pumped his legs, his heels digging and gouging the earth, driving him back, over the lip of the grave, onto grass, over the lip of another into . . . mud! Thick, gloopy mud that made each kick harder as the soles of his sneakers clagged with it, the piles of it rich with the scent of clay. And it wasn't just the breath driving him now but whoever had emitted that breath, the deeper darkness etched against what little light there was. For what had breathed out to extinguish a match had now risen. And as Sky's back hit another gravestone, as his legs struggled to move, so weighed down with freshly dug grave mud they could barely pump anymore, he saw that the black shape was actually a cloak that rose to a peaked hood. And he knew that, even if there had been light to see by, within the hood there would be nothing to see.

But he could hear. Another breath, an inhalation, painful, rasping, as if its lungs were full of liquid that air was being forced slowly through. The same rattling came again, along with words.

36

"Give me . . . ," it went. "Gi . . . ve . . . me!"

The cloak's sleeve rose. Skeletal fingers reached . . .

Maybe his scream woke him. Maybe it was his thrashing legs, carrying him off the bed to hit the floor with a crash. He immediately began to roll, over and over, until he reached solidity, until he could go no farther to outdistance that bony grip. And when he realized that what was behind him was not a tombstone but the wood of a wardrobe, he leapt up and ran for the light switch by the door.

His bed was a jumble, his duvet rucked up at the end like a pyramid, or the entrance of a cave from which he'd just crawled.

He left the doorway, threw the duvet to the floor, checked under the bed, inside his wardrobe. Finally satisfied, he lay down again, pulling the covers tight to his neck. Strangely he fell asleep quickly.

37

He woke when the sun had filled every corner of the room. "It was a nightmare," he said, loudly. "Just another bloody nightmare!" He lay there for a while, enjoying the warmth, the promise of a sunny day. His eyes were on the ceiling, his mind through it and on up to the attic, where his grandfather's legacy lay. The summer holidays were here and he had a mystery to solve. And there was no rule that said he had to solve it at night. He'd wait for his parents to go shopping. . . .

Smiling now, he swung off the bed, his feet automatically seeking his sneakers. They hit floorboards. He looked down, rubbed his eyes, looked again.

His sneakers were beneath the half-open window. He closed it, bent down. One shoe was rolled onto its side. He picked it up then dropped it, raising his hand to his face in puzzlement. His fingers were covered in mud. It stank of clay and was as cold as a grave.

"Now, you do remember about today, don't you, darling?"

Sky watched as his mother scurried around the kitchen, dishing out breakfast between the three plates. She was going through another vegetarian phase, so mushrooms and tomatoes were dropped to sit beside the eggs when Sky would really have preferred bacon and sausage.

"What?" he muttered, sipping tea, which he spilled because his father came in and shoved his shoulder. "Oy," he complained, but Henry just grinned and sat down. Turning back to his mother, he said, "Remember what?"

"It's the holidays—"

"Duh! I know that."

"—so Kristin arrives for two weeks."

Talk about good news, bad news! Sky kept his groan to himself, though his father mimed hanging himself by a noose, eyes crossed, tongue bulging. Sonja turned while he was doing it.

"Stop that, you!" she said, shaking her head. "I don't understand the pair of you. Especially you!" She brought the plates over, placed Sky's before him. "You

38

and your cousin used to be so close. Inseparable. What happened?"

Sky shoveled a big piece of mushroom into his mouth. "She changed," he mumbled.

"And you haven't?" She went to get her own plate. "And don't speak with your mouth full."

He chewed slowly, giving himself a chance to think. No, he hadn't changed. Well, not like her. And he could remember the exact moment when he'd realized just how different she'd become.

His father had taken a job in Abu Dhabi. They'd all moved to the Gulf, and he hadn't seen Kristin for a year. She'd been sent to a fancy boarding school because her mum, Sky's aunt, was always traveling on business and her father was long gone; also because her mum said it was time her daughter learned to be a lady.

Sky had laughed when he heard that. No school in existence was going to break Kristin the Wildcat. He'd gotten letters and e-mails to start with that confirmed her ongoing rebellion. Then he'd heard from her less and less, and finally not at all.

Still, he'd been looking forward to her arrival last summer. Another school for him, in London again, no new friends, the very few most recent ones left behind in the Gulf. He'd been so ready for Kristin, for the fun they always had.

And then she walked in . . . and he just knew. Knew by her hair, no longer a disordered hedge but coiffed

39

and colored. Knew by the makeup, by the subtle color of the lips, lips that immediately formed words that mocked the first thing he said in some very clever way that he didn't quite understand. Knew by the strange, posh voice she spoke in, though she barely talked to Sky the whole time, just to her friends on her cell phone in some incomprehensible school slang.

Her visit last year had been a nightmare! The worst kind, because it took two weeks to wake up from. He couldn't get her out of the house, at least not to do the things they always used to do. She'd grudgingly go shopping—for more clothes she couldn't possibly get dirty. And if the summer had been bad, the week at Christmas had been worse. He couldn't get her out of the house at all—she'd already done all her shopping! They'd stared at the TV for a week.

He'd finished his mouthful but there was still nothing to say, so he shoved in another. Sonja sighed and shook her head. "Well, I expect you to be a good host, Sky, and entertain her. Take her out of herself." Sonja leaned forward to fill his tea mug. "She'll be exhausted. She did eleven subjects at GCSE."

Eleven exams! That was just showing off. And she was only just sixteen too. Typical Kristin. He was less than a year younger, but he doubted he'd be able to do more than five.

His father was watching him try to keep the annoyance off his face. He crossed his eyes at Sky, then looked down at his plate. "Where's my blood sausage, woman?" he said, all mock gruff.

"You know what the doctor said, Hen." Sonja was dropping artificial sweetener into Henry's mug. "You have to watch your cholesterol."

Henry groaned, clutched at his heart, and began to eat. Despite the lack of fried meat, he and Sky cleared their plates fast, and Sky added three peanut butter toasts for good measure. When he was done, he pushed his chair back. "What time's she get here, then?"

"I'm picking her up from the station at quarter to eleven. Want to come?"

"Can't."

He was gone before he could be questioned further. If he only had a little time before the invasion, he might as well enjoy it alone.

41

He heard them return, ignored his mother's calls to come downstairs, grabbed a book. Eventually there were creaks on the stairs, the sound of the closed door swinging open. As usual, she didn't bother to knock. Something that never used to bother him.

He knew she was in the doorway. He didn't want to look at her until he heard her speak. Because there was still a chance, a tiny hope, that the last two visits had been . . . well, mistakes. That she'd been going through . . . some phase and had come out the other side. That she'd walk into his room and say, in a funny movie voice, what she'd said in every new room, whenever, wherever she had come to visit them:

"So, compadre . . . where can we go git into a whole heap of trouble?"

And Sky would grab her hand, pull her outside, and show her. One summer in Cornwall it had been air-mattress surfing, catching waves and riding them toward the rocks, first one to bail was a loser. One autumn they'd slowly destroyed what remained of a greenhouse with air rifles and fireworks. Then, the summer before Abu Dhabi, in London, they'd sneak out of her window about midnight, climb onto the garden wall . . . and just walk! The walls all connected to others, and they could go the length of the street, staring into people's houses. The things they saw wall-walking— funny, bizarre . . . often quite disgusting! They'd been chased more than once, each had fallen off. But they had a rule, a catchphrase borrowed from some movie poster: "No one gets left behind." So the other always came back, helping to distract the furious neighbor or the raging dog till both of them could escape and they could sit somewhere safe and laugh. Laugh and laugh.

"So . . ." She was speaking at last, and Sky held his breath. "So . . . you've really buried yourself in the boondocks this time."

He didn't know what a boondock was, but it didn't sound flattering to his new neighborhood. Especially not when delivered in that bored tone. He let go his breath, raised his eyes, and saw that her look went with the question. She was still pretty, always had been, he supposed. Or at least she had all the things that made up pretty. White-blond hair that fell in curly waves to her shoulders; a small ski jump of a nose; eyes of an almost steel blue beneath eyebrows that may not have been as thick as Sky's, nor in danger of growing together, but weren't far off; skin that seemed to catch any sun going and transform it to gold. But could she be pretty when the blue eyes held that so-bored look and her lips, which were wonderfully large, were twisted into what he could only describe as permanent sarcasm? He didn't think so.

"Well, cousin," she said, sauntering in and dropping onto the end of his bed, "how's tricks?"

He looked back to his book. "All right." He could feel her regarding him up and down, tried to concentrate on the words before him. When he'd heard her on the stairs, he'd snatched up one of the books he had to read by next term.

He saw her head tilt so she could see the title. "They're not making you read *that*, are they?"

Even though he was already struggling with it, her assault and its tone made him assume the opposite position. "I quite like Dickens," he said.

"'It was the best of times, it was the worst of times,'" she intoned. "Who can be bothered with an author who can't even make up his mind?"

She laughed, and he grimaced and tried to read. Her laugh had changed, too, turned into one of those musical ones. It seemed to run up and down an octave, hitting every note.

Getting no reaction, she sighed and moved to the window while he watched her now that her back was

43

turned. She was as nearly as tall as him, which made her tall for a girl. She usually moved very gracefully, lazily, so it was odd to see her moving stiffly now. He didn't want to ask. He tried not to . . . for about five seconds. Then he did.

"Hurt yourself at hockey?" he said, trying to put a little of her sarcasm into his tone.

She waited a moment before turning, and when she did there was a gleam in her eye, as if she'd snared him. "Oh, Sky. You really, really don't want to know why I'm stiff."

"No, I don't. It'll be another of your freaked-out, girlie, boarding school things," he said, head diving back down to the book. He knew she hadn't stopped staring at him, and after he read the same sentence three times with no success, he looked back. "All right," he said, in a tone that implied he knew he was going to find it the dullest thing in the world, "how did you hurt your leg?"

"Not leg, Sky. Legs. Actually"—her brow creased—"not even legs, really. *Thighs.*"

She said the word in a rather peculiar way, almost breathing it out.

"Oh God," he muttered.

"You want to know how I hurt my *thighs, Sky?*" She breathed out both the last words in that same annoying way now, moving across to the bed.

"Well, since you're obviously dying to tell me . . ."

She lowered herself onto the end of the bed, and

44

her voice dropped low. "We have a competition at the end of every term. In the dormitories. By candlelight. It was a hard struggle, let me tell you. But I won in the end."

Sky knew he was good at all sorts of games and was suddenly intrigued. "Bet I could beat you," he challenged.

She laughed. "I doubt it. But, anyway, you and I couldn't play this game, boyo. It's for girls only." She leaned in, her voice dropping still lower, so Sky reluctantly leaned in too. She went on in a whisper. "Two girls face each other on stools. The others form a circle around us. Then we pull up our skirts"—she began to mime rolling up a skirt over her jeans—"till they are up here." She mimed stopping. Sky looked at the imaginary skirt halfway up the leg. "Then . . ."

Sky looked up into her eyes. "Then what?"

"Then we take turns to . . ." She slowly raised her hands in the air, then slapped them down really hard on the tops of her thighs. The sound was louder than his air rifle firing, and it made him jump. "Not on our own, obviously. On each other's. Loser's first one to cry out."

"That's . . . that's . . ."

"Good, eh?" She laughed. "And I won! Beat the captain of hockey in a tense final."

". . . disgusting!" He shoved himself back up the bed, snatched up his book again. "I always said you were a bunch of perverts. All girls together."

45

"Why, Sky," she laughed, that run of notes again, "you've gone all red."

"Pervs," he muttered.

"Well," she said, standing, walking back to the window—less stiffly, he noted—"at least we *do* something at our school. What do you do at yours? Bet nothing remotely interesting has happened to you all term." Those lips formed into their sneer. "Smoked a cigarette behind the bike sheds yet, have you?"

Suddenly he wanted to tell her. Not just to prove he wasn't the boring loser she obviously thought him. He needed to tell someone about all the stuff that had been happening. He knew what his parents' reaction would be. They'd just nod sympathetically while edging toward the phone. They'd have him back in front of a shrink in a blink, and he'd had enough of that over the years. Besides, he knew he wasn't going mad. The encounters in the woods and the attic. The . . . arriving at school before he arrived. Above all, the runestones and how they felt. Something weird *was* going on.

He got up. "Come with me," he said. "That is, if you want to see something *really* interesting."

She looked like she might refuse. But when he walked out of the bedroom and made for the stairs to the upper floor, he heard her following.

"Family albums? Is that it?"

She'd draped the mink wrap around her neck. Sky was glad to see no light in the creature's bead eyes, no hint that it was about to speak. There were things he wanted to tell his cousin, but the talking mink probably wasn't one of them.

He pointed at the albums. "Did you notice anything strange about them?"

"Not really." They'd been through them once, and now she flicked one open randomly. "Just holiday snaps."

"Yeah, but there are none of Grandfather Sigurd."

She shrugged. "Not surprising, really. He walked out on them when my mum was seven and yours, uh, six? And then he died soon after. I bet Grandma was furious with him. I know I would be. I mean, does your mum ever talk about him? Mine doesn't."

"Not much. Except to say I'm a bit like him. Lookswise." He flicked an album to the last page, to the family shot before the fjord. "I reckon that's him. Taking the picture."

"The shadow?" She traced the dark shape that flowed toward their mothers' younger selves. "Could be. So what? Is that all you've got to show me?"

"Not quite. I also discovered . . . this!"

He reached up into the roof of the chest until he found the end of the duct tape he'd resealed the hidden compartment with. He'd left a little tab clear and, grabbing it, he pulled it along. It gave with a ripping sound, and before he got halfway down the second side, the panel disgorged its contents, the bag and book hitting the chest's base with a thump.

47

"Wow." Kristin leaned forward, all mockery gone from her face.

He handed her the book. While she undid the drawstring and flicked the volume open, he took the bag, pulled out the silk cloth, laid it on the chest's base, poured the runestones onto it.

"They're runes," he said.

"I know what they are." She reached and pulled one out, holding it up to the sun coming through the skylight. A shape like an "H" but with a slanting crossbar caught sunlight in its red slashes. "Beautiful, isn't it? They all are." She peered down, her brow wrinkling. "So these are Momo's?"

"I think they were Sigurd's. The chest was his before it was hers, and stuff was just shoved into it after she . . . you know . . ."

They had a moment's silence, thinking about their grandmother's death. Then Sky pointed at the book in her hand. "This is Norwegian, yes?"

She peered. He knew she spoke some. "The notes are," she said, reading. "But I'm not sure about some of these words." She read aloud. " 'Thurisaz. Wunjo. Dagaz.' " She waved at the glimmering stones. "They're probably the names for these." She moved a few pages on. "Yeah, look, some repeat. Thurisaz. Raidho. Pertho."

Something sounded familiar. He looked at the book. Yes, she had managed to open it to the exact same page that the wind had fluttered it to the other night. He tapped the paper. "That looks like a runecast, don't you think?"

She nodded. "I've read about them. It's a bit like the spread of tarot cards—something else we do in the dormitories." She ran her hands over the stones. "You lay out tarot cards or runestones in a pattern and, depending on which ones are chosen, they tell a story about the past or present, or answer a question about the future."

He hesitated, then decided to tell her. "I found the runes from that page, laid them out . . ." As he talked he sifted among the stones, selected the same ones again. Soon he had four of the five laid out. "But when I picked up that one"—he pointed at but did not touch the diamond-with-legs stone—"I . . . I sort of passed out. Everything went black."

Kristin picked up the stone, put it in place, completing the runecast. She didn't seem to have any reaction, and Sky let go the breath he'd been holding. "So?" she asked. "What do you think this runecast means? Is it about the past, the present, or the future?"

"I get the feeling . . . ," he said, remembering the words of the fox, the mink, "that that rune . . . maybe the whole cast, is to do with ancestors. Maybe . . . summoning them in some way?"

"Contacting the dead. Very cool!" Kristin smiled, then began to root in the sea chest, tapping the lid and sides.

"I did that already. There's nothing else in there," said Sky.

"There must be." Kristin sat back, started biting at her nails, though there was little left to bite. It was her

49

one obvious imperfection. Her fingers were a little stumpy, and she seemed determined to reduce them still further with her teeth. "I mean . . ." Thwarted at not finding any nail to pull away, her fingers seized upon the duct tape dangling down from the lid. When that gave, she moved on to a piece of the lining paper, began picking at one of the panels with the walking Chinese woman on it. "I mean, he can't just have left these stones, with no other explanation, no instructions."

"He left the book. I was hoping you'd be able to translate it," Sky said.

"My Norwegian's more conversational. This looks a bit technical." She had begun working a strip of the paper loose. "What's this?"

"Lining paper."

"No, under it, there's . . ." She tugged a little more. "Look."

Sky peered in. "It's . . . newsprint. So what?"

"What's it doing there?"

"Well, I suppose they line the box with it, then put this Chinese paper on top. No, Kristin, don't tear it. Mum doesn't even know I've looked in here."

"And has she?"

"Don't think so."

"She won't notice any difference then, will she?"

His cousin had stuck the top half of her body into the box to pull away the strip. Sky winced as he heard the sound, said, "Kristin . . ."

"Well, well, well," she said. "Look at this."

She emerged, enough for him to see in. She'd pulled the covering paper away. There was a black-and-white photo, but the cousins' bodies blocked out the light. So he reached back to the shelf, grabbed the little lantern, flicked it on.

The photo was of a man in a dark uniform, bright buttons down its front. Under one arm he held a cap with braiding. His other arm was around a woman wearing a mink wrap—identical to the one Kristin wore now. Standing before the couple were two small blond girls.

They looked at it for a moment in silence. And then Kristin read aloud, "'Kapitan Sigurd Solness, his wife, Aase, and their daughters Inge and Sonja on his'—I think it must be 'promotion' . . . 'his promotion to captain of the M/V Hardrada.'"

It was strange being face to face with him at last. Stranger still seeing the similarities to the face he regarded in the mirror every day. The blur of old newsprint had flattened his grandfather's features, but there was no mistaking what they shared—the same set-back eyes, same straight nose, same unruly blond hair that Sigurd obviously had tried to tame with oil as Sky tried with gel. Yet it wasn't so much the features, it was more the way each held their head, chin up, eyes regarding life down the longish nose. It spoke of challenges, offered; taken. And he had the weirdest feeling. He knew it was just because his grandfather had stared straight down the lens when the photo was taken, while his wife

51

and daughters hadn't, not quite. But the eyes followed him as he shifted under their gaze; left, right. Sky suddenly felt that he and Kristin weren't the only ones looking, that the photo was somehow . . . looking back.

And there was something else. Something Kristin, peering closer, spotted. "What's that?" She pointed.

"What?"

"That. Between his eyes."

"Ink smudge," he muttered.

But it wasn't. What Sky always tried to remember to do, Sigurd obviously didn't bother with—he just allowed the space between his eyebrows to grow, letting the two become one.

But Sky was spared further questioning by a series of creaks on the landing. They'd been so engrossed that they hadn't heard someone coming up the stairs.

"Sky? Are you up there?" his mother called.

"Quick!" he hissed, reaching for the strut nearest him that supported the lid, gesturing that Kristin should do the same. They each struggled as they heard Sonja's foot squeak on the attic ladder.

"Yeah, Mum, just a sec!" he called, pulling and pushing at the metal. Kristin's side gave, but his stuck for one agonizing moment longer before the lid slammed shut. It was only then that Sky realized that the furs and the albums were still out. He snatched up the silver fox coat just as his mother's head crested the trapdoor.

"Sky!" Sonja reproached. "I thought we were going to look through the trunk together."

There was an awkward silence. It was broken by Kristin. "My fault, Auntie," she said, smiling. "He said there were furs and things up here, so naturally I had to look at them." She lifted the head of the mink, threw it back over her shoulder. "Do you think it suits me?"

Sonja looked, laughed. "Very much. I remember my mother wearing that very one to many parties." She colored slightly at the memory, then smiled at the fox fur in her son's hands. "And you, Sky? Are you playing dress-up too?"

" 'Course not! Wild animal, me!" He slipped the coat over his shoulders, let out the high-pitched bark of a fox.

His mother smiled again. "Well, you were so occupied, you never heard me call for lunch. So if you can leave your games for a while . . ." She was about to descend when she saw the albums. "And bring those," she added. "We can go through them later."

53

She descended. Sky and Kristin regarded each other, wrapped in animal skins, still holding their poses. "Dahling," she said, as if she were in some old black-and-white movie.

He threw his head back. "Ow! Ow ow ow!" he replied, and they both burst out laughing.

He lifted the lid again, and they dropped the furs into the trunk. "Listen, these albums," she said, as she began her descent. "This is a good chance to find out more about Grandfather Sigurd. We should pump your mum for information."

" 'Kay," he said, reaching back to grab and pass down the albums. He heard her reach the landing, but he didn't immediately follow. Instead, he sat there and smiled, trying to remember the last time Kristin had wanted to do something as "we."

CHAPTER FIVE
THE CAUL

"So, Aunt Sonja, why are there no photos of Grand-father?"

Sky flushed. Here had he been trying to subtly steer the conversation round and Kristin just comes right out with it! He wondered how his mother would react to the bluntness.

"Well." Sonja looked down at the albums. "When he left us, Mother was obviously furious. She said that since he'd cut us out of his life, we'd cut him out of ours. So all the photos went." She sighed. "That was the toughest thing. If he'd just died at sea, it would have been bad but we'd still have been able to remember him fondly. But because he'd gone first . . ." She broke off, went to look out the window.

After a moment, Kristin said, "So you don't remember much about him?"

"*About* him or *of* him?" Sonja replied over her shoulder.

"Both."

Sonja came back to the table. "Well," she said, "there are lots of stories *about* Sigurd."

"Not stories, dear." His father had returned to his seat after they'd been through the albums. He sat with a sigh. "Legends!"

"Oh hush, Henry!"

"What sort of stories?"

"Oh, adventure ones. How he ran away to sea at fifteen and traveled the world. How, in the Second World War, he was in the Resistance and fought the Germans." She looked from one cousin to the other. "Then, of course, there were his special powers."

"What kind of powers?" Sky asked.

56 "Well." She leaned down, resting her forearms on the table. "To begin with, he was psychic."

"You mean like . . . see the future, tell fortunes type thing?" said Kristin.

"Hmm, in a way. But more . . ." Sonja was staring above their heads as if searching for the words. "In Norway, there's something we call *vardogr*. It's like a . . . sending ahead of oneself."

Sky went cold. "What do you mean?"

Sonja clasped her hands before her. "You'll probably scoff at this, but . . . here's a Sigurd story." She cleared her throat. "He's back from a voyage to Africa and he goes to report at the shipping company offices in downtown Oslo. In those days there were elevator operators to take you up and down. So Sigurd walks into the elevator, says, 'Good day, Johan. It's been a long time.' And this man turns white. 'But, Captain S-S-Solness,' he stutters, 'I took you up just five minutes ago.'

Henry grunted. "The man was obviously drunk."

Sky's jaw had dropped. "How . . . how did Sigurd do that?"

"I don't think he *did* anything. It just happened." Sonja sighed. "I think that was the first time, as well. Because my mother, when she told me the story, said Father was never the same again. He left us a year later."

"But if . . . if he was somewhere else, then who . . . or what was it that was sent ahead?" Sky was thinking about the last day of school. "What did the elevator man see?"

"Well, in Norway, we'd call that my father's *hamr*. It's a . . . a body double of oneself, an exact carbon copy."

"'Hammer'? Like . . ." Sky mimed driving a nail in.

"No," Sonja replied. "H-A-M-R. But in England I think it's called your 'Fetch.'"

"Wow!" Kristin was looking above her aunt, staring at possibilities. "How cool would that be! You leave your body at home and go do stuff. You could steal. Murder someone. But you'd be at home, with witnesses." She shivered and laughed at the same time. "It's like the perfect alibi, right?"

Henry laughed too. "Now you're talking. At last,

57

a practical use for all this"—he flapped his hand—"mumbo jumbo."

"Except," Sonja replied, ignoring her husband, "I don't believe you can control your Fetch. It acts independently." She smiled. "So no getting away with murder, I'm afraid."

Sky was still too stunned to speak. So it was his . . . Fetch that had preceded him to school, sat in class, held his pen. His Fetch he'd seen silhouetted in a doorway.

"So that's *about* Grandfather, Auntie. What do you remember *of* him?"

"Well . . ." Sonja pulled a hair away from her forehead. "I remember his laugh. It was one of those laughs that just took over the whole body, you know? And when Sky was born—"

"Oh no, Mum, not again!"

"What?" Kristin was looking between the two of them.

Sky groaned, but his mother continued anyway. "Sky gets embarrassed when I talk about it." She reached out and tousled his hair. "But it's just that when he was born and I heard his first cry, I felt I . . . knew him immediately. Because in his cry I heard my father's laugh."

Sky groaned again while Kristin cooed. "Oh, that's so sweet. So Sky is like Sigurd, reincarnated. Or maybe it's like his—what did you call it?—his Fetch lives on in Sky."

"Oh no, no." Sonja was still playing with Sky's hair. "But maybe Sky has some of Father's better bits."

"Get off," muttered Sky, moving his head away. His mother left her hand in the air where it had touched him, staring at it. Then she said, "Just a minute," got up, and left the room.

"Well, well." Kristin was smiling. "Perhaps we'll have to rename you, Sky. How about Sigurd Two?"

"Oh, I do hope not." Henry leaned forward and tried to punch Sky's arm. "Only room for one legend in any household, eh?"

"Leave off," he said, dodging, as his mum walked back in. She was holding something in one hand.

"All this talk"—she gestured at the table, the albums on it—"about Father and your birth . . ."

"Yes, we know, Mum. The laugh and cry. Please."

"But there's something else I haven't told you about that day." She looked at the object in her hand, then laid it down carefully onto the table. It was a little suede bag, the kind that might hold a piece of jewelry.

His father stood up. "Oh, Sonja. Really."

"It's time, Henry. I always said there would come a time. . . ."

"Yes, well. I've things to be getting on with." He was marching out the door as he spoke.

Sky stared after him. "Is Dad upset?"

"No, not at all. He's just . . . an engineer. Prefers things that are logical, that can be taken apart with tools. Like pumps. Funny, he wasn't always like that."

She smiled at a memory, went on. "Anyway, this sort of 'mumbo jumbo'"—she said it in his voice and flapped her hand the way he had, and they all laughed—"well, it drives him crazy." She pointed at the bag. "Go on, Sky. Open it. It's yours. I've been keeping it for you. For the right time."

The pouch was old, brown, a little stained. Like the runestone bag from the chest, it had a drawstring, which Sky unfurled and discovered was quite long. He loosened it at the neck, reached inside.

If he'd been hoping for an earring—he'd been nagging his mother for months about getting his ear pierced—he was disappointed. At first he thought the sack was empty, then he pulled out a piece of what looked like shriveled leather. He dumped that, rooted further with a finger. Nothing!

"It's not . . . not that?" he said, pointing down.

"Yes, Sky. That's it. That . . . is your caul." She was smiling at him in a very strange way.

"My what?" He picked it up.

"You know, where you were born . . ."

"Please, Mum!" Sky flicked his eyes again to Kristin.

His mother ignored him, turned to her niece. "Henry and I were living back on the land . . ." Sky groaned again. It was one of the most embarrassing things, this neo-hippie rubbish his parents had gone in for. ". . . and when Sky was due, there was no time to go to a hospital. And I didn't want one anyway. It was

60

a beautiful, hot summer, and I wanted him to be born outside. And he was. Hence the name Sky."

"That's lovely." Kristin's voice didn't seem too sarcastic, though Sky was sure she was storing this up. "But wasn't it a little . . . dangerous?"

"I was very idealistic and a bit naive." Sonja sighed. "And yes, it did turn out to be dangerous. The women on the commune weren't as experienced as I'd thought. And there was one big complication." She looked down at Sky. "You were born with the amniotic membrane stuck to your face."

"What do you mean? Like afterbirth?" Sky was revolving the contents of the bag between his fingers. Now that he was studying it, it was less leathery, more like a bit of steak gristle you hadn't been able to swallow. And it was surprisingly heavy, as if it had many layers, compressed.

"No," Kristin broke in. "The amniotic membrane holds the waters in. When it ruptures, the waters burst and thus begins the birth process." Kristin grinned smugly when he looked at her. "Biology's a breeze."

"So a membrane was over my face?" Sky shivered. "Gross!"

"Gross . . . and dangerous," Sonja continued. "It stops the baby breathing. The women there knew nothing about it. But luckily I'd read about it and wasn't too out of it with the pain. I pulled it off you, put it aside, and once it had dried"—she smiled, pointing down—"I put it in that bag."

"You mean . . ." Sky looked at the gristle he'd just been contemplating tasting and dropped it on the table. "Yuck! You mean this is my . . . amnio whatsit? That's disgusting!"

Sonja picked it up, replacing it in the leather pouch. Softly she said, "It's not disgusting, Sky. It's the mark of destiny." She smiled. "My father was born with one as well; and in Norway, in other places, too, they say those born under the caul are born with a gift. For it is the mark of those who can 'travel.' Like Sigurd did that time in Oslo."

Like I did at school, Sky thought, amazed.

"I think if you do have this . . . ability, then it will come out sometime. And I also think that perhaps your sleepwalking might be connected somehow. The first flutters, perhaps?" She raised the bag. "That's why I want you to have this. It might . . . help." His mother drew the drawstring tight, sealing the mouth of the pouch. "Just no running away to sea, eh? Not until you graduate, anyway."

As she spoke, she unraveled the cord, then spread it wide with her fingers and slipped it over Sky's head. She still held the pouch in one hand, and it was only when he looked up at her that she smiled and let it go. It seemed to Sky that the little bag did not drop as gravity dictated it should. It fell slowly, as if Time had run down or the caul had no weight, though he knew from before that it did. Yet it was when it reached his chest that he got the weirdest sensation. It didn't feel like it stopped at his flesh but that the caul pushed through, through its leather container, through his skin, to settle finally somewhere close to his heart.

CHAPTER SIX

SÉANCE

They emerged onto the landing simultaneously, with the last toll of quarter to midnight still vibrating from the grandfather clock downstairs. Neither had slept since their whispered conversation after they'd said good night to his parents.

Sky led, guiding Kristin over those stairs that made especially loud creaks—the third, seventh, and tenth—up to the third, top floor where his father had his den. His dad had shut the attic up, so he fetched the pole with its hoop and spike and reached up to the hook set in the trapdoor in the ceiling. He had done this often since they'd moved in, striving to eliminate all noise, a game of war and secrecy. He did it now, pulling the trapdoor down till it caught, unlatching the lower section of the attic's metal ladder with the spike, lowering it to the ground. He gestured "after you," and Kristin climbed up swiftly, silently, despite the cloth bag over her shoulder. Following, he stretched down from the top, used the spike again to snag the bottom part of the ladder, pull it up, and drop it into its latch with the faintest of clicks. Then he pulled up the top section gently till the whole folded snug into the attic floor and they were cut off from the world below.

"Brilliant," Kristin said, though he didn't know if she was praising his commando-like skills or the space he'd carved out of the jumble earlier in the afternoon. He turned on the camping lantern, and they looked around.

His parents' belongings—battered suitcases and rucksacks, Sonja's various craft projects, Henry's home brew equipment—had been pushed back under the slope of the roof. His own stuff he'd put in a circle to form the walls of a cave in the center. He felt slightly embarrassed by some of it now—too many relics of the boy he'd been, with the toy gun collection, the rack of war comics, the gas mask. And the old bookcase, stuffed with the adventure books he'd read all his life. Flush against this was their grandfather's sea chest. Maybe that was what his cousin had praised, the way the moon shone through the skylight, placing the trunk in a spotlight that transformed the tattered stickers from all those exotic ports into silver.

Kristin soon revealed skills of her own. In their whispers earlier, arranging this rendezvous, she'd said that she'd brought something with her that would help them, something she never traveled without. It

65

wasn't just sore thighs she'd acquired in her dormitory, apparently.

"Have you ever done this?" From her bag she took what looked like a board game, placing it on an empty suitcase she pulled over. Sky peered down. At the top center of the board a woman's face was drawn beneath the word "OUIJA." To the left of the face was the word "YES," to the right, "NO." The entire alphabet stretched in a slightly curving line near the board's bottom edge. Just below the letters was the word "GOODBYE."

On his head shake she continued, "It's easy." She delved into the bag again. "A plastic reader came with the set, but Celia sat on it. Anyway, I prefer . . . this!" With the distinct air of a conjuror she produced a small, squat shot glass with a cactus painted on its side. She inverted it, then placed it in the center, above the line of letters. "We each put a finger on it, like so"— she stuck a forefinger on top of the glass—"then we ask, 'Is there anybody there?'"

Sky couldn't help laughing at her spooky tone. Looking offended, she ignored him, carried on. "If we contact someone, the glass moves to 'YES'"—she demonstrated, moving the glass up to the word at the head of the board—"then he or she should spell out their name. After that, it's quicker if you ask questions that have a yes or no answer. Get it?"

Sky nodded again. It seemed that all moisture had left his mouth.

"And it's not just the Ouija board," she continued,

66

"but what surrounds it." She pulled a purple silk scarf from one pocket, draped it over the camping lantern, produced a candle from another pocket, lit it, and placed it on the toy gun rack behind her.

While she did that, he busied himself, too, lifting the lid of the chest till the struts locked, pulling out the runestones. He found the five from the cast and laid them out on top of the red cloth in the same pattern as before. And as before, when he put the last one, *Othala,* in place, he had the feeling that it clung to his fingers. It didn't burn this time, but he had to shake it off.

Meanwhile, Kristin reached into the lid. He'd put back the flap of paper concealing the photograph, in case his mum came up and started rooting around. Now she pulled it away and more of it to each side so the photo stood out, slap in the center. Then she cracked her knuckles, an explosion of bones. "So . . . you ready?"

Sky found enough spit to form words. "This Ouija thing. We're going to . . . contact spirits through it, yes?"

"Correct." She leaned toward him, into the light pool. He could see the excitement in her eyes. "But not just any spirit, Sky. You can get some dead bores, believe me." She laughed. "No"—she raised her arm, pointed—"we are going to conjure . . . him!"

Sky looked at the photo. The candle's flames shifted over all the faces, but because Sigurd's eyes looked straight out, into the lens, it was his stare that flickered, followed Sky wherever he moved, no matter how he tried to lose it.

"I'm not sure," he muttered, looking up at the sky-light. The moon had disappeared behind a cloud, and the room was that little bit darker. He shivered; but he wasn't cold.

"Come on! What have we got to lose?" She stuck her finger on the glass.

"Aren't we supposed to wait till midnight or something?" he mumbled.

"What? Why? No, no, that must be a whole . . . five minutes away." She jerked her chin, pointing it toward the glass. "Let's go, man!"

Cross-legged on the floor, they leaned over the board, Sky adding his finger to the glass. He looked at his cousin, her eager face, the blond hair flopped forward around it. Looked away, licked at his lips. Why didn't I bring some water? he thought.

"Right." She cleared her throat and, after a pause, said, softly but clearly, "Is there anybody there?"

Sky didn't laugh at the tone now. They sat. They waited. Nothing moved apart from the candle flame, nothing sounded except the old house and, from outside, a slight breeze passing through the oak tree.

His finger felt heavy on the glass; the caul in its leather pouch, which she'd insisted he wear, seemed to drag his neck down.

Silence. "Is there anybody there?" she repeated, more firmly.

Nothing for a long moment. Then the tumbler gave a lurch and began to slide up toward "YES."

68

"You're pushing it!"

"I am not!"

"You are. I can feel it. Look!" He took his finger off. The glass kept moving, then stopped.

"All right, maybe I was," she said, with a grudging smile. "Just to see if the surface wasn't too sticky. Rebecca Miles dropped cider on it last week, the idiot! Put your finger back. Go on!"

Half reluctant, he did. The house settled again into its clicks and scratchings, leaves rustling faintly beyond it; while the moon, which had been playing peekaboo in the clouds, now hid completely, the attic given over to the shadows with one tiny cave of light.

Silence again, all still. Then suddenly, through some quirk of the ventilation system, they heard, quite clearly, the grandfather clock downstairs begin to toll the hour.

Dong. Dong. Dong, it went, quite slowly.

"Go on," Kristin whispered. "*You* ask."

Dong, dong . . . dong . . . dong . . .

Was it him, or was the space between strikes lengthening?

He cleared his throat, was about to speak, when, suddenly, there was a scream. It was so piercing in that quiet, they both jerked back . . . yet their fingers stayed tethered to the glass. The scream had come from outside and now it came again, this time closer. It sounded like a woman in terror or terrible pain; but Sky, with relief, realized it wasn't.

"It's a fox," he said. "They make that . . ."

Dong . . .

"Never mind the bloody fox. Ask!"

Dong . . . . . . Dong . . .

Was that nine? Ten? Sky tried to speak, couldn't. Finally he croaked, "Is there anybody—"

Dong! The note vibrated in the air, echoing there. And then the candle flame lengthened, shot sideways, went out in a snap of smoke at the exact same moment that the lantern's bulb pinged, popped, died. It was black-dark, yet the blackness lasted a mere moment, just long enough for one last, drawn-out toll of the bell, and then the moon broke from its cloud prison, dowsing the room in silver . . .

70 . . . and the glass began to move. Not toward "YES." Straight for a letter.

"'S,'" breathed Sky.

It moved again. "'I,'" whispered Kristin.

"'G,'" they said together.

"Do you think it's . . . it's . . . Sigurd?" Sky had barely got the name out before the glass shot up to "YES" with a force that pulled him from his haunches. But it didn't rest there. It moved straight to "H," then "I," then "M," back to the middle, then "M" again, then "E," then "L." Only then did it pause. They could feel it quivering under their fingers, as if waiting.

"H-I-M-M-E-L," said Sky. "That's not a word." When Kristin didn't reply, he looked at her. Her face had gone so white, it looked like marble.

"But it is." She looked back at him now. "In Norwegian, *himmel* means . . . Sky!"

As she whispered the word, the glass leapt again to "YES," this time so violently that his grip was torn away. Yet the glass kept moving with just her finger upon it.

"Stop pushing it, Kristin. It's not funny." Sky was furious. He had fallen back, his eyes now level with the moving shot glass. He was clutching the leather pouch around his neck. Not for comfort. If he held it, then the caul wouldn't keep rising and thumping into his ribs.

"I'm not, I swear I'm not," Kristin gasped. "And I can't . . . can't take my finger away. It hurts if I try, like it's superglued." He leaned across, reached to grab her arm, to rip it away. But she stopped him with a whisper, shaky, desperate. "Don't! Please! Don't!"

He looked down. The glass was moving again, pulling Kristin swiftly around the table. The first word it spelled out was R . . . U . . . N . . .

"Runestones?" said Sky.

"YES," went the glass, then moved to spell another word. O . . . T . . . H . . .

"*Othala?*"

"YES," went the glass again.

"What the hell's *Othala?*"

The glass was moving faster and faster, so fast that Kristin barely had time to call out the letters.

"B-O-O-K! Do you think it means the journal?"

71

"Yes!" she cried out as the glass shot to the word. "Quickly, Sky, look in the book. Look!"

He fumbled it up. It was still open at the page it had always flopped to, the one with the runecast. The moon was bright, but it was still hard to read the letters scrawled beneath each inked rune. And suddenly he knew which one it was, anyway, just as the letters came clear.

"*Othala*," she croaked, "rune of ancestors. Rune that summons." Her voice didn't sound like hers anymore. It was deeper and was . . . was that an accent he heard?

He couldn't look at her, could only look down. At the runestones. They all glowed. But one glowed brighter than the rest. The one that had made the mink speak. The one that made Kristin speak again in that harsh, slow voice.

"Pick. It. Up."

He looked at her now. Had to. Her face was still white, the bones of it standing out, as if she were freezing; yet sweat was running down it in lines.

"I don't want to," he said, suddenly very scared.

"You have to!" Her eyes flicked up to him. They were desperate. And her voice was again like her own. "Please, Sky! Please. For me."

He supposed that, in a way, he had waited all his life to do something for her. He could do this. He could pick the runestone up.

He picked it up.

It was all gone in a moment, less—attic, Ouija board, Kristin's face—gone in an explosion of white. He felt he was falling backward, braced himself for the collision with the hard wooden floorboards, as he had hit them when he'd first touched that stone . . . until he realized he was not falling at all but already lying down with the ground soft beneath him and the runestone in his hand. And the light . . . it wasn't white anymore but yellow, and if it still blinded, that was because he was squinting into a sun that dazzled in a cornflower-blue sky.

He sat up so suddenly the blood went to his head. Steadying himself, he dropped the stone into the pouch at his chest and looked around. He was sitting on a grassy hillside that dropped away from him toward a river. On its banks stood a huge tent, a canvas pavilion. Some children played outside it, and from within came the sound of an old-fashioned brass band. People were walking toward it, drawn by the music. Rising, brushing grass from his skateboard shorts—he didn't know how he was wearing those or how they were so clean—he joined the procession.

Inside the tent, men and women mingled, dressed in the lightest of summer clothes, drinking champagne from crystal flutes. As he entered, it seemed to him that all conversation paused, that everyone was turning slightly toward him, that the orchestra took a half beat. Then the moment passed, the music picked up again, conversation resumed. He strolled amongst them, seen but ignored.

73

A hand on his shoulder, pressure turning him. He looked up. . . .

Why had he thought his grandfather would be an old man? He knew Sigurd had died in his fifties. Maybe it was because Sonja was getting on, so her dad had to be ancient. But before him stood the man from the photograph, though dressed not in a naval uniform but in the same light cotton as the others. Sigurd's face was very much like Sky's own—except his grandfather had not tried to tame the One-Brow into two, had let them meet and meld. Under it, the blue-gray eyes could have stared back at Sky from his own mirror.

The voice was low, gentle. "Welcome, Sky, welcome indeed. We have many things to talk about, you and I." As he spoke, Sigurd steered Sky out of the pavilion and down to a crescent of green that overhung the river. They sat, and even though he was bursting with questions, Sky looked at his grandfather, did as he did; took a moment to just stare at the shimmering water and delight in the swallows that swooped to skim its slow-moving surface, taking sips, snatching at insects hovering lazy in sunbeams. It was so peaceful, it almost made him feel drowsy.

But the questions had to return. "Grandfather," he said, at last, "where . . . how . . . ?"

A hand was raised, halting his words. "There is so much that you must learn, Sky. This"—Sigurd waved at the water—"is just a place between worlds. A haven where you can begin that learning. Begin to learn how

74

to fulfill your destiny." Sky made to speak, but his grandfather interrupted, gently. "I do have answers for you, Sky. But will you allow me to begin at the beginning . . . well, near it anyway? Because we do not have much time. You can only stay here a short while . . . this visit. Your gatekeeper grows frightened."

He pointed to the river. Sky looked, and on its surface . . . through its surface . . . he could see down into the attic. Kristin was there, finger still on the glass, staring wide-eyed at Sky . . . well, at Sky's body, lying on the floor, arms thrown back, mouth open.

"I have to say"—Sky shook his head—"*that* is a bit weird."

"It will not seem so for long. Not compared with what you are going to see." Leaning forward, Sigurd stared intently into Sky's eyes. "Have you not felt something of this before? When you feel as if you've left your body?"

Sky nodded. "I've had . . . troubled sleep all my life. Talked, walked. Seemed to live another life after I've gone to bed. And then, the other day at school, I . . . I was there before I was there. People saw me. I . . . saw me, I think."

A smile had come to his grandfather's face. "Good, Sky. You have already experienced vardogr. Your Fetch has walked. And that is nearly forty years before mine did. I knew I was right about you." His voice lowered. "People fear this Fetch, lad, our Double. They ignore him, pretend he doesn't exist. Yet they will look in a

75

mirror every day, or watch their shadows dance in the sunlight. Soon, you will think it as normal as that." He reached up, touched the One-Brow between his eyes. "This is one sign. Let yours grow, Sky. Be proud that you are chosen. But the very first sign is—"

"The caul!" Sky burst out excitedly. He had looked down, seen the leather pouch under Sigurd's shirt. "My mother says that we were both born under a caul. That it proves we are . . . gifted."

Sigurd sighed. "Often I have wondered—is it a gift or a curse? To find out you are . . . different. It is like discovering you have any talent; for music, sports. Will you ever be truly fulfilled if you don't use it? Yet, if you do, you must devote your life to it. The first time my Fetch preceded me, my world changed forever." He shook his head. "And once you learn to control it, you are able to leave your body, take on the form of an animal, cross the world in a heartbeat, leap a thousand years in a blink of eyes, travel—"

Sky interrupted again. "But Mum . . . your daughter, Sonja . . . she said that you *can't* control the Fetch. That it acts independently."

"Ah." A slight smile came again to Sigurd's mouth, though Sky could now see a sadness, too, in his eyes. "And that's why you are here, Sky, taking the first step along the path. Most with the gift never even acknowledge it, let alone learn how to use it. For such a gift comes at a price . . . and every journey demands a sacrifice. Odin, Allfather of the Gods, hung on an ash tree for nine days, frozen by the northern winds, starved. Finally he gave one of his eyes, and for his suffering he received knowledge. He received . . . the runes." Sigurd's voice fell to a whisper. "And I? I gave up my 'normal' life, sacrificed my home, my family . . ." He shook his head. "Often I wondered if it was worth it. In the end, I decided that it was." He leaned closer. "But you, Sky. Are you ready to sacrifice what must be sacrificed to gain what must be gained?"

Sky knew that, in another place, another time, when pushed to a major decision, he might have hesitated. But not here. Not now. "I'm ready. I have always felt . . . different, anyway, so I may as well have a reason for it." He leaned forward excitedly. "So where do I go? Or is it 'when'? Past or future? And how?"

Sigurd had sat back, was staring across the water. "Our people—the Norse—did not believe in these false divisions of Time as a straight line. There was only 'Time that is and Time that is becoming.' The past is the present is the future, different points on the same path along which the Fetch can travel. Your destiny lies ahead, but first you need to discover what is back down that path. You need to travel to your ancestors."

Now that he knew, Sky wanted to start at once. "How do I get there?"

"Through your caul. It is the blood and the skin that once joined you to your mother and, through her, to all who went before. You can return to them through it and return to your body the same way. The caul is the doorway. And it is the runestones, your inheritance from me, that will power you over the threshold."

Sigurd gestured down, to the water. Kristin was still there, her arm stretched out to touch the glass, her body as far away from the Ouija board as possible. Before her, the five runes laid out in their cast glowed, like embers in a fire. Five—which was strange, because Sky had one in the pouch at his chest.

Sigurd continued, "I brought you here through *Othala*, rune of ancestors. All journeys must now be taken through the runestones and only through them, not through those letters and that glass. Don't worry about the whole cast for now. Take the runes one at a time—for even the hardest journey is but one step followed by the next." He stretched out a hand, laid it on Sky's forearm. "Understand this: Each runestone is like . . . like an atom. Small but possessing infinite energy. Find the trigger and you will release that energy." He smiled. "And when you have experienced all five runes in the cast, you will know what you have to do."

Sky stared down at the runes floating within the water. "But how . . . *how* do I use them?"

Sigurd shook his head. "You will discover how. For 'rune' means both 'secret' and 'whisper.' You simply must learn to hear the secrets that whisper in your blood."

"'Simply?'" Sky couldn't help but ask. "Can't you give me a hint?"

"No, lad. Words cannot teach it. But I will tell you

78

this: At exactly midnight—that time which is not yet tomorrow, no longer today—you will travel again. Use *Thurisaz*, the rune at the top of the cast. Learn its meaning, but do not worry too much about words. Feel it! And you will travel, not to somewhere like this, somewhere between, but to a time and a place. Where one of our ancestors waits."

"Who is he?" Sky swallowed. "Is it even a he?"

"It is," Sigurd replied. "This I can tell you. There are ancestors we are drawn to most, so close to us it is as if we were born of the same womb, though a thousand years apart. I have been drawn to two such. I have even met the one you now shall meet. So I do know when and where you shall go. . . ." He raised a hand, halting Sky's interruption. "But I do not know what shall happen to you there. That is for you to discover."

As he spoke, Sigurd was rising. His hand was still on Sky's shoulder and he pulled him up, started pushing him gently toward the water. Sky resisted slightly, sensing the end of conversation. There were a million things he still could ask. But there was one thing he had to.

"Are you a . . . a ghost, Grandfather?"

A smile came. "In a way. Though it is a crude term. But if you learn to master your Fetch during life, you retain some power over your . . . spirit double after death. Those who don't learn to do so and die unhappy for some reason . . . well, they can only go 'boo' in the night, poor souls."

79

Sky suddenly remembered a graveyard at midnight, icy breath, skeletal fingers reaching out. "I think I've met one of those. He wears a hood but doesn't seem to have any head inside it." A shiver came, the first touch of coldness in that warm world. "He . . . he seems to want something from me."

The music, which had been playing under their whole conversation, stopped. Sigurd had turned pale. He took a long moment before he spoke. "What you have met is called a *draug*. The Unquiet Dead. Maybe he didn't die in the way he was meant to. Maybe he was not burned at his death, his bones consumed with flame. Or maybe"—he swallowed—"maybe someone meddled in the spirit world, raised him up, did not know how to send him back to his rest. Many draugs do not even know they are dead. They seek the companionship of the living. They seek . . . life." Sigurd's grip on Sky's shoulder had grown hard. "Keep away from this creature, Sky. He's only a danger if you let him get too close."

With a last look deep into Sky's eyes, he released his grip, took Sky's hand, stepped into the river. The gentle wind had returned, the orchestra had struck up again. The water was cool about Sky's ankles, delicious on such a hot day. He wanted to sink into it, fall toward his body in the attic and his cousin waiting there, terror on her face.

"She's pretty, isn't she?" Sigurd said. "Like all the Solness women. Well, nearly all." He laughed. "Give her my greeting and tell her . . . tell her not to be frightened. Explain what I have told you. If she is intelligent as well as pretty, let her seek out information for you both. You need her strong and brave, Sky, which she should be, for she, too, is blood of our blood. She must watch over you again. It is vital that when your Fetch walks, your body is not disturbed. And you must never, ever be woken."

His grandfather now released his hand. Instantly Sky began to sink. He felt no fear; he was a good swimmer. Yet this did not feel so much like swimming as flying.

Just before the water covered him he thought of one other question, and he shouted it up. "This ancestor I visit. I only have to watch him, yes? I won't have to *do* anything?"

Sigurd laughed. It was the laugh his mother had talked about, the one that took over the whole body. "I told you, Grandson. It is not enough to *understand* the meaning of each runestone. You must *experience* the meaning."

That was the last he heard before water filled his ears, closed over his head. He was falling, sinking, flying. He was between worlds, between himself and his Fetch. They were the same. And they were different. So different.

CHAPTER SEVEN
EVE OF DEPARTURE

The cry woke him, if it was indeed sleep that held him; pulled him, anyway, back from the falling, through the water, onto the hard floor of the attic. He jerked upright, his eyes drawn instantly by the only brightness in the dark—Kristin's face, as white as he remembered it, twice as frightened, her mouth still parted in the cry that had dragged him back, the sound still coming and starting to grow. Even in the moment of return he recognized the type of cry from his own nightmares. Starting small, it would build and build until it was a scream that could wake a town.

He was across to her in a moment, knocking the Ouija board off the suitcase, the glass rolling off to smash against a floorbeam. He put an arm around her shoulders, a hand up across her mouth to halt the sound. Her arms rose to try to stop him but had no strength to do so.

"It's OK, Kristin. Kristin! You're fine. Everything's fine."

She squirmed under his grip, her eyes still not settling on him but staring out, down, as if into some terrible vision. A hand rose, slipped under his at her mouth, tried to push him away. He could still hear the wail building underneath it, couldn't release her.

"Kristin," he whispered, "please. *Please!* My parents!"

It was enough; a beginning, anyway, a word from a normal world. He felt the vibrating sound slacken against his palm, saw her eyes focus before her, not beyond.

"I'm going to take my hand away now, yes? Will you be all right?"

Her eyes finally looked back into his. She nodded. He removed his hand.

She took breaths, sharp, shallow, a series of them. Now that she'd met his eyes, she was looking at him so hard. "You . . . ," she said, "you . . ."

"It's OK. I'm OK. Just take your time."

She reached out, gripped the hand that was still before her. Her strength was returning with her breath, and he was glad she bit her nails. She'd have drawn blood, so hard did she suddenly squeeze him.

"I . . . tho-thought you . . . were dead," she shuddered out.

"What? Why?"

"So cold." She gasped, took a deeper breath. He tried to rub her hand, but she snatched it away. "Not

83

me, idiot! You!" She pointed to where he'd been lying, continued, "And your eyes, rolled back, like—" She showed him the whites of hers. "I was going to go for help, but that . . . that . . ." She kicked the Ouija board, which had landed on its end, and it flew into the darkness beyond the moonspill. "It started spelling out what would happen if I did. It told me that if I woke you, you . . . you would die!"

A sob came then, her hand clamped over her mouth to hold it in. Sky moved over to the trapdoor, pushed it open a little, listened. The old house was as quiet as it ever was, and beyond the creaks and shiftings there was no noise of parents approaching. He let the door swing up, returned to his cousin.

"Are you all right? I mean, can we talk? I'll tell you what happened, OK?"

After a long moment and a longer breath, she nodded but then said, "Not here. Let's get out of here, eh?"

He let the ladder down as silently as he'd pulled it up, helped her over the stairs that creaked, passed their bedrooms on the floor below, went all the way down to the kitchen. He didn't speak until he had two cups of very sugary tea and some chocolate cookies before them. Then he told her all that had happened and everything their dead grandfather had said to him.

Her breath was coming evenly by the time he finished, and some color had even returned to her face, mainly in two red patches glowing on her cheeks. He wasn't sure he was explaining it very well. It had all made sense by that river. Here, in the cold kitchen, it was sounding crazier with every detail.

"OK," she said quietly when he'd blurted out the last of it, "let me see if I've got this straight—you've gone to the far side of consciousness. You've met our grandfather's ghost there. He's told you that you are going to become a time traveler. That you'll visit our ancestors, experience their lives, have amazing adventures. Learn the ultimate destiny of your life." She cleared her throat. "And he wants me to be your . . . *research assistant*???"

The last words were roared out with such venom, Sky could only laugh. Kristin was back. "And gatekeeper, remember," he said. "You have to watch over me, keep the . . . whatever . . . *channel* open. It's a very important role."

"Oh yes, you always remember the *gatekeeper* in every film, don't you?" She banged the table. "I have his blood, too, you know, just as much as you. What about the secrets that 'whisper' in mine?"

"Shh! Shh!" Her voice had risen in pitch and volume, and he waved his arms to try and bring her down. But it was too late. His mother didn't know to step over stairs three and five on the last flight down if she didn't want to be heard.

"That's Mum," he whispered, then stuck a finger to his lips. "Not a word, eh?"

"No, no, let's tell her we've been raising her father's ghost in the attic!" she hissed, just as the door opened.

"What are you lot doing up?" Sonja stood there in her dressing gown, rubbing her eyes.

"Couldn't sleep," they both said simultaneously. Then Kristin got up, yawned, and said, "But I can now, I reckon."

"Me too."

As they passed Sonja in the doorway, she reached out, fondled Sky's head. "You know, all that talk earlier? I was having the strangest dream. About my father. About you. Your faces kept . . . blending. I couldn't tell who was who half the time." She smiled sleepily. "It was a nice dream."

Kristin and Sky walked up the stairs together. They could hear his mother dumping their cups in the sink, running the tap. On the landing outside their doors, Kristin whispered, though it was more of a hiss, "All right, I'll do some research tomorrow. But just so I won't have to be terrified like that again. Bound to be some stuff on the Net."

"Fetch.org.uk?" Sky said. "Werunetheworld.com." When she didn't smile, he grunted. "Um, we don't have a computer."

She looked at him as if he'd just descended from the planet Tharg. "No . . . computer?"

"Our last one broke. Dad's planning on getting one soon, but . . ."

He didn't want to say that the computer wasn't the only thing that was broke. The move to this house had cost a lot, and with Mum not yet working . . .

"Never mind," she said briskly, "local library will have one. I'll go there in the morning."

"I'll go with . . ." He never finished the sentence because his words were spoken to her disappearing back. She went into her room and shut the door, none too quietly.

Sighing, he shut his. He suddenly felt as tired as he'd ever been. Not so tired, though, that he didn't check the wardrobe, look under the bed. Only when he finally climbed in did he realize he'd left the light on. Which was just fine.

Exhausted, he slept late. She was gone before he woke up.

"So hardworking, your cousin," his mother said when he came down for breakfast. "Goes to the library on the first week of her holidays. That's how she got so smart. You could learn from her, Sky."

"I hope so," Sky muttered into his cereal. His sleep had been disturbed, dream strewn. Nothing he could remember, just a feeling of discomfort that had only grown as the clocks ticked and sounded, their arms marching evenly and relentlessly forward to midnight. Of course he wanted to go, but . . . did it have to be tonight? Sigurd had said he must make another journey then, visit this ancestor, but . . . where? When? Above all, how? He knew virtually nothing about runes. He certainly didn't know how to use them to "travel" anywhere. It wasn't like buying a train ticket. He needed to "do" something. What? The confidence he'd felt the night before had evaporated with daylight and rough sleep.

Kristin found him later in the orchard. Since his parents had gone shopping, he was amusing himself taking shots at last autumn's deadfalls.

"Want a go?" He held the air rifle out to her. They'd had lots of competitions over the years. Though Sky practiced more, Kristin often won.

She shook her head. "We've got better things to do." She waved her bag at him. "I've found out stuff."

"Like what?" He took aim at an apple, missed.

"Well . . . OK, which do you want first? The bad news . . . or the bad news?"

He groaned, which made her giggle. "No, don't worry, Sky. There's good news too. Apart from the fact that you're cursed, of course."

"What you mean?"

She pointed at the bulge under his shirt. Both knew the leather pouch with the caul lay there. "You can't help doing what you are going to do."

"I can," he said angrily. He'd never liked being forced into things. "I don't have to do anything. I can keep away from the attic and chuck this caul and those poxy stones in the pond."

"Well, from what I've been reading, your Fetch would still go a-walking. And Sigurd's ghost would not stop a-calling."

"Would you stop a-speaking that way. It's not a joke!"

She looked a little sorry, though a smile still hovered

in her eyes. "No, you're right. Maybe I'm just trying to laugh it off. It is all a bit creepy, I have to say."

"What did you find out?" he sighed, exasperated. "Stop the jokes and hints and just tell me, will you?"

He'd walked away, to a tree that had a thick branch low to the ground. She followed, sat beside him. There was a creak but their seat held.

"OK, so here it is." She reached into the bag, produced a notebook, opened it. "Pathetic little library didn't have a working printer, so I had to take notes. How do you live in the countryside?" She was flicking through the pages. "Ah, here it is."

She crossed her legs, cleared her throat, and Sky, despite feeling unsettled, had to smile. *Kristin!* She was just so . . . together!

"So. Sigurd told you your Fetch is like this other . . . being in you, that can go a-"—she stopped herself—"can leave your body and travel around, yes?" He nodded. "Well, what he didn't tell you was that there's not just one Fetch. There's two."

"Two?"

"At least two. But the ones that are written about most—and they seem to appear in most cultures in the world but especially in the northern European ones—of those two, one is physical, can actually appear and do things. A body double."

Sky nodded. He was thinking of what had happened at school.

"That one, apparently, can also go into animals.

Like, take them over. Run around as a wolf but retain the human brain."

"And the other? The second Fetch?"

"Ah, now! That one doesn't have a body, it's just a spirit, invisible to sight. Our ancestors called it a *fylgya*. That's the one that can appear in dreams, the one that can disregard both time and space. And when the person dies, it's that spirit, that awareness, that goes on as—"

"As a ghost!" He finished her sentence for her. "He did talk a little about that. His spirit double that survived death. So that's what Grandfather is now. This . . . fylgya."

"Correct."

Sky bounced slightly on the branch, making it creak loudly. "So . . . that must be what left me and went to see him last night."

"Also correct. Your 'living' fylgya met up with his dead one." She grinned. "It's well creepy, isn't it?"

Sky nodded, shuddered. Something twisted and dived through the air. He thought it might be a bat but then realized it couldn't be. Not during the day. But the thought of a bat reminded him of the mink in the attic, the fox in the wood. "Can this fylgya, the dead person's one . . . can it go into animals too?"

She looked at her notes. "Dunno. Don't think so. Why?"

"Oh . . . nothing." Sky stared up, searching for whatever had flown above them. "OK, so was that the end of your research? What about runes?"

"Now, that is the weird . . . well, the start of weird*er* things." Her voice lowered. "So I type 'rune' into the search engine and . . . what do you think came up?"

"Seven hundred and eighty thousand entries?"

"Nothing."

"Nothing?" He frowned. "That can't be right. There must be rune pages."

"I'm sure there must. But nothing came up because the computer crashed. Soon as I hit 'enter.'" She lowered her voice. "And the librarian said that hadn't happened in six months."

"Coincidence," he muttered. Then he felt both disappointed and strangely relieved at the same time. If he didn't know more about runes, there'd be no traveling at midnight. He wanted to go, of course he did. But he needed a good night's sleep first. "So you didn't find out anything? Shame."

He started to rise from their perch. She pulled him back down. "Oh, but I did." She was reaching into her bag again. Like most girls' bags, it was overflowing with rubbish, and she seemed to be having difficulty finding what she wanted. "There's a secondhand bookstore across the road from the library, yeah? So I went in there, wandered down the stacks, and . . . ah!" She was pulling something up from the bag's depths. "In the farthest corner, *this* was lying on the floor."

A book came out of the bag. It was old, Sky could see that immediately. Both covers were missing and someone had bound it with pieces of cardboard, held together with yellowing, fraying tape. Maybe that same person had scrawled the title on the front in ballpoint. Or maybe someone else had. . . .

Rune Magic, it read. And Sky felt coolness on the back of his neck like someone's breath in a graveyard at midnight. He jumped up, looked around, looked back at her. "Cut it out," he shouted. "The book couldn't have just . . . just been lying there."

"It was." She squinted up at him. "Of course it was."

"Well, who put it there, then?"

"I don't know. Stop shouting. No one did. It was just there."

"Just there? For you to find? Very likely." He suddenly had a terrible thought. "Is this *all* a setup, Kristin? The runes, the chest, everything? Maybe you've been studying hypnosis or something at your posh school, along with Ouija and . . . and . . . thigh slapping! Maybe you decided your holiday project was going to be tormenting me?"

"What? Where's all this coming from?" Her voice matched his in anger now if not volume. "I *did* just find the book, thank you very much. It *was* just lying there. And you want to know what else?" She began riffling through the pages. "It's full of diagrams, charts . . . incantations! It's exactly what we need for you to take your journey."

"Oh, of course it is." His sudden fear, that cool breath on the back of his neck, made his tone even more sarcastic.

"Well, don't believe me, then." She held the book toward him as if she wanted to be rid of it. "Wasn't that my job, as *researcher*"—she stretched the word out bitterly—"to find out how to get you on the path? And this is the thanks I get?" She waved the book at him. "Go on. Take it."

He didn't want to take the book, he didn't and at the same time . . . he did, more than he could remember wanting anything in the world. It was as if his hands fought a war, one reaching toward the book, one wrapping around the tree trunk as if to not let him. He was being pulled apart.

Tires rolled onto the gravel of the drive. His parents were back. Gesturing to the book, he said, "You keep it. Till later."

"Why should I?" She thrust the book closer to him. "I mean, if you don't believe me . . ."

"I do . . . believe you. I'm just . . . a little freaked out by it all, OK? Look, I've got to go and hide this." He lifted the air rifle. Then he noticed how annoyed she still looked, so he reached out, touched her hand holding the book. "I'm really grateful, Kristin, honest. But put it away, please. We'll look at it later. Tonight. Tonight! In the attic."

Above him he heard wings again, the faintest of shrill cries. He looked up, but he still couldn't see anything.

93

CHAPTER EIGHT

BLOOD SHED

"Look, he must have said *something* else."

"He didn't! I told you everything he told me. I'm to journey to my ancestor and use that rune to do it. *Thurisaz.*" He pointed to the runestone at the top of the cast. Its meaning was "a thorn," according to Kristin's book, and it looked like a thorn on a rosebush. "But he never said how!" Sky had slumped back, his knees sore from kneeling on the floorboards of the attic, his eyes tired from staring down at the runecast they'd laid out, the one that was in Sigurd's journal. They'd been up there over three hours, ever since his parents went out to their dinner party. There were just ten minutes to go till midnight, and they had not a clue what they were going to do when the clock struck twelve.

"He must have said who this ancestor was."

"No. Just that he was a he and that I'm drawn to him."

"Yeah, but when did he live? What did he do? Was he a farmer? Road sweeper? Children's entertainer? What?"

Sky groaned. "He didn't say."

"Well, you're not much help!" Kristin did not seem as tired as him. "OK, let's go through it again." She ignored Sky's next groan, reached for the rune book, lifting it into the little light that his electric lantern, with its new bulb, gave out. There was no help from the moon tonight; rain had fallen ceaselessly against the skylight. They'd stuffed a plastic bag in the broken pane to keep the wet out. She had draped the mink wrap around her shoulders because it had gotten cold again, the bit of warmth they'd had during the day a tease of summer. He was trying to ignore the creature's beady eyes.

"So the one you used before," she said, pointing, "is *Othala*, rune of ancestors . . ."

"Rune that summons," he said with her. He had been scared to handle it, thinking it might burn him again or whip him off fast somewhere like it had before. At her urging he'd finally lifted it . . . and nothing had happened! It wasn't even hot anymore, as if its energy had been all used up.

"But he did tell you to ignore the other runes for now, concentrate on this *Thurisaz*, yes?"

"He said to take the runes one at a time. Sort of 'Don't run before you can walk,' I suppose. *Thurisaz*," he called from his prone position, "is the rune of attack, right?"

"Yeah, but according to the book it's much more than that. It's also a test. And a journey." She leaned over him. "So you travel to find something out about yourself. To be tested."

"By attacking someone? Being attacked?" He groaned again. "Anyway, if it's a test, why don't you go? You're the one who's done all the exams!"

"I wish I could, believe me."

He pulled himself up to sitting, snatched up the rune again. It did have the faintest touch of warmth to it, but none of the shock he'd felt on handling *Othala*. He sighed. "Your book's not much use. Doesn't it tell you anything about how to . . . get into this?" He waved the stone at her before replacing it in position.

"No," she said defensively, "it doesn't talk about 'getting into' individual stones, but about how to do runecasts and then how to interpret them. Doesn't talk about how to interpret one someone else has already laid out either." She snapped her fingers. "That's it! We have to do one of our own."

"What, in"—he squinted at the watch he kept on the bookshelf—"in seven minutes we'll unravel the mysteries of the universe?"

"Maybe not. But even in the little I've read I know it's not about knowing it up here"—she tapped her head—"but feeling it in here." She placed a hand on her chest.

"That's what he said too." He came back onto his knees, rubbed his eyes. "Right, let's try. What do we do?"

She was flicking through the book, stopped at a

page. "There's a simple runecast, the simplest. You pull out three stones, lay them out side by side. First one tells you—"

"Let's just do it," he interrupted. "It's nearly midnight. How do we begin?"

"Turn 'em all upside down so we don't know which is which. Yeah, do the ones from his cast as well. We need them all."

Sky did, mixing in the runecast too. Soon they were lost in the black-backed stones. "Now?"

"Shuffle them. You know, mix them up but . . . you have to do them in one direction, like a swirl." One hand held the book, and she circled her other in the air above the stones. "And go counterclockwise."

"Why?"

She was still reading. "They used to call counterclockwise 'widdershins.' It's the Left-Hand Path, apparently. Better for a certain kind of question."

"Which kind?"

She looked up from the book with a faint smile. "The scary kind."

Grunting, Sky did as he was bid. The stones clacked and swirled together, and though he was quite forceful, none spilled over to show their faces.

"What next?"

"It says here you must focus in. Try to clear your head of stuff. Go blank. And then refocus only on the question. Then pull out three stones and lay them down. Don't turn them over yet."

He shut his eyes. But instead of a desired blankness, his mind filled with colors and light, spotlighting everything he'd been thinking about—Sigurd, the sea chest, runestones, the talking mink, creaking steps, gravestones, grave mud, hooded men. The more he tried to shut them out, the more they poured in, took over. *Question?* There were dozens, each jostling for space between his ears, shoving each other to fight for prominence as if they were contestants in some competition, aching to be chosen. His life had become *all* questions in the few days that the sea chest had been in the house . . . well, there were a few before that, he supposed. But since the discovery of his grandfather's legacy it was the stones that had led him on.

And she wanted him to choose just one?

Even with his eyes fast shut he was aware of her attention on him, willing him to choose, and that only made it worse. Himself he could let down . . . but Kristin? It was like when the two of them wall-walked: You always went back if the other fell. You always—

Went back! Sweat broke onto his face, though his skin was cold. Images cascaded, never staying long enough to latch onto, pin down. He suddenly felt a little faint and realized he'd forgotten how to breathe. His hand rose up, as if to knock his chest into life, and touched something dangling there. A leather pouch, something firm within its softness; something that had been with him all his life . . . no, from before his life. Something that had connected him to his mother and through her blood, back to . . . forever. It was his caul and Sigurd had had one, too, and as he touched it, all the frantic images swept from his head and gave him the question.

"How do I return to my ancestor?" And saying it out loud, he opened his eyes and, in the same moment, reached forward and pulled three stones from the swirl before him. There was nothing to distinguish them from any of the others. Yet he knew instantly that they were the only ones he could choose.

He laid them down in the order that he'd picked them up, then looked at his cousin. She was staring at him intently.

"Are you sure?" she said.

"Oh yes."

"Then turn the first one over. This is the rune of . . . 'what is already.'"

He turned it over. He knew it.

"*Raidho,*" Kristin said. "Wow! A rune from the cast. How likely is that?"

"Quite likely." Sky had been surprised too. But now he'd chosen, there was a part of him that wanted to deny his choices, any significance to them. "I mean, there are twenty-four runes, right? And five in the cast? So the odds are better than one in five of getting one of them."

Kristin nodded grudgingly. "Well, I still think it's exciting. And we know what it means. 'A journey.' So the first rune shows what has already been decided:

the journey you need to take." She looked up, past him to the skylight. "What's that?"

"What?" He'd been so focused that he hadn't noticed the noise coming from behind him. Now he did, and he turned. Something was scrabbling at the panes of glass.

"It's nothing. There's ivy up there . . . ignore it," he said impatiently. "I'll turn over the second rune." He reached for it.

"It's not a plant," she said, stopping his hand en route. "The scratching's too regular. Have a look."

"Oh for God's sake." He lifted the lantern, raised it to the sloping roof. The faint beams ran across the roof slats, glanced across the panes . . . and caught eyes, staring, contracting in the sudden light.

"What is that?" Kristin had jumped back.

Sky looked closer. "A bat."

"A . . . bat? Eugh, all that leathery skin and . . . yuck! They're disgusting!"

"They're not, they're quite clean actually. And they're not going to bite you or anything. He's after moths drawn to the light, that's all."

"I thought bats were tiny. That one's . . . huge." She shuddered. "It can't get in, can it?"

"Of course not." If Sky was amused by this sudden and rare display of weakness by his cousin, he was mostly just annoyed at the interruption. "You've been watching too many vampire movies. Can we please get on with it? Its three minutes to midnight and . . . look, anyway, it's gone."

The bat, after a couple more flutters against the glass, had indeed flown off. Sky turned back to the runecast. Reaching, he flicked over the next stone. "Now, that . . . that is a little strange."

"What?" Kristin, who'd still been staring at the skylight, looked down.

"*Thurisaz,*" he said, "another rune from the cast."

"Not just another." Her fear was gone, her attention totally forward. "*The* rune that Sigurd said you would travel with. The rune of attack, of the test. So what are the odds against two runes from the cast coming up, Mr. Against All Odds?"

"There's . . . less chance," he admitted. "And what's its position mean?"

She looked down at the book, read, " 'That which is coming into being.' So, what is going to happen, basically."

"We already know that." He studied the two. "So what will the third rune tell us?"

"That's the one that will tell us *how* it's going to happen."

"I'll turn it over then, right?" Now he was there, he was no longer sure he wanted to know. His hand, halted about an inch above the stone, felt like it was being pushed down *and* pulled back. "What if it's another rune from the cast?" he whispered.

Her volume matched his. "Then we'll know. This"—she gestured to the runecast—"is what is meant to be."

He reached forward again, that last half inch, his fingertips hovering over the stone's black back, which no longer seemed dull but full of depth, of movement and light. He could feel heat rising from it. Then, as he willed himself to push that last impossible half inch . . .

Dong!

Midnight had come.

They both jumped. The clock downstairs, by that quirk in the ventilation system, seemed as if it were in the attic with them. Sky sat back, pulling his hand from the heat, and as he did, the caul, which had been dangling down, fell again onto his chest. But it didn't rest there. It began to bounce, moving out and then back to hit him, moving slowly and in time with the chimes of midnight. And it suddenly seemed to possess an enormous weight, heavy on his neck, tugging him forward again toward the runecast.

"The last rune, Sky," Kristin said, her voice strained. "Pick it up."

"No," he whispered, even as he tried to resist the tug forward, even as his fingers reached and he snatched up the stone. And the same searing flash and heat he'd had from the other came now but with double strength, not just held in his hand but shooting through his whole body.

With a cry he managed to shake it loose. It dropped straight into the position it should occupy, the final position of the runecast, the one that should tell him how to journey this night. It wasn't a rune from the other

102

cast. This one was an inverted "U" but with straight sides, the right one shorter.

But he had no time to be relieved. No time for anything because Kristin was whispering. It took him a while to understand what she was saying.

"The bat." Her eyes were wide, staring above him. "It's back."

He glanced up, though the effort it took to drag his eyes from the runecast hurt. The bat *was* back, the claws at the ends of its black wings beating frantically against the skylight. The plastic bag, shoved in the hole to keep out the rain, was being twisted, jerked.

"Forget it," Sky said angrily. "It's on the other side of the glass. Tell me what rune this is." He looked up. Her eyes were fixed above. "Tell me now," he shouted.

He had to know. The chimes still sounded, and it was the world's slowest grandfather clock. But seven had already gone.

Somehow she looked down, flicked pages, read. "*Uruz,*" she croaked, "rune of sacrifice. The slaying of the beast."

"Sacrifice?" he echoed. Sigurd had talked about that, how something had to be given up for knowledge. The ninth bell sounded, and the scratching at the window stopped for just a moment, a tiny one, not even long enough for another chime before something smashed against the glass, smashed it in, shards and splinters tumbling down on them, something else falling, flapping, growing larger as wings spread wide and claws reached out. Not for him. For Kristin.

She had no time to move, to even raise a hand to ward it off. The bat was onto her, in her hair, leathery wings spread wide, black against blond. Her shriek was almost muffled by the furred body. It spread over her face, and seeing that, Sky realized that it was bigger than any bat he'd ever seen in England, realized it as he leapt across the short space between them, stuck his hand in the fur on the back, pulled it away. It came, but he could see the scratch marks it left on Kristin's cheek. Then those same claws ripped into him, sinking into his hand. He cried out then, used his other hand to yank it off and throw it, hard, into the roof. But the blow it took didn't stop it; it dropped down onto him again, headed for his face.

He shot up a hand, met it, grabbed it, didn't try to throw it this time, despite the agony as razor teeth joined claws to pierce him. Didn't, because with his other hand, his left, he stretched past a sobbing Kristin to the shelf behind her, grabbing the knife whose blade he'd never folded in. He slammed the biting, squirming, furred body into the floor, lifted it again, slammed it down again, pinned it. Raising the knife, he brought it down hard, driving the point into the center of the bat's chest, skewering it to the floor of the attic.

The creature spat blood, claws raking him as he jerked his hand away. Then Sky was up, over to the other side of the attic, where Kristin had flung herself.

"It's all right, Kristin, it's dead. I killed it."

He felt no elation saying it. And no guilt. He'd shot squirrels, some birds before, with his air rifle till guilt had made him stop. But this killing felt nothing like that. It felt different, and he didn't know how until Kristin told him.

Her hands came away from her bloodied cheek. He'd expected her voice to be panicked, but whether it was shock or courage that made her speak so calmly, he didn't know. "You didn't kill it, Sky."

"I did. I . . ."

"No, you didn't. Look!"

He turned, and her words came as he took in the sight. The bat's wings had dropped down, released by death. The body, pinned by the blade, sprawled over the runecast.

"Sacrifice," she said, her voice a fragile whisper. "You sacrificed it."

And he realized she was right, just as the last stroke of the clock sounded, realized, too, that Time must have paused while he fulfilled the promise of the rune, *Uruz,* rune of sacrifice. It was still midnight, the moment that Sigurd had told him was no longer today, not yet tomorrow. All this he knew in a mind shading into darkness and a body falling through a floor that was no longer there.

Only the rain was the same. Except now, it fell not on the roof above, or through a shattered skylight, but directly onto him. Turning his head to the side, Sky was puzzled by the drops that ran from his long— *long!*—soaked hair.

Before him was a reflection in metal. A shield hung there, at its center a boss of iron. This was odd, but not as odd as the fact that it was not *his* face looking back. There were similarities glimpsed in the streaked metal— the set-back eyes, the fairness of hair. Yet this face didn't have just a trace of hair above the nose. This One-Brow was full, prominent.

A shout came from close behind him. "For Odin's sake, pull your weight, Bjørn!"

He looked back at the shouter. Standing with his arms wrapped round the tiller of the longship stood a huge, bearded man. He was glaring down at Sky. Despite the beard, the furs he wore, the gold dragon brooch at his shoulder, Sky recognized him. In another time he had known him as Sigurd, though he knew the man was not called that here.

"Aye, Father," he said, his tongue forming words he couldn't know in a voice he had never heard before.

Grappling with the oar, he glanced once again into the metal beside him. Bjørn looked back. For the smallest moment, each saw the other. Then something faded in each pair of eyes. No, not some*thing,* he realized, the last thing Sky realized. Some*one.*

Himself.

CHAPTER NINE

VIKING

"Off wandering with the spirits again, Brother? Or just dreaming of Sweet Gudrun?"

Thorolf thumped onto the oar bench beside him, pulling his gaze away from the shield boss, from the strangeness he'd seen there. For those moments, Bjørn had almost believed he was someone else. It wouldn't have been the first time. But the teasing brought him back to himself. His brother had no one as pretty as Gudrun of Holmdal awaiting *his* return; and as for wandering with spirits . . . well, there were those who could walk when their body slept and those who couldn't. Thorolf was just jealous . . . on both scores.

Yet before he could reply, match jest to jest, their father roared again behind them and they bent fast to the oar. Thorkell the Swift was not going to lose his title because two of his sons slackened. His skill in navigation had brought them to the river mouth before all the Norwegian fleet, while the strength of his oarsmen and his own handling of the rudder had kept him ahead even of the king's longship. Three times, King Harald Hardrada's captain had tried to pass him at points where the river widened. Three times, Thorkell had swung his ship out, forced the king's back. At the last, Harald himself had roared, laughing across the gap, "Go then, Thorkell Grimsson. Be the first to land. And take the English arrow that's meant for me!"

Bjørn knew that the king was content. His father had raided up this very river for a score of years. He would guide the fleet to the landfall, where the riverbank sloped down and the longships could be beached. Once ashore, though, Harald Hardrada would follow no one. He had come to claim a kingdom, and you didn't do that from the rear!

Despite again putting his arms and back into the pulling of the huge oaken oar, Bjørn's eyes were free. They moved everywhere, most often to the riverbanks of the land they had come to conquer. England! It was the first country other than his own that he had ever seen, and it was as different from Hareid as . . . well, as he was from the huge lump of a brother who pulled and puffed beside him. On his island, the land rose steep from the harbor to the bleak fells. Any cultivation was done on scant patches of fertile soil. But in this England, well-tended crops stretched away in strips on either side of the water as far as he could see— which was far indeed, for he had the long sight. There were huge pens for animals, whereas on Hareid any family that possessed a single cow kept it safe in the house beside them for most of the year. These pens were empty, though—the English had already driven their animals far from the river as soon as word had spread of the coming of the dragon-prowed ships. But the richness of the land was clear even to one like Bjørn who had not traveled. And that richness they were there to take.

His eyes returned to the ship, his mind to gold. The men had been promised a mighty bounty from this land their king claimed as his right. And Norway had responded to his call to arms—it was said that this was the mightiest war fleet ever to sail and row from its shores. Yet his family—father, mother, brothers, and all—had tried to stop him coming! Too young to go a-Viking, they'd all said. Too young, at fifteen summers!

As at night, when his fylgya would often slip from his skin and go flying, so during the day his mind would leave and be where he wanted it to be. It was a useful trick, especially when tasks were painful—such as the pulling of this oar! Now it went back, to the contest he'd arranged. . . .

"Come, Ingvar," Bjørn cried, pulling his brother from the table where he rolled dice against some other men. "I've better sport."

His brother shook him off, wished to stay at the

hazard. "Go boil your head, Bear Cub. If I do not start to roll better, all I gain on the raid to come I will have to give to these oafs."

The oafs jeered. Bjørn leaned down, whispered, "I've caught a goose. It's yours if you will but come."

He knew his brother's appetites. And a goose supper would pay for many a roll with the bones. Also, Bjørn was his favorite brother, the closest to him in age if five summers younger. So, reluctantly, Ingvar rose. "Back in a moment," he muttered, to more jeers.

Outside the hut, Bjørn led him swiftly to the edge of the village, where a solitary spruce grew that was a favorite for practicing with arrows. Several lads were gathered around it, plucking their latest shots from the bark.

Ingvar halted as soon as he saw where he was being led. "Where's the goose?" he asked suspiciously.

"Safe." Bjørn's eyes twinkled. "Did I not tell you that you must shoot against me for it? I am sure I did."

"Bjørn." His brother groaned. "How many more times must I beat you before you learn? I am the best shot in Hareid. Probably the best in the west of Norway."

"Then I am the second best," said Bjørn. "And the day will come when you miss."

"That day will not be today, Bear Cub."

"Then why should you worry! You'll be eating goose by nightfall." Bjørn smiled.

Ingvar licked his lips, looked around. "Where are my bow and quiver?"

One of the village lads brought them forward. "Ten flights?" Bjørn said.

"We'll shoot till you miss, as always." Ingvar yawned, tested his bowstring's pull, checked his arrows, reached for one. With the speed for which he was famous, Ingvar placed it to the string, pulled. Almost at the same time, it seemed, a shaft quivered from the tree.

"Hurry up and miss," Ingvar said, stepping away.

Bjørn was slower. After all this preparation he wasn't going to rush. He pulled, sighted, let fly. An arrow sprouted beside his brother's.

"Again then." Ingvar lifted, shot, with that ease Bjørn envied. He would probably never be as fluent with the bow as his brother. But that didn't mean he couldn't win.

He shot again, hit again. The arrows flew, until the tree was studded like a hedgehog. Ten were shot, then another five. It took time, and the boys shouted, loud enough to draw a crowd. Bjørn had never lasted past twelve before. Soon, he was aware that his other brothers, Thorolf and Eirik, were there. Finally, even his father, come from the beach where the trees they'd felled were being turned into a ship that could carry eighty men.

"I need water," Ingvar grunted, striding over to a rain barrel beside the nearest hut. "Ah, these boys," he shouted, waving at the crowd. He always enjoyed a crowd, Ingvar, and he decided to walk the last ten paces to the barrel on his hands.

111

It was the moment Bjørn had waited for, the one he'd trusted would come. While eyes were elsewhere, it took but a moment, a reach inside his tunic, a bend at knee. The arrow looked no different from any other in Ingvar's quiver. And his brother had already checked those.

"Come," Ingvar said, wiping his mouth, walking back. "Let us put an end to this foolishness."

He reached, placed the arrow's notch, pulled with that lazy ease, loosed.

The arrow missed the tree by the length of a man's arm. Skittered away down into the rocks by the fore-shore.

There was a gasp, not least from Ingvar. "That arrow was not one of mine," he spluttered. "It did not fly true." He looked at the crowd, at his father, in appeal.

It took a long moment before Thorkell spoke. "Let the boy shoot," he said.

Ingvar looked as if he would protest, then silenced himself. No one argued with his father when a decision had been made. But he whispered out of the side of his mouth to Bjørn, "You'll miss!"

He wouldn't. He couldn't. Cheating was frowned upon by the White Christ's followers. There were many of them in the crowd watching now, including the priest man. But Bjørn, like his father, like Ingvar, still followed the old gods; and Loki the Trickster was his favorite. He wouldn't feel too bad about tricking a brother. But he'd feel terrible if he cheated then missed the tree! Because then his plan to persuade his father to take him to England would be ruined!

He stepped up to the mark. His fingers had run slick with sweat, and he wiped them on his breeches. The tree, in the late-afternoon sunshine, seemed to shimmer and sway. A light wind had sprung up. He licked his lips, took a breath . . .

A last arrow sprouted in the tree.

Somehow amidst all the shouting he heard his father softly say, "Not bad, boy." High praise indeed. Ingvar, meanwhile, in a fury, had taken off for the beach to find that last arrow. But if Bjørn's friend Anders, hidden in the rocks down there, had done his bit, there'd be no arrow to find.

There wasn't. But later, a furious Ingvar sought him out. "I know what you did, you cur."

"Me?" Bjørn kept the table between them, moving now this way, now that, the opposite to his brother's moves.

"You shaved one of my flights."

Bjørn shrugged. Cheating was one thing. But since Ingvar was also a follower of Loki, it was not that big a thing. Lying was something else.

Ingvar halted, so Bjørn did too. They regarded each other for a long while. Finally, in a softer voice, Ingvar said, "Well, Bear Cub. Can I at least share the goose?"

Bjørn's One-Brow bunched in the middle. He waited a long time before he said it. "What goose?"

The roar brought half the village to their doors, in time to see Bjørn running from the village ten paces ahead of his screaming brother. But if there was now some doubt as to who was the better shot, there was none about who was the faster. Bjørn lost him half-way up the path to the fells. . . .

A roared order from his father brought him back to the present, and he raised his oars with the rest of the East-men so that the ship could pass a tangle of logs with ease. It allowed him to turn and look ahead, to Ingvar leaning on his oar three benches closer to the prow. He winked at him, and Ingvar winked back. His brother had finally forgiven him. Partly because, with Bjørn re-placing him in the handling of the bow, it meant that he could take up the role he truly desired, as Thorkell's second spearman. And partly because, like any Norse-man, he admired a good trick, well executed.

But it alone had not been enough. His mother's voice could sway Thorkell when no one else's could. And she argued hard against her youngest being taken, the one who had come so late in her life, whose own life she had saved even at his birth by pulling away the skin that covered his face. This skin, this *hamr*, marked him as a seer, one of those who could travel to the spir-its and the ancestors and seek help there for his people. She had also begun to teach him the secrets of the runes. She said he had the sight. You did not waste one so gifted on an English sword.

There had been one more thing left for Bjørn to do. And as his father ordered them to pull again, as his body bent to work, his mind once more was free. . . .

It was the night before the war band was due to sail for the rendezvous with the king. *Ravager* was on the water, its sail furled, waiting. He came to his father, who sat brooding on his choice.

"I know the village is short of good weapons, Father," Bjørn said, laying something heavy and wrapped in cloth beside Thorkell's mead horn, "so I have brought you this."

The ax shaft poked out from the back sling he had crafted for it, the wood glistening even in the scant light the dung fire gave off. That was partly the result of the night hours spent polishing it, rubbing it with precious oil. Mainly, though, it was from the quality of the wood; for Bjørn had hunted for months for a suitable ash tree to give up a branch. And when he'd found it, he'd sacrificed an edge of one little finger, given the tree wound for wound, mingled blood with oozing sap. Then he'd spent days with his adze, shaving the branch down until it was ready to hold the axhead the smith had promised him—in return for Bjørn's work at the forge for a week and all the beer he could steal.

His father lifted the weapon in one huge hand, turning it this way and that into the light. "This blade," he grunted, "is of an older style, maybe from my grandfather's day. Where did you get it?"

115

"Gray Arnstein," said Bjørn, naming the smith. "He told me it had lain in a corner for a lifetime and more, as everyone wants the heavier heads now, like your Skull-splitter." Bjørn pointed to his father's mighty ax, resting within an arm's length of the table. "But he said its lightness and curves might suit my youth, my size."

Thorkell hefted it in the air, adding his second hand, the blade passing a nose's length from Bjørn's face. He didn't blink. "Arnstein is right, it would suit one such as you. Until you put on some more muscle, like your brothers. It's well balanced." He lifted the ax-head closer to his face, squinted. "And what's this?"

Bjørn knew what his father studied. He himself had etched them into the metal. "The bear claw is my mark. For did you not name me after that fiercest of creatures?"

"And this?

"That is the rune I shall travel by, if you permit me. *Uruz,* rune of change, of sacrifice." He looked his father in the eye, made his voice stronger. "The boy is ready for sacrifice, Thorkell. He is ready to be reborn as a man."

It was the first time he'd ever used his father's given name. The eyes raised to him, blazed for a moment. Then that light died and another look came into them. Somewhat sad, Bjørn thought.

"It may be useful to have a rune reader with us," his father muttered. He looked back down at the ax. "Have you named him?"

"When he tastes his first blood, he will be called 'Death Claw.'"

His father nodded. Then he threw the weapon up in the air. As his son caught it, he leaned forward. "You understand you may not get to use this weapon. If it comes to a fight—and that is by no means certain; the cowardly English may just flee at the sight of so many Norwegians—you will be my bowman. Your ax will rest in its sling while you shoot over the shield wall and bring down the first of my enemies. Is that clear?"

Bjørn knew enough to show no emotion, no joy. "May I go and prepare?"

Thorkell nodded, reached for his mead horn. Bjørn was at the door before his father spoke again. "And Bear Cub?"

"Yes, Father?"

"If you've found Ingvar's last arrow, leave it here, eh? I will need yours to fly straighter."

Bjørn had a smile as he left the hut. But it lasted only as long as it took him to walk around the corner, until he heard his father's voice through the wooden walls and the first of his mother's wails.

Bjørn now looked down at the ash ax handle at his feet, poking out from its sling. And suddenly he had two clear yet opposite thoughts. He hoped the weapon would get the chance to earn the name he'd chosen for it—you could not name a weapon until it had been blooded. But a part of him hoped it wouldn't. Hoped that the English would just melt away in fear, as all suspected. That each Norseman would win a kingdom for his king, share in all the plunder, without having to draw blade or blood. And then that he could take his share of the plunder in fertile land and bring Sweet Gudrun here.

These thoughts—of glory, of fear, of love—danced through his mind as he and his brother pulled hard upon the oar while his two other brothers and the eighty men of Hareid who had joined the expedition pulled hard too. *Ravager* skimmed the water as lightly as Bjørn skimmed the iced lakes of his home on sheets of birch bark. And though the work was wearying, Bjørn did not slacken. No man would betray another by not pulling his weight.

The banks began to narrow, the land blending into water. The river bent, and as they rounded the curve, they all could see it was a promontory that sheltered a bay beyond.

"Eastmen, hold," his father cried loud, and the men on the ship's right dug their oars in, then raised them.

"Westmen, one more pull," he called again, and those on the left, Bjørn and Thorolf included, gave theirs one more hard tug before lifting the blades clear of the water. *Ravager*'s prow swung around, forestem aimed like an arrow at the shore. The ship flew of itself now, a hawk with its wings folded, stooping onto land as if land were prey. The keel grounded on shale and mud, leaning slightly to the side as it did.

His father had timed it perfectly. Yet if the Vikings were surprised to be so suddenly in touch with the land again, their surprise was as nothing to that of the men on the slopes of the riverbank less than an arrow's shot away. Four of them, Englishmen . . . and soldiers, too, for they lifted helmets as they rose, grabbing spears, one a bow. Yet none raised the weapons they hefted against the men who invaded their land. Indeed, each did nothing more than yelp, turn, and stumble back up the slight slope to the four horses tethered there. To the jeers of the Norsemen, the men scrambled into their saddles and, with desperate kicks, were soon away over the rise of ground.

The hoofbeats fading over the greensward, mockery died away. Men studied this piece of the country they had come to help take for their king. It was a wide stretch of shale beach, enough for a dozen vessels at a time to disgorge their crews, then be replaced by the next ships. Even Harald Hardrada's mighty fleet—some said it numbered no less than three hundred vessels—would have its men ashore and swiftly.

But for now there was just one. For this small moment, the land belonged to Thorkell the Swift and the men of Hareid alone.

"Bjørn." His father startled him with the sudden, loud calling of his name. He turned.

"We have a tradition. An honor given to the youngest amongst us, one who has not gone a-Viking before. It is he who will set foot first upon the land. The king's

119

son, Olaf, wanted to claim that right for the whole fleet. But we of Hareid have proved ourselves the finer seamen. We claim the right."

There was a roar up and down the benches. Men who had already begun reaching for spear, ax, and sword now began to thump them upon the crossbeams where their feet had rested. "Grims-son! Grims-son!" came the two-beat chant of their leader's name. And the youngest man there rose from his bench, scared, proud. To the beat, the chant, he stepped over the benches and progressed the length of the ship, laid his hands there on the curve of the forestem. He turned, and the voices dropped to a murmur. One man near him leaned forward, touched his knee.

120

"You are not baptized, lad. This is your chance to come to the White Christ."

Bjørn looked at him, startled. Then he looked back down the rows of men who stared at him. Most leaned back, their oars tipping again into the water. Though Hareid was far from the center of Norway, still half the shipmen had come to the God from the south, taken his water. His mother had, even if she had not put aside her runes; and two of his brothers, Eirik and Big Thorolf, under her influence. He'd thought of it, too, thought that one day, when he needed the White Christ's gentleness to raise a family with Sweet Gudrun, wish fertility onto his wife and his fields, maybe then he'd do the same. These were things that the southern God seemed suitable for. But for now, he needed the protection of someone more suitable.

"For Thor," he yelled, turned. Just before his hands left the wood, he was aware of noise, a shouted command, and movement, a sliding; but he did not allow himself to be distracted. It was only a fall of twice his height, less; he'd jumped from tree branches far higher. He knew to brace his knees against the ground beneath the water, taking the fall, rising up. He was determined not to stumble but to land and stride forward in one movement. As he fell, he saw himself doing this, felt pride in the vision. He was the first Viking ashore in this the greatest of all invasions. . . .

He landed, but his knees did not brace him; had nothing to brace against. For water, he realized, would not hold you up, even if he'd heard that it had once held up the Christ. He sank through the surface, continued falling on and on, down and down. His feet did touch eventually, but by then he had an arm's length of water above him. Kicking off, he reached the surface swiftly and spluttering. The cry of "Thor" had taken all his air.

Once the water cleared from his ears, he heard the noise. The entire crew were lined up, the Westmen leaning on the ship's sides, the Eastmen standing on their benches. All were laughing at him, roaring their pleasure. The oars were once again out of the water. They'd only dipped in the once, on that command Bjørn had heard as he leapt, his father's command to row off the shore.

Thorkell was leaning out over the water, one hand on the afterstem, a huge grin splitting his beard. "Now remind me, Bear Cub, for I can't remember . . . did I ever teach you to swim?"

CHAPTER TEN

BERSERKER

The brothers sat together, a group within the larger group of the men of Hareid.

All unscathed. All hung over. All pissed off.

If Bjørn was in less pain than his brothers—as the youngest by five clear years he had managed to get a far smaller share of the beer and mead the city had sent to the conquering army as tribute—he was probably angrier. They had all fought before, at least; each had been taken raiding by their father in previous years. But Bjørn felt that the battle that had just taken place might be the only one he'd witness in his lifetime. And the men of Hareid had been kept in reserve by Harald Hardrada, a reserve never used because the English army had collapsed so quickly. So by the time they had reached the battleground, they had found just bodies, stripped of everything valuable. No swords, axes or spears, helms or brooches. Few clothes even,

and those that remained no better than the impover-
ished ones he already wore. For four days they'd squatted outside York, close to where the battle had been
fought, while the city negotiated its surrender. The king
had chosen not to sack it because it would be the capi-
tal of his future kingdom—another opportunity for
plunder gone. In those four days all they could do was
look at those who had fought swagger about in their
finely dyed and cut English cloth, listen to them boast
of the brooches they would be taking to their wives
and sweethearts back home. They had sat and watched,
listened and drank, feeling ever more like starlings
amongst eagles.

"What's Father doing again?"

Big Thorolf had already asked this question three
times, but he had the memory of a herring.

Bjørn sighed. "He and the other leaders are with
the king. The city surrenders and sends hostages and
ransom."

"They better send mutton and mead." Ingvar was
trying to squeeze a last drop from a mead skin. He
threw it down in disgust. "I'd go for just water now.
My tongue feels like the floor of the sheep shed." He
groaned and lay back, a hand to his forehead. "Go get
me some water from the river like a nice young brother,
Bjørn."

"Father said we were to all wait here." Eirik, the eldest, laid a hand on Bjørn as he started to rise, eager for
an excuse to be off. "So wait here we will."

"Oh come, Eirik," Bjørn pleaded. "The river's just over that rise. I'll fill these"—he lifted the four empty skin sacks—"and be back in a shake of a horse's tail."

Eirik licked dry lips. He had drunk as much as any of them. As the eldest, probably more. "Go then, boy. But do not dawdle. You'll feel this if you do." He lifted a fist.

"If you think you can catch me." Bjørn laughed as Eirik reached for him, missed, and lay back with a groan and a curse. He turned and considered his route. There was a rough passage ahead of him, made up partly by a little furrow in the ground, mainly by the way the soldiers had their legs thrust out. It was not the most direct way to the water, but it was preferable to trying to pick his way between all the sprawled bodies. You didn't want to step on a Viking on the best of days. On one like this, with a hot September sun in the sky and the beer long run out, you truly didn't want to step on one!

Yet having seen his passage, he immediately didn't take it. Instead, he stumbled, tripped on Thorolf, landed half on him, half beside him. His huge brother cursed, a hand raised to push off. Then he saw Bjørn's face, followed the direction of his gaze. And all words fled.

There was someone walking—limping, one leg dragging—along the rough and narrow line toward them, someone whose approach had caused that line to instantly widen. Bjørn had heard of magicians who could part a river to get across, and that was the look of

125

it here, of water drawn rapidly back. Feet were jerked away at this man's passing, held above the ground long after he'd passed.

"Feign sleep," Eirik whispered, and all the brothers did, even if Bjørn was half sitting on Thorolf's shins.

If they could not see him, there was no mistaking the sound of his approach. It came from the one leg, a stiff and wasted thing that dragged along the ground as the other moved the man forward; came from the gnarled ax handle, pitted with a hundred cuts, that was used to steady him, digging into the wetter mud, scraping across the drier. It came also from the man's breath, wheezed up from a chest whose bones had been broken badly and badly set. And whenever this man passed, another sound always came with him, of voices hissing a warning as Eirik had just hissed.

This man only came down from his cave on the fells twice a year for the supplies the land would not yield. These were given, never paid for. Any sheep he took up there was considered a gift to the gods and never missed, the bones scattered to the winds. When the dogs started to whimper and curl their tails between their legs, when mothers ran into the street to pull their crying children indoors, when even the boldest of men would slip into doorways and clutch the sign of Christ-Cross or Thor-Hammer at their chests and mutter incantations for protection, all knew who was coming. And those same mothers, when a child

126

would not behave and sleep, would raise this man's name as warning, the worst of threats. "Hush, child, and sleep," they'd whisper, "or Black Ulf will come down from the fells and take you!"

The dragging, the wheezing got closer, closer. Bjørn's own breathing came ever more shallow. He knew he must be crushing his brother's legs under him. Both were in pain. But neither moved.

Closer . . . closer . . . and he was there, beside them, and each of the four took a breath, held it, praying silently—two to the White Christ, two to Thor—for Black Ulf to pass them by.

The dragging stopped. The wheezing did not. But the sounds Bjørn longed for, of scraping foot, of ax shaft dragged, never came. Something else did. A voice, unlike any voice he had ever heard before.

127

"Thorkell's brood."

It was the whisper of wind through the marsh grass in the coldest time of winter. The last croak of a bird, suddenly dying as the hawk hit it on the wing. An otter trying to gnaw its own leg off to escape the snare. It was all these. And yet within these sounds was another—a voice, unused to use, conjuring a human quality long forgotten—mockery!

"Brave sons of Thorkell," it came again, barely above a whisper. "Are you dead that you do not breathe?"

They exhaled as one, each then sucking in air that had turned suddenly sour. They coughed, three of them feigning sleep still, feigning it badly. So it was just Bjørn who opened his eyes, though there was nothing willing in the opening. It was as if the lids were forced up.

He had only seen Black Ulf as a shadow limping down a street, or sliding into a cleft of rock on the fells at that time each year when the sheep were gathered. In Bjørn's mind he had become a mix of animal and of something fresh dug from a grave. But what—who—stood before him was undoubtedly a living man, though unlike any he had ever seen before. He was older than belief, his face a mass of wrinkles like scars, as if someone had taken a bone comb and run it again and again from crown to chin. Strange patterns had once been stained with needles into the flesh, but if these had ever stood distinct they were now smeared into a mass by the man's aging. Such hair as remained hung in wispy, gray hanks down the face, and looking closer, Bjørn could see that it was woven with objects—a sparrow's skull, the leg bone of a weasel, the jaws of a fish. Beneath the face, a body thin and twisted was wrapped in black cloth that was full of tears, the flesh revealed traced in scars, great and small, like bloated worms, writhing. On his back was an old and mangy wolfskin.

128

All this Bjørn saw in the moment before he could see nothing but the eyes, which glowed through the scant hair as if through a veil. They were the bright green of a waterfall up on the fells, and when they fixed entirely on him, everything stilled. The whispered warnings down the line, his brother's tension beneath him, even the wind from the water. All gone. It was as if he were suddenly alone with Black Ulf, his mother's whispered threat come into life.

"Bjørn, the Bear Cub." The voice came again, faint, a birdcall in a high wind.

"You know me?" Bjørn tried to make his own voice level, challenging. But it rose and dipped, like that of a boy shading into manhood.

"Know you?" On the face, the wrinkles around the mouth shaped into what could have been a smile. "Know the Viking who was the first ashore in England? Oh, yes." A sound came, like dry leaves rustling. Almost a laugh. "I watched your first step."

All had known Black Ulf was on the longship. All aboard had cursed the fact. He had not rowed, but had lain beneath the decking in the small hold, where sails, arrow sheaves, and spare weapons were stored. "And I remembered my own first time. My . . . baptism." That rustle came again. "Remembered in your swimming, my own. A time . . . before. Before I was . . . before I became . . ."

The voice sank, vanished; a pale fist, gnarled with scar and age, emerged from the tattered cloth to gesture at himself. The green gaze left Bjørn now, yet it was the relief of only a moment for when it came back, the hand came with it, almost touching Bjørn's face. He wanted to draw back, look away; but he was held, as if bound with metal. For clutched in the hand was a leather pouch.

Many men wore them. It was the safest place to store what was most valuable—coins, a God-sign of cross or hammer, a ring-token from a lover. But Bjørn knew that the man before him had never possessed anything most men would consider precious, knew that what was within the pouch had been with him all his life. From before his life. Knew this because a pouch rested against his own chest and contained the same thing—the skin that had covered his face at birth, the skin that had marked him as blessed. Or accursed.

It was clear in the wreck of man before him which way Black Ulf's caul had marked him.

His fist moved, tracing shapes in the air, and Bjørn's eyes followed it. Indeed, it suddenly felt as if sight was all he had, and the voice, when it came, did not slip from behind the veil of gray hair, from the gash of wrinkles that formed the mouth. The voice seemed to speak in his head.

"Remember this time. This time . . . before. And if you have a chance not to fight . . . take it! Let your caul rest, the doorway remain unopened. For then . . . then you will never know!"

The hand slipped back inside cloth, emerged empty. Other sounds returned—the grunt and cursing of men idle and hot, the wind blowing up from the river. And the sounds that had approached them now began to move away, the drag of foot, the wheeze of breath, the clump of wood pushed into the earth. When they had gone far enough, the brothers lying on the ground exhaled as one.

"Thanks to the Christ, he didn't stop." Thorolf had sat swiftly up and was rubbing his legs where Bjørn had sat on him. "You nearly broke my shin, you lump."

Eirik and Ingvar were both staring after the black-swathed figure. Both now muttered in agreement.

"But he did stop."

They stared at Bjørn, mouths wide. Bjørn looked at each, continued, "He spoke to me. You must have heard him."

His brothers still stared. Then Eirik, ever the swiftest, followed by Ingvar and finally Thorolf, all began laughing. "Good try, Bjørn," Eirik said, leaning over to punch his youngest brother on the arm. "And no doubt he invited you up to the fells so he could suck the marrow from your bones, eh."

He punched again, sat back, and Bjørn looked at each of them in turn. They didn't hear, he thought. Black Ulf spoke only to me.

The thought terrified. "Why did Father let him come?" he asked, trying to keep his voice level.

"Because he's a berserker, of course." Eirik replied.

"Him?" Bjørn could not have been more astonished. All knew of the berserkers. They were the fiercest warriors and much prized in a war band, for they had no fear of death, none. Indeed, they sought it—for the warrior who died in battle was guaranteed swift passage to the hall of the gods, Valhalla, where he would feast and fight forever. Many men fought valiantly, succumbed to the red battle mist, strove till the killing was done. But most men stayed themselves, however fierce they became. A berserker . . . changed, transformed into a beast that possessed him utterly, only human in the form, in the wielding of ax or sword. And some said even that was not always true—that those about to be called to the gods did change fully into the beast within, into wolf, into bear.

That is why he has a wolfskin on his back, Bjørn thought. But the terror of the man's words made him wish to deny it. "He can't be! How can you have an *old* berserker? It isn't possible. They go unarmored, naked apart from their skins, to where the fight is fiercest. They die young, then live forever in Valhalla."

"And that's why Father let him come on this voyage." Eirik had leaned in so his words were only for his brothers. "They were youths together—"

"Youths?" interrupted Ingvar, shocked. "How can father and that . . . that wreck be the same age?"

"It's the life each has lived that's done that, I think." Eirik shrugged. "Nevertheless, together they went a-Viking for the first time. But on that raid, the Wolf came to him. Black Ulf went *berserk*. And on the next and the next. Yet each time, no matter how terrible the wounds, he lived. And then there were no raids for a while and he drank and he drank and his woman threw him out and he went to live on the fells. And when the war horn sounded, he was too drunk to hear its call.

Years went by, till he became as you see him now."
Eirik's voice sank to whisper. "But if a berserker does
not die in battle, if he dies drunk in his bed or his cave,
there will be no Valhalla for him, no feast until eternity.
He will live forever . . . but as a draug . . ." Eirik shuddered. "A Shadow, who can only watch as humans love,
live, fight, die. A walking corpse that does not even
know he is dead. So Black Ulf, when he heard of this
invasion, came to Father, begged to be taken. And how
could Father deny his old comrade, however low he
had sunk, this last chance for paradise?"

Thorolf's voice was awestruck. "But . . . he can
hardly lift the ax handle he leans on. How will he be
able to lift a weapon?"

"He won't need to," Bjørn said softly, seeing it, "as
long as he can lay himself under the stroke of an English one."

133

As he spoke, he rose, snatched up the water sacks,
and turned away. The passage that Black Ulf had opened
had not yet closed. He began to walk down it. He needed
to be alone.

No one knows if they have this animal within, he
thought as he walked, *can* know only when the warriors join and blows are given and received. It was something that the gods, mighty Thor, Odin the Allfather,
gave. It was both blessing and curse. But he knew that,
if he had a choice, he would not be so chosen. He
wanted to fight, fight fiercely beside his brothers, before his father. But he wanted to win glory and booty

and go back home with it, to marry Sweet Gudrun of Holmdal, to raise a family of his own. That would be paradise enough for him.

Maybe it is good that we have conquered a kingdom with just this one battle, Bjørn thought. Maybe it is good that I missed it.

Ashamed of the thought, relieved by it, he pushed down the passage of pulled-back legs. It brought him to a rise. The river wound below him, but the banks here were steep, so he followed the little hill along till he came to a path down. The hill rose above him, and he knew that from its crest he would be able to see York. Knowing that his father had gone with the king to receive the tribute and hostages from the city, he decided to climb to the top and look down. Perhaps he would see Thorkell returning with goods, beer, gold.

But when he got to the top, he saw something else.

CHAPTER ELEVEN

THE BATTLE OF STAMFORD BRIDGE

It was hard to tell what it was at first, other than a mob of men. Those in the foreground were on foot, those behind mainly mounted; all were moving fast toward the gap between the hill Bjørn stood on and the one beside it, toward the valley he'd come from. Many were shouting as they ran or rode, and Bjørn thought immediately that they must be shouts of excitement, joy; the tribute had been paid, part of it in horses, and this mob was bringing that tribute back to the Viking camp to share. This thought held while he scoured those below him for his father, always distinguishable because of his height. But when he spotted him, with an even taller man beside him, he realized that something was wrong. Very wrong.

Thorkell Grimsson was running beside Harald Hardrada. And less than an arrow's shot behind them, the men on horses, with chain mail on their chests and spears in their hands, were slaughtering King Harald's men.

"Father!" Bjørn had no hope of being heard above the screams. So he dropped the waterskins and ran down. There was only one way for this crowd to come, through the gap between the hills below.

He stayed just up the slope, watched men he knew sprint by, men from his own island who had no eyes for him, no ears, either, despite his calling. Only when his father, matching the king stride for stride, ran by did Bjørn descend. It felt immediately like he was caught in a surge of sea, buffeted by jabbing elbows, nearly knocked to the ground. Somehow he kept his feet, struck out himself, forced his way to the gray-gold heads that towered above the rest.

"Father!"

Thorkell glanced down. Eyes widened for a moment. "Bjørn!" he gasped. "Where are your brothers?"

"Ahead." He struggled to keep up. "Father, what—"

"The English king . . . Godwineson . . . came through York while we waited for . . . for our tribute." Thorkell's words came in gusts, wrenched out.

"He hunts me as they do the deer . . . in their fields." King Harald's breath was less forced despite his greater age. "But let me get to my spear and my house-carls and we will show him that . . . that this stag can fight!" His voice, despite the running, boomed like a wave smashing into a sea cave. He looked behind him as he ran, so Thorkell and his son did too. Bjørn could see that men had fallen there, causing others to trip and fall in their turn. The gap between the hills was suddenly a mass of bodies, with the English on their rearing horses, stabbing down with their long spears.

"Good," said Harald Hardrada. "That will delay them for a while." He slowed, almost to a walk, as panickers still fled past them. "Thorkell Grimsson, can you . . . muster the men here, hold them off till I have got across there"—he gestured to the opposite bank of the river, where the bulk of his army lay—"and can bring my men to your aid?"

"I can, my lord. No, I will."

"Good." The king glanced down at Bjørn. "So this is the Bear Cub who was first ashore?"

Thorkell nodded. "Bjørn, youngest of my house."

"Do your father proud, boy," the king roared, and was gone, sprinting once again, this time toward the river, to the narrow bridge there, buffeting aside smaller men who blocked him.

The cries and shrieks grew louder behind them, another look back confirming that those who had fallen were dead or dying, those who had survived were coming on. Most of these were English and on horses.

"Your brothers?"

"This way, Father."

Bjørn led, darting between men who were staring past them at the pursuit. Most had weapons, shields strapped to their backs. Almost none had their mail shirts and coats; after the victory, they had sent them back to the ships as too heavy to carry around or wear in the hot autumn sun.

Thorolf, when they found him, had his on. It had been made for him for this raid and had taken every piece of silver he'd earned on the last. He'd refused to be parted from it. Like Ingvar beside him, he held a great spear across his chest. Eirik had his father's shield at his feet. In one hand he grasped his father's huge ax, Skullsplitter, the haft end resting on the ground. In his other hand he held his father's helmet, a cone of heavy metal, a strip of steel down the nose.

Thorkell took it, shoved it hard onto his head. Then, lifting the ax, he waved it two-handed above his head and, in a roar that pierced even the milling mob's yells and shouts, cried, "Men of Hareid. To me! A-Grimsson!"

Skullsplitter was recognizable to all from their land. Men started to rally to it. Keeping it hefted high, Thorkell, with his sons around him, began to march toward the river.

"There's a rise just before the bridge. There we'll stand."

Bjørn looked up the valley. The bulk of the English horsemen had pushed through now, were scattering among the Vikings, who fled, bloodied spears rising, falling, rising again an even deeper red. His fingers felt slick on the bowstring, for he had notched an arrow as soon as he had his weapon in his hand. He was his father's bowman; he had his role, but his arms felt as if they could not pull with the strength required. Maybe it was the weight of his own ax on his back in the sling he'd made for it. Like Thorolf with his suit of mail, he'd refused to be parted from his weapon. It had no name yet, for it could only be named in battle. So if he lost it, how would he be able to call for it?

His father was at the top of the small hill in three strides. Once more Skullsplitter was shaken in the air, now drawing forth a cry from the eighty men of their village. "A-Grimsson!" With a single sound like a door bolt driven in to shut out the night, the Hareid men locked shields. Men from other villages, other parts of Norway, fled past them, crowding the bridge that could take only two abreast. But they were getting across. A glance back told Bjørn that the king had raised his raven banner, Land-waster, and men were mustering to it.

139

On the hill where Bjørn had stood only moments before, horsemen had gathered. One was alone at the summit, slightly apart, the men below looking up at him. With a gesture, he waved to something behind him, on the other side of the hill. Four last horsemen heeled their horses away from the gap. And the army of England marched through it.

"May Christ watch over me this day." It was just one whisper that went down the ranks of Hareid, though all the gods were called upon, and none. Rank upon rank of men were advancing, as thick as bees clustered on honeycomb.

The front ranks halted before them, though more and more kept arriving, spreading around their slight rise. Axes, spears, and swords glimmered in the late afternoon sun. All these men had mail shirts while, among the Vikings who faced them, Thorolf stood out as one of the very few who had not sent his away. Still, when the vast English host cried the name of their king—"Godwineson!"—and beat their weapon butts upon their shields, the men of Hareid answered back with "Grimsson!" in a shout nearly as loud.

Then the silence came. Bjørn had heard the tales. There was this moment, before the battle commenced, as men stared at other men whom they would soon try to kill, who would try to kill them in return. A moment that could break a war band who felt themselves outnumbered—as the Norsemen were—or in too impossible a position. A moment when lesser men would turn and flee, take their chance on the narrow bridge, in the dark water.

Such men did not come from Hareid.

"What do you wait for, Godwineson?" Thorkell's deep voice rose above his ranks. "After so many stabs in the back, does the thought of looking in our eyes daunt you?"

An English voice, but speaking the tongue of Norway, came from a man still mounted on his horse, the same man Bjørn had seen sending his army through the gap in the hills. Their warlord and king, Harold Godwineson. "We wait to let you see what you face, Norseman. You have no armor and a river at your backs. We have three men to each one of yours, and more coming. Lay down spear and ax. You will have life, at least."

A murmur passed down the Norse ranks. Each man there was a trader as well as a fighter, and all offers needed to be considered. Even dishonorable ones, like this offer of surrender and slavery.

"Life?" The voice that spoke was not the trumpet blast of Thorkell Grimsson. It was closer to a whisper; yet it carried still, up and down their own ranks, across to their enemies. Bjørn had heard it only once before, and it chilled him now as it had then.

"Life?" asked Black Ulf again, slipping between shields like a dark wraith to stand before his countrymen. "What's so wonderful about that?"

He stood there, swaying, his thin, black clothes lifted from his scrawny frame by the breeze. In one hand he held a sword, though it looked more like the sword held him, propping him up against the ground.

The silence lasted a long moment as the Norwegians looked in some terror at what their ranks had disgorged, the silence ended by English laughter.

"Look, they have sent forth a champion!" someone called, and in a moment a man came smiling out of the English line, striding the five paces to where the frail figure leaned.

"Come, Grandfather," the Englishman said, "let us to the fireside and get you a bowl of warm milk."

As he spoke he offered an arm—and Black Ulf took it. Took it in a movement as swift as all his others

141

had been slow, took it in a rise and fall of sword so fast that few people saw it. Certainly the Englishman didn't, Bjørn thought, or surely he would have moved his arm out of the way, not stood there and let it be sliced off at the elbow, standing there a moment longer as the blade returned to once more link Black Ulf to the earth.

Then the screams came, the Englishman's loudest, reeling back to his ranks, spraying them in red. Screams, too, from the Norse ranks as all doubt was swept away, all offers rejected by blood, spilled. And another scream from Black Ulf, not of triumph, not of fear. A scream that began part animal, then became all wolf. Driving the sword into the earth before him, he ripped at his clothes, their thinness no obstacle to his frenzy. In a moment he was naked, covered only by the wolfskin on his back and the froth that was beginning to run from his mouth.

A shout came from the enemy leader, Godwineson. "Enough! Kill him now. Kill them all."

As their mass moved forward, two men came first, half his age, twice his height. And two men died, Black Ulf's blade carving "S" shapes in the sunlight. Then Bjørn lost sight of him as the English advanced and the Norse readied themselves. He had arrows to stab into the ground before him, so his eyes were busy. But his ears could still take in the rising howl of wolf, the shouts of men, the clash of steel. This task done, he looked up, heard the wolf howl suddenly cut off and, just before the shield walls smashed together, saw something flying over all their heads. He thought at first it must be a waterskin, an odd thing to hurl, spinning, over your enemy. Until he noticed gray hair and the skin racked by age, drawn with inks, bones of animals in the hair. And the wild smile on the face of Black Ulf.

He'd always thought he'd be terrified by battle. But though fear was there like an animal burrowing into the walls of his chest, he had no time for terror. He had his job, for his family fought as one—Ingvar and Thorolf with their spears, stabbing at men if they could, reaching to drag down shields if possible so that their father could leap out with Skullsplitter and let the ax live up to its name. The great weapon needed two hands to wield it, and so he would have been open to thrust and jab if Eirik, the nimble one, did not leap before him, taking any blows aimed at the axman, deflecting them away, leaving the enemy open. And then Bjørn would shoot, in the half moment that flesh was revealed, aim for a face beneath the helm, an armpit when sword was raised. He shot and missed, shot and hit, knew he'd killed, knew he had no time to glory in it. The arrows he'd shoved into the ground were soon gone as the English wave stormed on, broke against the rock of Norwegian shield, stepped back to storm again. He found others, jerked from the bodies of men who fell beside him, snatched from the arrow sheaves of those less lucky than him, face down on the reddening earth. His fingers burned and bled from the bowstring, and still he shot, still Thorolf and Ingvar stabbed

143

and snagged, still Eirik spun and blocked, still their father smote down. And a pile of bodies began to build before them.

It could not go on. The English had the numbers, and their men had mail armor. One of their warriors could take a cut and not be hurt, but the Vikings had only flesh. The ranks began to sag as shield men fell and were not replaced. To their left, three men suddenly died. The line bent, broke.

"Thorolf!" Bjørn screamed as his brother stabbed forward, not noticing the gap in the line at his side. There were two Englishmen in it turning to him, and Bjørn only had an arrow for one. That one fell back, clutching at the feathered stick suddenly sprouted in his eye. But the other English warrior raised his ax up high to where the death strokes begin, and Thorolf's mail shirt, which he was so proud of, was no proof against it.

"No," Bjørn screamed, leaping forward, snatching up Thorolf's spear, thrusting up in his turn. The Englishman threw himself back, beyond the blade, and Bjørn stumbled, his hands slipping to either side of his brother's head, watching the light that had lingered there flee.

His tears blinded him; and it was as if they flooded his ears, too, so little did noise come in. Faintly, he heard his father, the battle cry "A-Grimsson!" Vaguely he was aware of that father above him, of his other brothers there, too, formed over him now, over him and dying Thorolf, spear thrusting, shield blocking, Skullsplitter striking down. He looked up and a man was running at him, spear drawn back. Bjørn saw his death in the blade. He would be joining his brother soon. Perhaps he had done just enough to earn a seat beside him in Valhalla.

And then his father was before him, his ax raised high. But Eirik, slipping in reddened mud, was not able to ward the blow—so the death meant for Bjørn took Thorkell instead. The spearhead had been driven with the force of a running man; it plunged through his father's chest and out the other side. And his father's death cry, that mighty voice sinking to nothing, drowned in blood, brought the noise of battle back full force to Bjørn's ears; and with sound returning came . . . something else.

145

He'd thought the burrowing at his chest cage that he'd felt from battle's start was fear. He was wrong. He knew it as he rose slowly from his crouch, looking at the Englishman who was trying to jerk his spear back from his father's body. Knew it as he reached up behind him to the sling on his back, as his hands touched the ash handle he'd carved so lovingly. Knew it as he slid the ax out, at the same moment that his enemy pulled his weapon free. And knew it best when he brought the axhead over in a cut that would have cleaved the thickest log, his hands sliding down the shaft to meet so that both took the force and blade bit through helmet as if it were a whorl of butter.

The burrowing wasn't fear. It was a bear being born.

There was only a little of himself that he kept. Bjørn's clothes he shredded with his claws so that he could feel the breeze and the blood of his enemies on his skin. But he kept Bjørn's knowledge that if tooth and claw were strong, this ash stave, tipped in steel, was stronger. His enemies learned it, too, before they died. And the little bit of him that was still Bjørn knew one more thing: that he was alive as he had never been alive before. He could die now, now that he had discovered who he was, what he was.

He was Bjørn the Bear. And he was a berserker.

It could not last. No matter how many Englishmen he killed, there were always more, while there were less and less of his kind. Though he howled and struck and tried to drive forward, those around him were being forced back. And since a bear is cunning as well as fierce, he knew he needed help if he was to keep on killing. So he let himself slide back with the others, all the way to the banks of the river till there was nowhere left to go. Still, he would fight on. But swords struck from left and right, axes from above, spears from everywhere. One cut his leg, one his arm. Then a swung shaft hit him hard in the side of his head and he was over, tumbling backward down the steep slopes, into the dark water.

It closed over his head, so cold that the shock started to bring the bear out of Bjørn. And the first thing he realized . . . he was not alone in that chill darkness; something bumped and nuzzled at him. With his unwounded arm he reached up, tried to fend it off; but his fingers snagged in what felt like strings of seaweed. Caught, he drew the thing toward him just as he broke surface, gasping for air.

Eyes the green of waterfalls! Berserker held berserker, and Black Ulf's eyes, in his severed head, gleamed.

CHAPTER TWELVE

REFLECTIONS

With a shriek, Bjørn hurled the head away from him. It bobbed for a moment on the surface, then sank, teeth still parted in that wild death smile. On the riverbank, the Vikings' final resistance had been broken, the last men tumbling into the water to escape the thrusting English blades, joining the bodies that floated there, already dead, and the others, like Bjørn, striving desperately not to drown.

He was a strong swimmer. But he swam now with one leg and one arm slashed, the other two hard-pressed to keep him afloat. And something was pulling him down, as if hands grasped him. He thought, It's Ulf. He wants me to join him. But . . . no, the pulling was coming at his neck, as if a heavy stone were tied there.

His head dipped below the surface. He forced it back up, gasped air, glimpsed a huge Viking on the tiny bridge holding back the English horde; glimpsed a head pushing through the water toward him. If he'd had air, he'd have screamed. But it wasn't Black Ulf. It was Ingvar.

"Bjørn!" his brother cried. "Bjørn! I come."

He could not wait. Each time his head sank, each time he forced it up, Ingvar seemed farther away. His one good arm and leg were weakening. The weight at his neck was growing heavier.

What was it there? As he went under again, he reached, grasped. A leather pouch was in his hand, held by a cord around his neck. He was about to take it off, free himself of the burden, when a voice spoke in his head. He had heard the words before, though he didn't know where, when, or who had spoken them.

"The caul is the doorway," the voice said.

"Bjørn!" he heard Ingvar cry.

He let the caul go. The pouch sank against his chest, weight returning, twice as heavy as before. He could resist no more. Even as his brother's hands reached for him, he began to sink.

For the longest time there was no bed to the river, nothing to kick off against. A part of him wanted to climb the ladder of bubbles that emerged from his mouth, for he knew they led to the air he needed. Yet no effort lifted him and none could halt his falling. He thought then that this was to be his doom, to rest among the reeds until his body bleached white and became bloated with foul-smelling air. Eventually,

149

perhaps, he'd float to the surface. Bjørn had seen men the sea had taken returned that way. If the English were a civilized people like the Norse, they would take his body and burn it. Set his spirits free. A berserker needed that.

Then he did hit earth, mud first that sucked him in, sealed the mouth that was open and searching. But the mud did not slow him, only slid him on, down. And as he accelerated into a fall, Bjørn felt—*Bjørn felt!*—other things sliding. First, any part of the animal that he'd been, receding into the cage of his chest. Then that . . . that something he'd glimpsed in the shield boss on the longship the morning they'd landed, that had appeared to be both him and yet not him . . . that feeling returning now as he fell, faster, hurtling down, no longer in water, in air, wonderful air, night air, gasping it, shrieking into it . . .

Sky shot from lying to sitting to standing in one moment. The next, he fell again, one leg collapsing under him as if all its tendons had been suddenly cut. But this fall was short, a few feet only to the floor, and it hurt like river mud and black air had not.

Still, Sky thought, it hurts a lot less than being stabbed with a spear.

He knew where he was! Knew it in the jab of runestones in his back, in the rain falling through a broken skylight. He was in the attic. His attic! And someone should be in the attic with him.

"Kristin," he called, his voice quavering. "Kristin?"

No one! She had left him. Alone. How could she have left him alone?

He needed light, had never needed anything so much. His hands, scrabbling around, swept the rune-stones out from under him. They made a din, crunching over . . . was that broken glass? Yes, that was it, the bat. He had killed it, the room still held the iron-tinged reek of its blood. No, he hadn't killed it. *Sacrificed it,* she'd said.

Where was she?

"Kristin?" he whispered.

Then there was a thump against the trapdoor, a scrape across its wood. Someone was about to climb up. Someone? Or something? Had Black Ulf followed him from beyond? This was the trouble with the night terrors that had haunted him all his life. Just when you thought you were out of one . . .

He backed away to the edge of the floorboards. The trapdoor opened, the folded metal ladder lowered down. Then the steps creaked as weight was put upon them. Someone was climbing up. What if that some-one had a hood and no head within it? What if . . . ?

A shape appeared. It had a head. "Kristin!"

"Sky!" She scrambled up. "You're back."

"*I'm* back? You . . . you . . . where have you been?" He had never so happy to see anyone. He'd never been angrier with anyone in his life. "You left me!" he yelled. She tried to hush him, but he went on. "You're not sup-posed to leave me. Ever!"

"Shh! Sky, I'm sorry. I had to. Calm down!"

"Calm down?" he screamed.

"Shh!" She flicked on a flashlight, shone the beam briefly back down the steps. "Your parents came home about five minutes ago," she whispered, "and I heard them go into your bedroom. Then they began to shout because you weren't there. They've been running around downstairs, have checked all the rooms, the garden. . . . I said I'd look in the attic. . . ." Her voice became strained. "But I thought I was going to have to . . . wake you up or something."

"You can't. Don't ever . . ." Sky shuddered. He knew his grandfather had been right: If Sky had been disturbed while his Fetch was walking, he would never have found his way back to himself, caul or no caul. Been stuck forever in . . .

152

He turned away from her, tried to contain the sob that came with that thought.

"Sky . . ." She reached out, touched his shoulder gently. "What . . . what happened back there?"

"I went . . . saw . . . it was . . ." He shook his head, his hand going to cover his eyes. In the house below, he could hear his parents' ever-more agitated calling.

"Like a nightmare?"

It was so inadequate a word that he almost laughed. Instead, he whispered from behind his hand, "What have you done with the bat?"

"The bat? Nothing." She swept the flashlight's beam around the attic. "What have *you* done with it? It was here when I went down."

He looked. The knife was still plunged two inches into the floorboards. But the runes were no longer stained in blood. And the bat's body was gone.

"Your face," he said, reaching a hand toward her. "It's . . ."

Kristin ran her fingers across her cheek. "Nothing," she said, looking at her fingertips for traces of blood. "How can that be?"

He looked at his own hand. The scratches had vanished there too. Then he heard his mother call again, nearer. She was coming up the last flight of stairs.

He swung his feet onto the ladder, began to scurry down. His cousin's words halted him.

"Sky, I'm so sorry. I promise next time . . ."

His neck was level with the floor of the attic. He imagined how he must look to her: disembodied. "There won't be one. So you can do what you like," he said. "Because I am never going back again. You understand? Never!"

For three days, he didn't even go to the floor below the attic. And he barely spoke to Kristin, grunting at her at mealtimes, avoiding her after them. His mother *tsk*ed and said it was a shame they'd had a falling out, as she was here for a while yet. But Sky didn't make any effort to be with her. It wasn't that he really blamed her; he understood why she had left him in the attic. But whenever he did look at her, she was usually buried in the book about rune magic. Or another one; she'd

153

been back to the library, got out others. She'd look up, aching to tell him stuff; aching most to hear what he had to tell her. But he wouldn't. The less he said, the quicker it would all fade. He thought.

He was wrong. He could sometimes hide from his memories, in a book, in football on TV with his dad. Strangely, his few dreams were ordinary to the point of dull. But the pain in his arm and leg grew every day. There was not a mark on his skin. Yet he could barely lift the one, move the other.

On the fourth morning, his mother had had enough. "I'm taking you to the doctor, my lad," she said.

What could a doctor diagnose? He listened when Sky said they were skateboard injuries, even though there was no bruising or scrapes. He nodded, and hummed as he bent the limbs back and forth. Then he sent Sky for X-rays, which almost made him laugh. Was there a machine that could pick up thousand-year-old spear wounds?

"We'll send these to your doctor, Mrs. March," the X-ray technician said, putting the sheets into a brown envelope. "He should have them tomorrow."

They drove into the town. It was market day in Ludlow, and his mother wanted to do some shopping. "Do you want to come with?" she said, when she finally found a place to park in a road not far from the castle.

"No, thanks." He hated shopping at the best of times. And his leg was really throbbing. "I'll just wait for you here."

"Won't be long." A quick—and painful—squeeze of his arm and she was gone. He sat there, trying not to think. He'd forgotten to bring a book or some comics, and since she'd taken the keys he couldn't even put on the radio. The only distraction was to watch people scurrying by.

Townsfolk and visitors bustled up and down the street. It was a lovely day, one of the first hot ones of summer. Watching them in their T-shirts, dresses, and shorts made Sky shrug deeper into his coat; he hadn't felt warm since . . . since "he" fell in the river. And his own skin had felt slimy ever since, as if mud still clung to it.

He watched the crowd in the car's side mirror. To amuse himself, he began to think of it as a camera lens. People came up the hill toward the car, passed in close-up, disappeared out of shot, were replaced immediately by the next piece of action. He started making up little films.

Here was a girl about his own age, jabbering on her phone, obviously excited about the rendezvous she was heading to with one of her three boyfriends. He envied whichever one it was while the girl was still down the hill, in long shot. Then, as she got closer, he saw that a lot of her prettiness was due to her makeup, that her glittery T-shirt was two sizes too small, and her heels too high, making her walk comical. She passed the car. She had no boyfriend but she wanted one, was off to a burger bar to discuss that with her friends.

He refocused in the mirror-lens, found an old man back down the hill who was struggling with the incline, though not as much as his little Scottie dog, who stopped every three paces to huff and drool. This did not seem to annoy the man as much as the passersby who kept tripping on the dog and its retractable leash. Sky was sure there was a wife waiting for him at some café near the castle, as fat as he was thin. He was late, and his wife would give him a hard time about it.

Eventually, even the man and dog made it past the car, and Sky looked back for the next mini-epic. Immediately he saw balloons, a bunch of them in every color, attached to a boy of about four, who was shrieking in delight as he swung them back and forth. They kept banging into the face of the mother, who could not protect herself because her hands were full of plastic supermarket bags. She'd jerk her head away, then say something to the child, who would shrug, laugh, and keep jerking the balloons. It had to be a birthday, but Sky decided that was too boring for a film so he made the little boy into a dwarf from the circus and the mother into his friend the Bearded Lady—that was what was concealed beneath the silk scarf she wore at her neck!

Laughing to himself, Sky enjoyed the way the balloons kept bouncing into the women's increasingly annoyed face. Each time they dipped he could see beyond them for a moment, little glimpses of other worlds that were coming his way, the next film to replace this one when dwarf and Bearded Lady passed by. Here was a man in a brown hat, a lady next to him in a beret—spies, obviously! Then the mother shouted something, stepped to the side, out of the frame of the mirror. Sky really wanted to see what she was doing to the "dwarf," so he turned, looked back. The balloons bobbled . . .

Sky scrunched down fast into his seat. It had been so quick. Nothing, really, he was sure, just a flash of what had been bothering him for a few days perhaps, nothing more. Not . . .

Cautiously, keeping low, he turned, pressed his face to the glass, waited for the balloons to part again and now they wouldn't, just dangled there, spinning on their axis because the mother had put down her bags and was holding on to the boy's arm. He shouted something and she reached her other hand across, grabbed his fingers. With a yelp, he pulled them away. One of the balloons came loose, floated free. There was a gap, and Sky saw through it.

The gap was filled with a gray hood.

His head just below the top of the seat, he looked in the mirror again, saw the boy now crying for the balloon that floated away, saw the mother say something sharp, then bend for her bags. Saw people behind her. None of them wearing hoods.

He suddenly didn't want to be in the car anymore. In a moment, he had the door open and had slipped out, was limping quickly up the hill. Beyond the line of shops stood Ludlow Castle, and laid out beneath its great granite battlements was an open square, filled now with stalls for the weekly market. The crowd was thick, but somewhere in the press would be his mum. He thought it would be good to see her. Help her carry the groceries back.

Traders were selling everything from fruit to meat to cheese. Swiveling his head from side to side, he couldn't spot her. Yet each time his head turned, something kept appearing at the very edge of his vision. He'd turn his head further, try to see whatever it was full on . . . and there'd be nothing there, just ordinary people. He'd turn back . . . and a shadow would edge in again.

He began to walk quicker. Food stalls gave way to ones selling electrical goods, CDs, pots and pans, secondhand clothes. Where was she? He looked back the way he'd come, the crowd as thick behind as ahead. He seemed to be the only person not moving. Just until he thought he saw someone else not moving.

On the edge of the square, closest to the castle walls, was a stall of mirrors. Small plastic bathroom ones, huge ones with fancy oak frames, funky modern ones with glass centered in a mass of twisted metal. A single freestanding one, oblong and nearly as tall as Sky, leaned back at a slight upward tilt. Caught, Sky looked at himself. Within the collar of his dark coat his skin looked paler than he'd ever seen it. Then, glancing around, he realized that every mirror there now held a double of him, that somehow all of them angled in to exactly where he stood now. All, that is, except one.

It was oval, antique, speckled with black corrosion at the edges, framed in silver. And it reflected nothing. Not gray walls, scurrying people, a smudge of cloud. It was empty, and Sky suddenly realized why. Maybe he'd read it somewhere. Maybe he just knew.

The Undead have no reflection.

He turned and looked straight into the gray hood. And as soon as he did, everything stopped. People froze—a woman offering coins to a stall keeper; a man shoving his arms into a jacket; a pigeon flapping up with a discarded crust.

He looked behind him. He had found his mother. She must have just seen him, because her lips were parted in the beginning of a smile.

Sigurd had said that their Norse ancestors didn't believe in Time divided neatly into past, present, future. They thought it more like a tidal river, one aspect flowing into the next, flowing back. And here was the proof. A man beheaded a thousand years before stood in front of him now. While a thousand years ago—and four days ago!—Sky had lived as Bjørn. And now they were together. Outside Time.

"What do you want?" Sky whispered. Yet in the hollow space made by Time's blending, it sounded like a shout.

The draug did not move. A breeze riffled the dark cloth.

"Why are you here?"

The wind blew stronger, taking Sky's words, scattering them. Around him, the frozen forms shifted, as if all the people there had breathed in. Behind him, his mother's smile had widened. Before him, the edges of the draug's cloak had begun to fray, blending into light.

Terror made him angry. "What do you want from me?" Sky yelled.

The bones of a hand appeared. The word emerged on a hiss.

"Death."

It was what he expected.

160   "Whose?" he whispered, half certain, hoping he was wrong.

A finger was uncurling from the skeleton of the hand. Yet light was already shining through it, bone becoming transparent. The cloak had gone from gray to white. Out of the corner of his eye, Sky saw the man slip on the jacket.

Voices. A coin clinking on another. A pigeon flapping past his face. A shadow where a cloak had been. Then that got lost, too, dissolved into a shaft of sunlight.

A hand on his shoulder. The smile on his mother's face.

"Got bored in the car?" She squeezed where her hand rested. "Feel up to carrying a few bags?"

"Sure, Mum," he said, bending and picking two up. As he straightened, he looked again into the mirrors. All of them were full of movement, of faces.

None of them held his.

CHAPTER THIRTEEN

THE FEVER

"Look, will you please slow down!"

Sky let go of the strand of barbed wire he'd managed to climb over. He didn't answer, just carried on, limping up the hill. His leg still hurt, but it hurt as much when he sat still. And every step took him away from the house, from the attic and all it contained. Out here, moving toward the woods, at least he could breathe.

"You act . . . like there's someone . . . chasing you." Kristin's words came in clumps of air as she fought to keep up.

"There is."

They were entering under the canopy as he said it. A fallen tree slowed him, and as he put one leg across it, she grabbed his coattail. "What . . . are you . . . talking about?"

She'd been shouting questions at him since he'd

dragged her out of the house on his return from Ludlow. He hadn't answered any of them. Hadn't been ready. Now perhaps he was.

He was straddling the oak, anyway, one leg each side, so he flopped down onto it. Gratefully, Kristin dropped onto the ground. "I'm being stalked," he said.

Kristin's head whipped round to where he was looking, back down the valley. They'd come quite high up, and the fields were spread before them. "Where? Who? I can't see anyone."

"He's not there. Except . . . he might be anywhere." He looked up at the trees. Shouldn't it be cooler beneath them?

"Who? Look, are you going to talk to me? You've told me nothing about your . . . trip . . . voyage to the other side. Whatever." She hit his leg. "Its been driving me mad. Tell me!"

He sighed. "Where to begin?"

"At the beginning, fool." She hit him again. "You killed the bat, then . . ."

He told her all of it. Nearly all. What happened, anyway. He couldn't begin to tell her how it had felt, not yet.

She listened, her face a frown of concentration. Now he had begun, he wanted to get it all out. When he finished, there was a long silence, a pigeon cooing in a nearby tree the only sound.

"I've got so many questions, I don't even know where to start."

163

"Believe me," he said, "so have I."

"The first thing I have to say is . . . bloody hell!" Her eyes were huge in astonishment.

"And then?" He could see her mind working behind her eyes, and he realized he should have told her before. If anyone was going to figure this out, it'd be Kristin.

"OK . . . how do you know it's this . . . berserker that's stalking you?"

"It has to be."

"Yes, but you said he died in the battle."

Sky nodded. "Had his head chopped off."

"And didn't you also say that it's only berserkers who *fail* to die in battle that become the Undead or these—what did you call 'em, 'draugs'?" He nodded again. "So if this Ulf finally died the way he wanted to, then surely he's gone off to this Norse . . . heaven."

"Valhalla. That's what they said. But how would anyone know?" Sky had finally stopped searching between the tree trunks to look at her. "Just because they believed it doesn't make it true. They also believed their bodies had to be burned to set their spirits free. I doubt anyone pulled Black Ulf's decapitated head and corpse from the river and cremated it. They were too busy dying." He shuddered. "No, you had to see him. If ever there was a candidate for the Walking Dead, Black Ulf was it."

"So he followed you back from the battle and popped up . . . in Ludlow?"

"No, he was already here. I'd seen him twice before but convinced myself he was a nightmare." He tapped his head. "Given my history, that was the obvious answer."

"You should get that seen to," she muttered. She chewed at the stubs of her nails but, finding nothing worth pulling, she began to pick at the fallen oak, stripping away bits of bark like scabs.

"I've tried. Or rather, my parents did. Took me to shrinks to try to 'cure' me of my sleepwalking and talking. But they were like that doctor today. Useless. Because it wasn't me who was stabbed and drowned. It wasn't me who went berserk. It probably wasn't me who used to go sleepwalking. It was my Fetch."

"Or fylgya." She ripped off another length of bark, distractedly. "Hang on. . . . Bjørn drowned, you said?"

"Actually, I don't know. I know I—he—was drowning. But he's meant to be our ancestor, right? So he couldn't have."

"Unless there was already some messing around with . . . whatsername?—Sweet Gudrun—before he left Norway."

"I think I'd have remembered that," he muttered. Kristin looked up at him and grinned. Sky blushed, hurried on. "Something else to ask Sigurd, I suppose. If I was to travel again."

"Which you won't."

"Which I won't," he said firmly, shutting his eyes, keeping them shut as he began to take his coat off.

How come he was now so hot, when he'd been cold for so long?

"Don't feel bad about not going again, Sky." Her voice came softly. "It must have been horrible."

He stopped, one sleeve off, and laughed, but there was no humor in the sound. "No, Kristin, you don't understand. It's not because it was horrible." He opened his eyes. "It's because it was brilliant."

She gasped, and he went on. "Oh yeah, part of me? Scared, sickened. But another part . . . Bjørn in me, the berserker in me . . . he . . . I . . . loved it! The power of it! It's as if that's what I was born to be."

"A killer?" she said, horror on her face.

"Yes!" He had reached forward, grabbed one of her arms. "It felt like it had always been there, this bear within me, growling in the dark, waiting for its chance. And when I found the key to its cage . . ."

He was gripping her arm like it was the shaft of a battle-ax. With a yelp, she jerked it away, fell back a few feet. He glared down at her, something stirring inside him, enjoying her pain, the fear on her face. Then, as suddenly as the feeling came, it went. "And *that* is why I must never go back," he said.

She stared up at him, eyes wide, rubbing where he'd gripped her. Another pigeon started up farther into the wood and they listened to the rise and fall of its calls. Two sets had past before Kristin pulled herself up, knelt before Sky. "Maybe that's why you have to," she said softly.

"What?" He shook his head. "Not a chance!"

"I'm not saying that you have to be Bjørn again." He groaned and she laughed, went on, "But you can't pretend he didn't happen, can you?"

"I can try." He still had an arm in one sleeve and he pulled it out now, though it was an effort. He dumped the coat over the fallen trunk.

"And spend your life fearing that you'll suddenly go berserk? Not to mention these wounds you have, in your arm, your leg." She nodded emphatically. "Oh, I think you do have to travel again, Sky. But not to Bjørn." She made him look at her. "To Sigurd. Or rather . . . to his ghost."

The thought disturbed and attracted at the same time. "Why?"

"He got you into all this. He's responsible. And he obviously knows much more than us. He'll have answers."

Sky thought for a moment. It was hard because his forehead was throbbing so much. "But how do I get to him? I don't think I can take another séance at midnight, or any more sacrificed bats." He paced, trying to get the stiffness out of his leg, circling his shoulder. The sun, breaking through the thinner canopy at the edge of the forest, was searing his forehead. "Look, can we go farther in? It must be cooler there."

She rose. "I'm fine, but . . . yeah, you do look a little hot."

They were climbing up the slope of the Wenlock

Edge, oak, ash, and beech giving way to pine, the forest floor rich in old needles that had gone from green to reddish brown. Maybe it was the climb, maybe it was the pain in his limbs that grew with every step, but he didn't feel the coolness he desired. Instead, movement brought more sweat.

He'd hoped to make the crest of the slope. But he was swaying so much that, when Kristin reached forward to help him, he stumbled, sank onto her arm and on down to the forest floor.

"What's the matter?" she asked anxiously. "You look . . . terrible."

"Don't feel so good," he wheezed.

"Do you want an aspirin? I think I've got one here."

168   She began rooting in her handbag, which, if he'd have been feeling better, he'd have mocked her for bringing to the woods. She pulled objects out, set them down on the floor of the forest. At first all he saw was girl stuff—a brush, hair bands, a compact. Then out came the tattered volume *Rune Magic*, followed by the runestones' sack and the journal. Her hand went in again, but he leaned forward, grabbed it. Gently.

"Forget the aspirin," he said. "Tell me about those. What you've been reading."

She looked up at him. "Are you sure?"

"I should be studying all that. I *will* study it. But . . . stuff's got in the way. You know, 'death by ax,' that sort of thing." He smiled weakly. "Can you . . . ?" He gestured down.

Swiftly, the cloth was spread, the stones tipped out upon it, the five from the cast selected, laid out in their cross. He watched her select *Uruz*, rune of sacrifice, the rune that had killed a bat—or had it?—the rune that Bjørn had carved onto his axhead. That she placed above the cast. The others she pushed aside.

Pointing at *Othala*, she said, "So this was the rune of ancestors, that first one that brought you to him or vice versa, yes?"

"Yes." He licked his lips. Why had he forgotten to bring water . . . again?

"And this one is *Thurisaz*, the rune of attack, of test. What you went through, with Bjørn . . . uh, *as* Bjørn? Anyway, back there." He nodded. "Well, according to my book, this one comes next." She pointed to the runestone on the right side of the cast. "This is *Ansuz*."

He looked at it: one vertical line, two slanting diagonally down from that, like branches off the right side of a pine tree. And just as each of the other two had drawn him before, so this *Ansuz* seemed to be the only one with life in it now.

"What does it mean?" he asked, his tongue thick.

"Literally?" She opened the book to a page she'd marked, read out, "'A mouth.'" Says here that it's to do with any form of communication, messages and the like. But while you've been snotty and not speaking to me, I've been studying. And my trusty book says you have to look at runes in pairs, how they are positioned with each other. This *Ansuz* is paired with *Othala*, which is opposite to it in the runecast. So it is communication . . . but with ancestors—"

"Which we're already doing!"

"Yes, but if you'd let me finish, together they also mean 'advice.'"

"So . . . seeking the advice of ancestors."

"Correct."

"Grandfather?"

"Unless you fancy Bjørn . . . yes, Grandfather." She shut the book. "Though I don't know how much choice you have in the matter. I mean, have you ever felt in control of this?"

170 He shook his head. Control? That's what Sigurd had talked about, promised: that Sky could learn to direct his Fetch. But it was like he was in a school play, with some teacher who thought he was in the West End or on Broadway, saying, "Move there! Say it like this!" Sky could do nothing for himself. Except choose not to go. But then what? Dodge draugs all his life? Wait to go berserk? He knew there was a pill for epileptics. Was there one for berserkers?

He looked at Kristin, at the certainty on her face. She was right. Sigurd had talked of the secrets that whispered in Sky's blood. He had certainly discovered some of those! And yet he knew it was only half the solution, like those equations Riddley had been teaching the last day at school. Sky had "X," but what was

"Y"? And why did his grandfather need him to learn all this? He had talked of "Destiny," his family's destiny, but had refused to explain further. It was true: Sigurd—Sigurd's ghost or fylgya or whatever he was—owed them some answers!

Sudden anger heated his head still further. Each breath had become harder to take, as if something were squeezing off his throat. He reached up. . . .

The cord that held the caul pouch had got twisted around his neck. He slipped his fingers into it, then let them slide down it, unraveling the string. When they reached the bag itself, he felt through to the hard lump of skin within it.

"What?" She bent over him. "What did you say?" Directly behind her was the sun, breaking through a gap in the pine tops. Her head was in a corona of light, each blond hair glowing red. Her face was lost to shadow, so bright was its surround.

"Doorway," he muttered. "It's a doorway." One hand wrapped tight around the pouch, he stretched with the other. He felt silk, then stone. He grasped one, could only hope it was the right one. It felt hot; but then, all of him did.

Concern was on the face that drifted in and out of his vision. "Should we go back, Sky? Sky?"

"Can't . . . move," he said, sinking back into the softness of pine needles. Above him, light and darkness merged around her.

"I'm getting help." She stood up, but it was as if she'd

171

leapt—she suddenly seemed far away. And he needed her to stay so badly.

"No! Don't leave. Guard me! Please!" Her shape blurred. He thought he was shouting, yet he wasn't sure she could hear him. "I'm going . . . going . . ."

Gone.

CHAPTER FOURTEEN

THE CAULDRON

Gone. Pine-needle softness changed to rock, sunlight to blackness, heat to a cold so intense that Sky had not one second of relief before sweat turned to ice and bit into his skin. He raised his head, pulled himself up to sit, to kneel, to stand. One step and he slipped, sending stones clattering off some edge, heard them falling far below him. His feet tried to follow, and he just managed to steady himself with a hand thrust out to a rock face.

He clung there like that, breathing heavily. There'd been that tiny moment when he'd gone into Bjørn before he'd lost himself completely in the Viking. He waited now—was he about to make the change? No. Nothing. He was Sky still, that much he knew. Though when . . . *where* . . . he didn't have a clue. Except that it was freezing!

His eyes were beginning to adjust, but in that deep

dark there was little to see—a rock face rimed with ice, some sort of snowbound path on which his feet just held him. His other senses compensated, feeling the way the wind lashed straight at him, driving ice crystals into his exposed skin, smelling salt in the air, hearing a crash and drag of waves below him. He had to be on a cliff, standing on a steeply angled path that cut up it.

Down or up? he wondered. The sea had to be below, and that offered little prospect of comfort. Up and there could be something. Someone.

He began to climb, leaning against the wall of rock, pushing off, head bent into wind and flung ice. He had no idea how far he'd have to go, but staying still wasn't an option. He wondered now if he'd ever been warm and why he'd taken off his coat in the forest.

It wasn't far, in the end. Far enough for the cold to have numbed every part of him, for his feet inside his sneakers to feel like lumps of ice that he somehow lifted and placed, lifted and placed, for his fingers to barely feel the rock they pressed into. Then came a change in the way the wind blew, gusting stronger now, almost forcing him back. He sensed a leveling, a wider space; and then the cliff face was gone and he was falling forward. From hands and knees he peered ahead. He hadn't used sight for a while, and he wondered if he'd gone blind. Then he saw it, the barest flicker of light, and he was up in a moment and staggering toward it, hands thrust ahead of him. Prepared for a collision with another rock face, the softness, the giving, took him by surprise. He fell through it—an animal-skin blanket over a cave entrance—to light, to heat.

To his grandfather.

Sigurd was rising up on the other side of what Sky saw to be a huge cauldron, his arms spread wide, hands holding up a fur cape with mink tails that dragged to the floor. It was a gesture of welcome, and Sky stumbled the last few yards, falling gratefully into warmth.

"Shh, boy, shh," his grandfather whispered, settling again to the floor, Sky clutching him.

It took an age for Sky's breathing to become normal, for the shakes to diminish, and during that time he could barely think. He knew that Sigurd reached forward to the cauldron, dipped a drinking horn into it, raised it steaming to Sky's lips. He drank and was warm almost instantly. The hot drink tasted of herbs, of sweet wine. It went straight to his head, made him dizzy, sleepy.

His grandfather's voice sent drowsiness away. "What is it you seek, Sky?"

Sky sat up, shrugging the cape off himself. Now that he was warm again, the fire was enough. And he needed to see Sigurd's face. He realized he was clutching a rune-stone in one hand. He laid *Ansuz* on the ground beside the cauldron, looked up. "Answers," he said.

"Did I not tell you they would be found at the end of the runecast? Have you completed it?"

175

"No. And I'm not sure I want to."

Something glinted in the old man's eyes. "Want to? It's not a question of wanting. It is your destiny. What has to be."

"No, it doesn't. I could decide not to . . . use the runes again. Just return to my normal life . . ."

"Normal?" Sigurd laughed. "Your life was never going to be normal, Caul-Bearer. And once you met your Fetch . . ."

It annoyed him, this idea that he was power-less. "Fetch or no Fetch, caul or no caul, I still have a choice. It's called 'free will,' in case you haven't heard of it!"

Sigurd leaned forward to look at him intently. "And if you do have a choice, what other would you make?" Flame light, licking up the sides of the cauldron, played on his face. "I know you have visited our ancestor, Bjørn the Bear. I don't know what happened there. But I can see in your eyes that it was . . . wonderful."

"Wonderful?" Sky gasped. "It was terrible! I . . . killed. Not once. Many times. I saw my brother, my fa-ther die. And in the end, I drowned."

Sigurd shook his head. "You did not. Neither of us would be here if you had."

Sky couldn't help himself. "Then what happened to me . . . him?"

Sigurd smiled. "We are drawn to those of our an-cestors we are most like. You to Bjørn. Me to both his father, Thorkell, and to one of his daughters. Oh yes,

176

Sky, you can be drawn to your female ancestors as well, if you are like them." He smiled. "And I know the story only as they knew it. Much of that changed with the telling over the years. Story becomes legend. Bjørn became 'The Last of the Vikings.'"

"And what did this legend tell?"

"You had a brother who lived—"

"Ingvar!"

"If you say so. He rescued you from the water, bound your wounds, got you back to the longship. You returned to Norway, to the arms of your love, and then . . ." Sigurd's voice had dropped to whisper. "Don't you want to learn what happened then, Sky? Don't you want to live that?"

"Yes! No!" Sky was on his knees now. "I don't want to be a killer."

Sigurd nodded. "I think you have already learned that lesson. Learned that you can kill . . . if necessary. For a cause. For a king."

Sky shook his head violently. "But I didn't kill for Harald Hardrada or for his cause. I killed because . . . because my brother had died, because my father was killed taking the spear meant for me. . . ." He stopped, seeing the smile that came to Sigurd's face. "What?"

"You have learned what you needed to, Grandson; that was the test in the rune, *Thurisaz*. You learned that sometimes killing is necessary. Your father's sacrifice, your brother's death taught you that."

Death! The word, an echo in his ear, reminded him.

177

He had heard that word whispered that day, but in another time and place.

"The draug. The one I told you of before? He's back."

Sigurd leaned away from the light. "You've seen him again?"

"Yes. And I think I know who he is."

Sigurd's voice came faintly. "Who?"

"Black Ulf. He was—"

"I know who he was," Sigurd interrupted. "Remember, I have been back, like you, drawn to Thorkell Grimsson. I know Black Ulf's sad tale. And I have one to tell you. It is not a nice one and it does not have a happy ending. But I think you should know it anyway."

178   Sigurd came forward again into the light, closed his eyes to it, drew a breath. "I discovered my Fetch late, far later than you. Immediately I wanted to know everything about it and I devoted myself to that. Ignored family, work. Nothing could bring me knowledge quickly enough. I made a mistake, fell in with some"—he placed a hand over his eyes—"some bad people. They said they could help me with my quest. But they only wanted to use me and the power in the runestones I was just discovering, to help them in theirs."

A silence came, broken only by the crackle of logs, the hiss of metal expanding. "And what was that, Grandfather?"

"Nothing less than the raising of the dead." He

brought his hand away, looked at Sky. "It is called 'necro-mancy,' and it is a terrible thing. It is not like talking to them through letters and glass, or becoming an ances-tor for a time. These were ceremonies performed to rip souls from their rest and drag them back to this side of the veil." He shuddered. "I helped them do it. Some came. Most returned. One stayed."

"Black Ulf?" whispered Sky.

"I do not know for certain. I only know it came through the person I was drawn to then, Bjørn's fa-ther, Thorkell. So if you tell me it is this . . . well"—he shuddered—"I can believe it."

Sky swallowed. "He found me again. He talked of death. . . ."

Sigurd leaned forward, clutching at Sky's hand. "I know that is one of the answers you seek through *Ansuz*"—he pointed at the runestone between them—"how to deal with this draug. And I tell you that *that* answer also lies at the end of the runecast. Trust me, Grandson. I speak the truth. For this reason, for so many others, you can only go on."

Silence came again. Both gazed at the shadows the flames cast on the cave's rough walls, listened to the gentle bubbling in the pot. At last, Sigurd spoke. "You *could* give up now. Deny your blood, seek a normal life—whatever that is. Live till your death, whenever, wherever. Live . . . with all you were born to do left un-done. That was my fate," he sighed. "Leaving my mor-tal body just when I'd had a glimpse of what I was here

179

to do. There was nothing left for me but to move through the realms of the dead. But you . . . you! Born under a caul, with the One-Brow"—a hand came out of the furs to touch Sky just above the bridge of his nose—"you have such possibilities open to you. Such wonders to explore."

He stood, huge in the cape he now spread wide. His shadow flickered vast on the rough walls behind him, and his voice, when it came, filled the space with echoes.

"Of course you seek an answer, Sky. And you are right to. But to what? Do you truly know what the question is? When you have not learned all your ancestors can teach you?" He shook his head. "You cannot. Until you journey through the runecast to its very end, I say you cannot."

180

Sky stared at his grandfather, conflict on his face. Sigurd gestured into the cauldron, to the surface of the liquid there. "You have said you have free will. That you have a choice. So, choose, Sky," he whispered. "Choose."

At first, all Sky could see was the steam rising from the darkness of the brew. Then something did indeed stir on the bubbling surface, shadows resolving into form, into figure.

"That's . . . that's Kristin." He saw her in the forest, kneeling close to his entranced body, staring down.

"See how she longs to have your adventures, Sky. What would *she* dare if she was you?"

There was something moving beyond her, farther

into the depths of the dark liquid. It was like a 3-D sculpture. Kristin and the runes sat on top of . . .

"A longship," Sky cried, seeing the beautiful curved lines of the vessel, the dragon prow, a black sail at the mast, courting the wind. He could see, with the memory of Bjørn, that this ship was even more magnificent than the one he'd sailed on to England. And that part of him—Bjørn in him—longed to be aboard it.

Sigurd spoke softly again. "There is another side to the runecast, one you have not yet seen. One you must learn. For Death is not an end. It is just one more marker along the way. And Bjørn"—a smile came— "Bjørn was not named 'The Last of the Vikings' for no reason."

Sky had leaned over the cauldron, yearning to see the longship more clearly, yearning also to see Bjørn aboard, grasping the tiller—for then this magnificent vessel would be Bjørn's . . . and somehow his too! Suddenly he realized he'd leaned too far. He toppled in, tumbling toward liquid, Kristin, the runecast, his own body on the forest floor. He shrank as he fell, almost instantly, the cauldron suddenly vast, the waters far below. He fell slowly at first, then built up speed, until he was rushing toward a surface choppy as a tossing sea. And as he fell, Sigurd's final words came to him, loud, echoing around the iron of the cauldron's walls.

"You have already learned to kill, Sky. Now you must learn to die."

181

CHAPTER FIFTEEN

THE LAST OF THE VIKINGS

There was a moment, such a brief one, when Sky saw Kristin. He thought it would feel like this if you leapt from a tall building and glanced into the various rooms as you fell. A snapshot. He saw her seeing him, her eyes wide, mouth already opened to shout. He was in his body on the pine needles and then he was out of it. Past her. Gone again.

Then there was Sky-becoming-Bjørn; and there was Kristin. Except now her name wasn't Kristin but Ingeborg, and she was no longer a cousin. She was a daughter.

And in the last moment he had as Sky, he felt one thing clearly—when he'd *been* Bjørn before, he'd been young, with a young man's strength, had felt it in the way he pulled at the oar or hefted the ax. Now he felt tired, so tired and weak. And not in the way a young man does when he gets sick.

Bjørn is old, Sky thought . . . the last thing he thought . . .

"Father?"

Bjørn's eyes opened to the voice, the gentle shaking. They'd closed to hold in the feeling, that strange one he'd felt once or twice before in his life when he was himself, and not himself. But it was certainly his youngest daughter, Kr . . . Ingeborg. Ingeborg, born in the autumn of his life, who shook him.

"Are they here?" he whispered. And his daughter nodded and tried to smile because she knew he could not bear tears.

"Then bring Edmond to me." As she turned away, he added, "Bring him, child, and stay. I need you both."

She lifted the cowhide that shut this room off from the other, larger one, admitting a hum from the people waiting there. She beckoned and held the curtain up to allow one of them to enter.

Edmond came straight to the bed, lifted Bjørn's hand, pressed it to his forehead. "How fares my lord?"

Bjørn never regarded his own face anymore, too disgusted by what he saw. But the man's before him told the tale for them both. It was thirty winters since he had seized the English lad in a raid, and they had shrunk the boyish cheeks, thinned the mop of fair hair, grayed what little remained. Only the light in the eyes remained, a dance that had charmed Bjørn from the first. He had made Edmond his body slave and he had grown as dear to him as any of the three wives he had lost. Dearer, perhaps, in some ways. And certainly the two people who stood before him now, slave and daughter, were the only two left who loved him. Those others who waited outside didn't. But he didn't need love from any of them for what he was planning. He needed obedience.

He used Edmond's hand to pull himself up, swing his feet slowly to the floor. "My bearskin," he said, "and my ax."

His daughter wrapped the cloak around him, fastening it at the shoulder with the fine gold dragon brooch he'd seized from the Moors off Sicily. Then Edmond handed him Death Claw. He lifted it, saw that his command had been obeyed. The edge was as gleaming and would be as sharp as it was when he took it to England in Harald Hardrada's invasion. The haft was new, aged and fashioned well. It was the fifth that had held the head; the others had shattered over the years in raid and battle.

His bearskin and his ax. They would remind those who waited what he had been, what he could be again if they did not do as he bid.

He thrust his still-huge chest out, raised himself to his great height, drew in a lungful of air. Ready, he nodded. Edmond went to the entrance, held the skin aside.

They all bowed, in their own ways, according to their desire or fear or allegiance. All except one, who barely inclined his head. But Bjørn could see the gleam

184

of hate undisguised in the black eyes, beneath the black hair. And it gladdened him. For what he planned, Finbar's hate was exactly what he needed.

He glared back and, eventually, the gaze dropped. He had broken a thousand sticks on this slave's back, and it had not diminished the hate in the look one jot. But it had at least made him a little more cautious at courting such punishment.

Bjørn looked at the others. The three elders of the village would obey him to the last, too frightened to do otherwise. It was his son and the priest man who might oppose, whom he must master.

Toki, third born but the eldest now, had only come back to Hareid two nights previously, after Bjørn's summons had reached the royal court. His son was dressed as was the fashion in the south, his trousers made up of squares of different colored wool, his tunic of a turquoise that could only have been dyed in Castile. His face had a carefully trimmed beard, a carefully composed expression; but his eyes were indifferent. He wanted nothing here but a speedy return to the court, away from the barbarous northerners he now despised. That, and the title and lands that would come to him when his father finally died. They would buy him many pretty tunics, finance many court intrigues.

For a moment, Bjørn looked beyond him, beyond the room, to other sons. To Thorolf, named for a slain brother, drowned these thirty summers, whose death caused that of his mother, Sweet Gudrun, wasted by

185

sadness. And to Leif, the best of them all, perhaps, most like his father. In love with the wild sea, he'd sailed to the west, never to return.

His mind came back. There was a last man there, not that he was wanted. But the priest went where he willed these days, so much did the villagers revere and fear him.

They all follow the White Christ now, Bjørn thought. All except him and the slave who hated him.

Someone coughed. He looked up, to the faces before him, realized that he must have paused and thought on lost sons for a while. It was one of the curses of age, this . . . drifting off. Now he would speak.

"I am dying," he said.

186   There was shifting, little more. Perhaps Ingeborg sniffed back a tear, perhaps Edmond. Perhaps Finbar gave a little laugh behind his veil of hair. The others just stared.

"I am dying," he repeated, "but I am not yet dead. I am still the headman of Hareid, still leader of the war band." He raised the ax, trying to make it seem light. "And Death Claw can still tear flesh."

That shifted them all. Toki spoke. "Is that why you ordered *Storm-Bringer* made ready, Father? Do you think to raid again?"

Before he could deny it—the ship was needed, but not to raid—his son continued, "Because we cannot just go a-Viking anymore, Father. Those days are gone. The king has alliances, is making peace as well as war.

None of his vassal lords can choose to go off on their own."

Once Bjørn would have shouted his son down, told him that no one, not even a king of Norway, would tell the lords of Hareid when and where they could voyage. But it was an old dispute and not worth the raising now. Not when there were more important things to discuss—to command—while his strength held. Already he could feel Death Claw begin to shake as he leaned on it.

As other voices came, he lifted the ax, brought its butt hard down upon the wooden floor. "Enough! I will tell you what is now to be." He continued into the silence his anger had brought. "You know what this bearskin means. I have worn it in too many battles to remember. Each time, when the fight was hardest, almost lost, the bear inside me growled, roared, filled this skin. And the fight was won, because I became what I am . . . a berserker!"

187

He looked at them on the word, and they all, to a man, looked away. He went on. "It is twenty years since he was needed, twenty since he last came and took me. My bear has slept. But it has been a long winter for it, and now my bear is hungry again. He must wake up one last time. For a berserker is not meant to be old, not meant to die in his bed. A berserker, above all other warriors, *must* die in battle, singing his death song, singing it loud so the Valkyries will hear and speed him fast to Valhalla. For if he does not . . ."

He did not need to say it. All knew of the draugs, the Living Dead, even if only a few still believed. He could see the sneer on his son's face; see the priest man make his cross-sign, warding off the heathen superstition before he spoke. "My lord, you have heard your son. You cannot go a-Viking again. You especially cannot shed innocent blood just . . . just so your 'bear' can live."

Cannot? The word irked him. But then he remembered—he did not need to persuade them. He only needed them to do his will. "Be easy, Priest. I doubt I could prize these lazy farmers and fishermen from their plows and nets, doubt any still know how to wield any blade but a meat knife. No." He paused. "I propose something different."

He had them now, he could see. In his youth, before he went with his father and Harald Hardrada to England, he had thought he would be a skald. He had told tales before the winter hearth, had held people just so, waiting to hear the next part of the story.

"Tomorrow, just before sunrise, *Storm-Bringer* will be anchored in the sea road, loaded with all I need for this last journey—mead for my drinking horns, weapons for the hunting, gold to buy passage from any spirits who request it. We will build a pyre of wood in the center of the ship for my last bed, lay my hunting dog dead at its base. The men of Hareid will row me to the ship, singing the old songs. Then all but three will row back."

"What three?" It was Ingeborg who whispered it, dread on her face.

He looked around, saw that dread spread to each of them, the fear of being chosen. Eyes avoided his. "I am the first," he declared. "Bjørn the Bear. Then there will be Edmond, my body slave, to see me laid out properly upon my pyre when the ship is aflame . . . for all know only in the cleansing flames can a berserker speed to Valhalla."

It was Edmond who interrupted, a beating offense for any but him. The fear was clear in his voice. "Master, kind lord, you know I believe in the Christ. I cannot hope to come to him if I die in this way."

The priest was beginning to speak, to protest also. Bjørn slammed the haft of his ax down again, commanding silence. "You will not die, unless you are unlucky. You are there only to do this last service for me. And when you have done it, when the ship is alight and my body burns, you will swim for the shore. And when you touch it, you will no longer be a slave but a free man, with gold in his pockets and a place set aside on a merchantman to England. This I declare will be done."

189

"And the other man?" Toki's voice came, a quaver in it.

Bjørn lifted the ax, swung the weapon. Everyone flinched as it passed over them. Until it rested before one. "Him."

All looked, saw. And he who was pointed at saw

last, raising his eyes from beneath his wild black hair. "Me?" Finbar's voice was croaky, his accent full of the Irish lands of his birth despite the ten years he'd passed in Hareid. He had mastered Norse mockery, though, his words rich in it. "What service can I render my kind lord that is not beaten from me with boots and sticks?"

"You will be given back your sword, Finbar, and the coat of mail I took from you when we found you hiding among your cows," Bjørn said softly. "And you will fight me. Even a cur like you should be able to kill an old man. Though I promise . . . I will not make it easy for you."

The gasps, the protests, came from all except the man who stared at him silently. Bjørn, staring back, saw the glint come into the eyes. "I will fight you, Thorkellsson, and I will kill you. I will cut out your heart and offer it to my gods. "

"And that," Bjørn said, "is the service I require from you. And for it, once you swim to the shore, you, too, will be free to return to whatever bog begot you." He looked up, then, away from the hatred, to the shock on all the other faces. "This is what will be. I command it." He shook Death Claw at them, since it was shaking enough anyway. "For this blade, for the beast within this skin, I command it."

His voice was a roar, his eyes fire. Family, sons, daughter, his body slave, all looked down. Only Finbar stared on, savage delight growing in his eyes. And the priest man, who had been struggling to speak and now did.

"Even you, my lord, cannot countenance such . . . heathen doings. Now, at the end of your life, now is your chance to forsake all that, to atone for your sins. Take the water of the Christ, his blood in wine, his flesh in bread. Your Valhalla does not exist. Only heaven is real, and paradise awaits even you. But you must forsake your gods!" he cried.

Bjørn smiled. It was the first time he had felt like doing so in a very long while, for now all was arranged. "Priest," he said, "surely this is not the time in my life to be making new enemies?"

When the rowers, with a last farewell shout, disappeared into the darkness, Bjørn let himself sag onto the longship's tiller. It had taken the remnants of his strength to pluck weeping Ingeborg from his neck, to walk in full armor between the lines of villagers, to stand proud in the prow of the rowboat as he and his two slaves were ferried out to *Storm-Bringer* tethered, like a straining hawk, five arrow shots from the shoreline. Far enough for no one on the shore to see, in the night-dark, how swift his ending came; close enough for the slaves, their duty done, to swim ashore. They were up ahead of him now; Finbar chained in his armor to the mast step, to be freed on Bjørn's last shouted command; Edmond readying the funeral pyre. But that darkest hour before the sunrise hid them;

that and his eyes, for he no longer had the long sight of his youth.

He lifted off his helmet, laid it aside, stuck a finger inside the mail coif, tugging it away from his neck. Breathing was difficult, anyway, but with this much weight upon him, it had become nearly impossible. And though it was mild for October, with only a slight wind coming over the waves, he felt cold. Suddenly, all he wanted was to be back in his bed, swaddled in furs, his sweet Gudrun—no, Gudrun was dead, long dead, dead from sorrow—his Ingeborg there, bringing him heated ale, the tenderest cuts of meat. And there was someone else who would tend him, rub his feet, which were always the coldest part of him, fetch him a basin of hot water to lay his aching hands in. . . .

"Edmond," he croaked, wondering how long he'd been sitting on the deck. Awhile, perhaps, because there was the faintest of lightening in the sky to the east, the mass of his island silhouetted against it. What he couldn't understand was why the stars, which had seemed so bright, looked now as if they were blocked by clouds.

Then he realized. They weren't clouds. What filled his nostrils was smoke.

He sat up, anger giving him a little strength. He had given no order yet! The pyre should only have been lit after the battle was fought. After Bjørn the Bear had returned to die.

He rubbed his eyes, peered. Flames were leaping

at the vessel's center, and he could see the smoke fast flowing now, filling the vessel like gray water, wind gusts pulling at the cloud, tearing it into sheets, wafting it to the sky. Then he heard a sudden cry, as suddenly cut off, followed by the sound of hammering, of metal cutting into wood.

He dragged himself up. This was wrong. This was not what he'd decreed. He bent, grasped the ax handle, could not lift the weapon. So heavy! But he had to. There was an enemy on this ship, and if the fire had been lit without his word, that could only mean the enemy was free.

And then he saw him. Just for a moment, as smoke shredded. A face twisted by savagery. Black, black hair. Then he was gone. Moving toward him, no doubt, sword thrust forward, stalking him in the swirl. His foe approached. He had to be ready.

Come, Death Claw! He had the butt end in his hands but he could not lift it, as if the steel blade was forged into the deck planks. Part of lifting was breath, but if he'd found that hard before, it was worse now, with nothing to fill his lungs but foul smoke. He coughed, again and again.

Then someone else coughed, and somehow he raised the ax, though it took all his strength to lay it across his shoulders. Gray shifted, he saw the face again, Finbar's face, though now it came at him side on, then, as he looked, turned upside down.

"No!" he screamed, and twisted away. He flailed

out with one hand, reaching for anything to hold him up, grasping only smoke. The ax slipped from his shoulder, and the weight of it and the weight of armor pulled him down hard upon the deck. His little air was driven out and he lay there, all his strength gone. And because his head was flat on the decking and because the smoke was rising, he could see beneath the bank of it. See two feet shuffling forward, getting closer, closer.

"Finbar?" he whispered, and the feet stopped, swiveled till the toes were pointing toward him.

"No, Master," Edmond whispered back, "it's me. But Finbar's here too."

And with that, something rolled across the decking toward him.

It was a head. Finbar's severed head. Eyes wide, wild, staring out, blood leaving a slimy trail on the planks. And yet . . . suddenly it was Black Ulf's head rolling there, and Bjørn was grappling it in a river in England, trying not to drown.

Then hands reached down for him through the smoke, seized him by the front of his mail shirt, began to drag him forward to the middle of the ship, toward the center of the flames.

Both men were coughing, flame and smoke searing their lungs. With a huge heave, Edmond had pulled Bjørn upright, held him with his back to the flames that began to cook his flesh inside its metal casing.

"Why?" Bjørn spluttered. "I thought you—"

"Loved you?" The fire in the Englishman's eyes was a match to any around them. "Do you see this dog whose body lies at the base of your pyre?" Bjørn looked down to Finbar's headless corpse, hands still shackled to the mast step. "This dog who showed you nothing but hate? Well, I hated you a thousand times more than he ever could." The smoke took him. He coughed, spat, then jerked the sagging Bjørn upright again. "Thirty years ago you stole me from my home, my family. For thirty years you kept me as a slave. I had to bathe you, groom you, nurse you, listen to your boastings of battle, put you to bed when you were drunk."

The ship shuddered, began to break apart. Bjørn could see a hole smashed in the deck planks, no doubt by the man who held him. And it reeked of the slaughter-house, the tarred animal hair melting between the planks, seawater bursting through, turning to steam on the searing wood.

195

Edmond looked around to the imploding ship, looked back. As he did, he pulled a dagger from his belt. "Time for me to go. But before I do, know this." He pushed his face right up to Bjørn's, his voice a hiss. "There is no death in battle for you . . . berserker! You will lie here, your throat cut like a hog in a pen, your body singed, not burned because the sea will take you, rot your flesh to feed the fish. And so my vengeance will last through all eternity." He tipped back his head and laughed. "Your spirit will not soar to Valhalla, Bjørn

Thorkellsson. Your spirit will walk for all time . . . as a draug."

On the word, Edmond slashed the blade across Bjørn's neck and then, with a yell of triumph, shoved him backward. Bjørn tumbled onto the pyre, his howls choked by the blood that poured down his throat. Yet somehow, even as his life bled away, even as sight faltered and sound was reduced to the whine and sizzle of his flesh within his armor, somehow there was enough of life left in him to see his killer run to *Storm-Bringer's* prow, to the dragon head carved there, see him leap to clutch at it . . . and see, just as he leapt, the ship shatter, planks detaching from the keel, crossbeams collapsing in. Water poured onto Bjørn, more liquid to add to the blood he was drowning in. Yet, in a hiss of steam, it extinguished the flames, bringing coldness, a new kind of pain.

And in that moment, time collapsed with the timbers. Bjørn was Bjørn still, but younger, much younger, it was him leaping off the prow of the ship, not Edmond; him plunging into the river in England, water closing over his head because his father had twitched the tiller and the men of Hareid had shifted their oars. He could hear their laughter again, all of them, even Black Ulf's dry rasp from below the deck.

It seemed too good a joke not to share. So he wrapped his arms around one of the men by him; not the dead, headless one but the one who had mistimed his jump and had tumbled, screaming, onto him as the ship broke apart. Grasping the body to him, he held him tight despite the shrieks, the desperate flailing. The weight of his armor, of his own immense body within it, pulled them both down. As they sank deeper and deeper, the one in his arms struggled less and less and at last lay quiet, as quiet as the sea.

CHAPTER SIXTEEN

BACK FROM THE DEAD

Perhaps it was the calmness of drowning, perhaps the quiet of the forest. But this time Sky didn't return to his body in a rush, no flailing. He came back peacefully, waking to birdsong, to sunlight through leaves. His fever had vanished. It was like going to bed with the flu and the moment you woke knowing it was finally finished. And the phantom wounds in his arm and leg . . . gone.

He turned his head, looked at Kristin. She had moved so she could put her back against a tree. Her eyes were shut, her chin reaching to chest; when it touched, she jerked her head up again. He watched her raise her fingers to her mouth and begin gnawing at her nails.

"Hallo," he said, and her eyes shot open.

She was across to him in a second. "It's OK, Sky. You're back. You're safe."

"I know I am. Apart from the fact I've just drowned

after having my throat slit. Oh, and the longship's fallen apart."

She began to speak soothingly, as if to a small child, patting his shoulder. "Of course it has. Now Sky, why don't you just lie back . . ."

He smiled at her tone. "I'm awake."

"Of course you are." She looked hard at him. "Are you?"

"Sure."

She held up five fingers. "Then how many hands am I holding up?"

"Five," he said, and they both laughed. "Really, Kris, I'm fine. And here."

"So what's all this about drowning and longships?"

Where to begin? All these images of what he'd just been through kept playing in his head like they were part of a jumbled-up film, or a dream where he just needed to snatch one image out to remember the whole thing. "I went back. Bjørn was old . . . ," he began, then noticed something about the way the sunlight was coming through the canopy. "What time is it?"

"Uh . . ." She pulled out her cell phone. "Five-fifty-five."

"Then I've been away for . . . what, four hours?"

"Yeah."

"That's a bit strange. Last time I was gone for only two hours, but it lasted a week back there. This visit only lasted a day, yet I was gone double the time." He scratched his head. "Ah!"

"'Ah' what?"

"It's that Norse-time thing again. No past, present, future. They just all blend in. 'Time that is . . .'"

"Never mind all that." She leaned forward excitedly. "Tell me what happened."

Instead of answering, he got up, offered her a hand. "Supper will be on. We should get back." Reluctantly she allowed him to pull her up. Immediately he began walking briskly down the track. "Come on," he called over his shoulder, because she hadn't moved, was standing there, hands on hips, obviously exasperated. "I promise—I'll tell you as we go."

She caught up, slipped into step beside him. "Well?"

"Well, for a start, I met *you* back there. Your spitting image. You were called Ingeborg."

"Yuck! What a horrible name!" Then she smiled. "Still, was I a Valkyrie? A warrior maiden in leather straps, a double-handed sword, killer abs?"

Sky shook his head. "No. But you were very nice."

"'*Nice*'?" She hissed. "Oh great!"

"*And* my daughter."

"Eww! That's vaguely disgusting."

"It gets worse."

"How can it get worse?"

"I think you were also Sigurd."

"What? Double eww!" She retched, then looked at him. "What *can* you mean?"

They'd reached the barbed-wire fence. Sky pressed it down for Kristin. She stepped over. "He said in the cave that he was drawn to ancestors either side of Bjørn—Thorkell and a daughter—

"Inglenook!"

". . . borg. Yes. He said that you are drawn back to the ancestors you are like, both men and women."

He ignored the place where she pressed the wire down for him. Instead, he leapt the fence in a standing jump and strode down the field. In the distance they could see the house.

"Look," she shouted. "Will you just tell me every-thing, from the beginning, right now, please!"

"I'll try. Bjørn was old, sick. So he . . ."

The longship had just broken apart by the time they reached the back gate. His mother was at the win-dow, beckoning them in. "Coming!" he called.

Kristin grabbed the arm that reached for the gate latch. "How *can* you just go in and eat?"

"I'm starving." He winked. "There's nothing like dying to give a man an appetite."

She didn't laugh. "I don't get this. Before you went on that last . . . journey, you were barely eating, you had a fever, pains in your arms and legs. You practically fainted up there. Now you're jumping fences . . ."

"I feel great."

"Why?" She punched his arm, and he yelped. "What did you find out? You told me what happened, but did you get any answers? And if so . . . what are they?"

She was shouting again. He shooshed her, waved to his mother beckoning again from the window. "There's too much to tell now. But I *can* tell you this: It's not about the answers, not yet. It's about the question! The question that waits at the very end of the runecast."

He could see so many things warring on her face: confusion, sarcasm, anger. She was shaking, and it made him laugh. "Later, I promise you, I'll tell you everything. Later, in the attic. When we tackle the next rune."

"When we . . . ?"

He grabbed her arm. "The attic!"

There was supper to get through first, Kristin and Sky both so quiet his mum thought they'd had another falling-out. Thus when Sky asked if they could go play a board game up in the attic, Sonja was so relieved, she didn't even make them stay and help with the dishes.

He'd already told her everything that had happened on the longship. Now he told her what Sigurd had talked about in the cave.

"Basically, he didn't give you any answers then?"

"No, he did. Well, he told me that I had to understand the question first. And that I'd only understand it once I'd reached the end of the runecast."

She shook her head. "He put you off. 'Understand the question'? That sounds like the sort of crap you get in philosophy class. You know, 'Am I a butterfly dreaming I'm a man?' type thing!"

"No, I don't know. I don't go to a fancy boarding school, remember. Philosophy? We barely get algebra!"

"All I'm saying is, it doesn't actually help you figure out what he wants you to do."

"But that's OK, Kristin. Because I'll find out once I've worked through the runecast. I just have to trust him."

"And do you?"

Sky stared above her, into the shadows under the eaves. "Yes," he said at last. "I mean, I've always felt different, yeah. The sleepwalking. The . . . waking dreams. Sigurd's shown me why. And I can't tell you how cool it is to go into another life. Terrible, sure, at times. Scary. But dead cool too."

"I wish I could find out," she muttered, nails to mouth. "So you want to go on?"

"Oh yes," he said, coming up to his knees, reaching for the runestones. "Let's go."

Five hours later and Sky's good mood was leaking away like air from a slow puncture. He banged the attic floor with his hand, then flopped back to rest on his elbows. "I just don't get it."

"Don't give up." Kristin was swirling the runestones around for the twentieth time. "We had trouble getting through before."

"Not like this."

They had tried the runes in a variety of casts. Nothing! They had laid out the runes in their familiar cast and he had held each one, especially the last two that had not yet been explored, *Raidho* and *Pertho*. Held

203

them, meditated on their meanings as supplied from Kristin's book, mumbled over them. Nothing! Just the coldness of stone.

"Shall I go into the garden and catch a small vole for sacrifice?" Kristin volunteered.

He looked at her. "You're not serious?"

"I could be persuaded." She shrugged, reached behind her. "Then we could try . . . this?" She held the Ouija box up.

"No."

"Why not? It worked before."

"Because he said we had to do it all through the runes."

"'He said'! 'He said'!" She shook her head angrily. "I thought we were tired of him dictating everything."

"Shh! Yeah. But I am sure he's right about the runes." He picked up the runestone with the "R" shape on it. It felt as cold as all the others. "*Raidho:* the journey," he intoned. Not a flicker! He put it down again, exasperated. "Well, I'm ready to travel. But where do I buy my ticket?"

Kristin was flicking through the pages of *Rune Magic* again. "You know, it does mean 'traveling.' But there's also a sense of . . . of transformation involved. You need to change—"

"Unlike what I *have* been doing?" He gasped. "I've only gone and been a Viking twice. I've killed, I've died. I've learned the lesson of each rune."

"Have you? Then tell me, genius. What was the lesson of the first rune?"

"*Othala*. That my Fetch—"

"Fylgya."

"Whatever. My *Double* could travel out of my body and meet dead relatives."

"Barrels of fun. And number two?"

"*Thurisaz*. Rune of attack. Proved that, if necessary, I could kill."

"If necessary, couldn't we all?"

"I don't think so. I couldn't have . . . before."

Kristin nodded. "OK. And *Ansuz*? Answers from ancestors, yes?" Sky nodded. "So why send you back to experience death? What answer's in that? Didn't sound like a very good death, by the way. Not in Viking terms." She shuddered. "Not in anyone's."

"You know, you're right." He came up to his knees. "And I don't think Sigurd knows that. I mean if he *was* Ingeborg . . . you—"

205

"Shut *up*!"

". . . watching from the beach. He . . . she . . . would only have seen the longship in flames, would have assumed it had all gone according to Bjørn's wishes."

"So Sigurd thinks you've experienced a good death. But why does he want you to have that, anyway? What for?" She grabbed Sky's arm, shook it. "What does he want from you?"

The very last of Sky's good mood fled. "It's true," he moaned. "I know nothing."

"And you said your body wasn't burned." She lifted the book. "It says in here that it was very important to the Vikings that their bodies were burned after death. Something about setting the spirit free."

"Yeah, well, I . . . sorry . . . *Bjørn* drowned. If the throat slitting didn't get him first."

"So?"

"So . . ." He sighed. "So . . . so . . . nothing! We can't know what Sigurd wants until he chooses to get in touch with us again." He gestured to the runestones. "We're helpless."

"What do you mean, 'we,'" Kristin snapped. "I don't know what you're complaining about. You're the great 'time traveler.' You get to do all the fun stuff."

"Fun st—?"

"While I . . . I get to do the bloody *research*!" she shouted, throwing *Rune Magic* across the room.

He shooshed her again. It was too late. There were footsteps on the landing below, then the creak of the metal steps. Sky threw his jacket over the runes just before his father's head appeared at the trapdoor.

"Look, you two, all this carrying on and"—he looked down, saw the distinctive box—"Ouija, eh? Now that brings back memories." He tried to look as serious as he ever could. "But since it's half past twelve, can all your little spirit friends please go home?"

"Sorry, Dad."

"Sorry."

His father climbed back down, and Kristin made to follow. Halfway down, she stopped, said, "There's a girl at school who's studied hypnotism. She's quite

206

good. Had Cassie Jenkins running around the dorm barking like a poodle. I'll call her, get her techniques— then we'll see if you can reach Sigurd that way. I'll send you into a trance."

She descended. He picked up his jacket, gathered the runes, slipped them back into the bag, tucked it into the big book, his old *Compendium of Horror,* that he'd hollowed out. He didn't feel safe with them in the chest anymore in case his mum started rooting around in it. Putting the volume into the bookcase, he took a last glance around.

Stupid me, he thought, reaching back. He'd left one of the runes out.

He wasn't that surprised when he saw which one it was. *Raidho.* He tried saying it out loud again, almost like a prayer. "Transformation," he intoned. But nothing sounded in the attic, and from outside, the only noise was a distant fluttering of wings. No bat appeared; the rune still didn't feel special, just as cold as any pebble. He was about to open the book, tuck it away with the others, when, for no particular reason, he dropped it into his pocket.

He had just climbed down the stairs and was putting up the ladder when a man's voice came from the shadows.

"Good evening."

CHAPTER SEVENTEEN

THE LIGHTER

The ladder fell with a crash. Sky jumped back. "Who's that?"

The man didn't move. There was a laugh, sinister, drawn out. Then the deep voice came again.

"Count Dracula," it said.

Sky gasped. "Dad?"

"If you are a vampire's son, then yes!"

"Dad! You scared the crap out of me."

"Revenge is sveet," his father said in what Sky now realized was an attempt at a Transylvanian accent.

"Is everything all right up there?" Sonja called up the stairs.

"Fine," they both replied.

"Bed, you two!" They heard the bathroom door close.

"What are you doing?" Sky saw the light was on in his father's den. "Working late?"

"No, no. I'm . . ." Henry pushed the door open. Behind him, in the center of the floor, Sky could see his father's home brew equipment laid out on newspaper. "Giving it a clean. Going to make a new batch."

"Ah well, have fun." Sky turned to the stairs.

"Sky?"

"Yeah?"

"Can you . . . uh . . . can you come in here?

"I'm off to bed, Dad. Bit tired." Actually, it was an understatement. Dying was hard on the system!

"It'll only take a minute."

With a sigh, Sky followed his father. He'd rarely been in his den. He looked around now at the ordered shelves, the rack of trophies Henry had won for cricket and tennis, designs for pipe systems laid out on the desk his father stood before.

"Yes, Dad?"

"I was going to wait for your sixteenth birthday, but . . . I . . . I wanted you to have something from your grandfather."

Startled, Sky thought it was something else from Sigurd. But then he realized what his father meant. "From . . . your dad?"

"Yes."

Sky knew very little about this other grandfather. He had died when Henry was very young, younger even than Sonja when Sigurd died.

"He was French, right?"

"Sort of. He was actually from Corsica. The island's

209

ruled by France, but it's closer to Italy. Your grandmother told me he considered himself Corsican, not French."

Sky struggled to remember the little-told story. "And you were actually born there, right?"

Henry nodded. It was a bit strange. His dad was just so . . . English. With his ale, his cricket. Even if he had dark hair and skin and was slightly built. Sky definitely took after his Norwegian side; he was already a couple of inches taller than his father.

"Do you remember him?"

"Not at all. He brought my mother and me to England when I was a baby. Then he went back to Corsica . . . and died." He reached behind him. "Got a picture, though."

Sky came forward as Henry flicked on the desk lamp. Laid out was a black-and-white photo of a man. A cloth cap on dark hair. A shirt open at the collar. He was sitting at a table and had a pipe in his mouth and a shotgun across his knees.

"Bit more powerful than your air rifle," Henry said, pointing.

"My what?" said Sky innocently.

But Henry was bending closer to the photo. "I went once. To Corsica. Hitchhiked there when I was seventeen."

Hitchhiking, Sky thought. Runs in the family, then!

"Did you like it?"

"Not really." Henry sucked at his lower lip. "Freaked me out, actually."

Sky smiled. He'd gotten so used to his father as the practical engineer, he'd forgotten he'd been a bit of a neohippie. Hitchhiking? Freaked out?

"Why?"

"Dunno. I felt threatened somehow." Henry shrugged. "But I did find where my father used to live. It was way in the south. And I met an old woman who'd known him. She was the one who gave me . . . this."

He held up a lighter. "You can see this in the photo. On the table in front of him?"

Sky looked down, then up at the object in his father's hand. It was the same lighter. All brass, a little over an inch high. His father used his thumb to push up a sort of arm that covered the wick. Then again to flick a flywheel. A spark came. A low flame.

"It used to be filled with petrol, but it works just as well with lighter fluid. You soak cotton, in here." He showed Sky a screw in the base. "And here's something interesting." He held the lighter so Sky could see the side. "See this here?"

Sky peered. "Looks like a stain."

"No, it's worn. A pipe's always going out, so you use one of these a lot. You're always rubbing it. So this"—he pushed the lighter a little closer—"this is really my father's thumbprint." He looked at it a long moment. "This is what I want you to have. All this talk of . . . cauls and sea chests. Well, here's something from my side of the family."

211

Henry held the lighter out. But as Sky reached for it, he had an odd feeling. Like his hand wanted it . . . and didn't want it! Like his hand had a memory of its own.

He took it, his thumb moving into the position to lift the arm, to strike. It covered his grandfather's thumbprint. It slid into it as if it were a track.

The floorboards shifted. The room spun. It wasn't like grasping a runestone, he wasn't "gone." But he was suddenly plunged into a cone of mist. It swirled around him, smelled of tobacco and some unknown plant or herb burning, acrid to nose and tongue. He heard a voice, a woman singing something high-pitched and sad.

Then three things came at him out of the mist: a wolf, teeth bared, neck tilted back, howling at a tall, carved stone; an old woman, completely bald, singing that same heartbreaking song; and last, some sort of cat, but bigger, wild, was writhing on the ground in front of him. He saw hands reaching down to the beast, knew they were his hands, Sky's hands, yet different, with scars on them his own did not possess. His hands lifted the wildcat's head, turning it . . . turning . . .

"Are you all right?"

He was sitting on the floor, his father bent over him. Before him, the lighter lay just beyond his fingertips.

Henry part lifted him, got him into a chair. He reached back, handed him a half-empty mug of beer, which Sky gulped at, coughed. "You know, it's strange," Henry said, patting his son's back, "but when that woman gave me the lighter, I did exactly the same thing. Fainted, I mean."

Sky looked up. "Was she bald?"

"Bald?" His father looked puzzled. "No. Why?"

"Nothing." He coughed again, then drained the mug. "Can I have some more beer?"

"Definitely not. You're mother would kill me. And it's bedtime." Sky pushed himself up from the chair. "Do you need help with the stairs?"

He took a few steps. "I'll be all right, Dad." He wobbled to the door.

His father's voice halted him. "Don't you want this?"

Sky looked back. His father was holding up the lighter. He only hesitated a moment. "Oh, yeah. I do. And thanks, Dad. It's . . . great."

"You're welcome," Henry said, coming to the door, his hand stretched out.

Sky took it. There was no mist. No flashes. It felt warm. But he supposed a lighter would.

When he got to his room, his legs still felt weak. So he put the lighter down on his dresser and lay on the bed without bothering to undress.

What was that all about? A wolf? A cat? A bald old woman? Didn't he have enough stuff going on? He stared at the shiny brass, then got up, opened a drawer, dropped the lighter in. "Another time," he said.

He lay down on his side and immediately felt something digging into his thigh. Rolling onto his back, he pulled the runestone from his pocket. He glanced at it, then shoved it under the pillow. That could wait as well; he'd find some way into it, but not until he'd had a good sleep. What was Kristin's last offer? Send him into a trance?

"Yeah, like I'm going to let her hypnotize me." He had a sudden vision of this girl at her school, barking around the dormitory. His cousin would love to get him to do that. In a week he had already been enough things. He could do without entering the animal kingdom, thank you very much!

CHAPTER EIGHTEEN

THE HAWK

". . . and, anyway, a dog can't fly."

"Who said that?" He'd sat up fast, so fast his head hurt. In fact, he wasn't sure if the pain was caused by the waking or had been there for a while; then again, he wasn't even sure if he was awake.

"Hallo?" he said, as much to himself as to anyone else.

"Hallo." It was like an echo, his own voice coming back at him. Yet it wasn't an echo. It was a reply.

He looked up. When had someone put a mirror on his ceiling?

He looked down. The mirror was on his bed, had to be. Didn't it have to be, since he could see behind himself, to the lamp shade, the ceiling above his outstretched wings?

Wings? Sky didn't have wings, not last time he looked. Arms were what he'd always used, had gotten by with. The boy on the bed, the one just falling back down, just closing his eyes, a runestone slipping from his fingers . . . he had arms, stretched the length of his body.

Arms? How useless! Arms couldn't keep you hovering. Arms couldn't be tucked, letting you fall like a stone to the earth, stopping you just above it, just where prey was squirming. They couldn't be fitted to the wind, letting you glide along the earth.

He dropped onto the windowsill. There was just enough of a gap to squeeze through.

Sky soared. He'd flown in dreams before, thought he knew what it would be like. It had been nothing like this. The power of it! Adapting to each pulse of wind, harnessing it, tiny adjustments of angle and tilt, a flap here, a curve there, and . . . *whoosh!* Up, up he went, higher and higher to a dead stop, wing tips as far apart as they could go, the world so still below because he was still. The sun was just cresting the rim of the world, and he could see for miles, the villages and hamlets, the dark smudge of a forest splitting two valleys, the hills called . . . who cared? The boy back on the bed would know their names. But why should Hawk care about anything else now, now when he could see the square iris of a sheep's eye and every petal on a rose? See a badger thrust through its favorite gap in a hedgerow, an otter dive and scrag a fish. And . . . there! There in the next field, that mound of earth cascading clumps down itself, something pushing up from beneath the ground . . .

No, not something. *Breakfast!*

Timing was everything. Swooping lower, directly above the spot, he hovered till he saw the tiniest glimpse of pink snout thrust itself clear. Then he dived, talons reaching, razor curves sinking into velvet skin. He rose, swept to an oak at the edge of the field.

The mole quivered under him. It was the matter of a heartbeat to stab down with a beak as sharp as his talons. The quivering ceased. And Sky-Hawk began to feast.

It took a moment to remember why he was there, why he had become bird. It was not this, to kill, to eat. He wasn't even hungry. Leaving the carcass on the branch, he rose again, then dived, weaving between the trees, deeper and deeper into forest on the long hill.

He knew where the rendezvous had to be. There was an ash tree he'd fallen from before he'd learned to fly. He glided up to it, reached, landed. Tucking his wings around him, he looked down to the clearing.

A fox sat there. Grandfather Fox, who opened his jaws and said, "So, you have come."

"As you see." Sky—the hawk—fluttered his feathers. "It was harder this time. I could not come to you through the runes."

"But you did. A rune brought you. *Raidho,* rune of transformation. Remember that, Sky—there are many different ways to use the stones." The fox tipped his snout up. "I did not know in what shape you would

217

come. We cannot always choose what form our Fetch will take. This bird of prey suits you, my grandson."

Sky-Hawk stretched his wings out, shook them. "I could stay like this forever. But I know it is only a dream."

"It is not a dream. It is another part of your Fetch's power—to borrow another shape and form. It is something you can . . . *will* learn to do."

"But I don't feel . . . entirely like me." A shiver ran through feather and claw. "I just killed something. For no reason. For . . . pleasure."

"Not pleasure, Sky. Instinct." Grandfather Fox extended his neck up toward the branch. "The creature is in you as much as you are in it. You have its feelings as well as your own. Its needs. Its desires." The fox's voice—Sigurd's voice—came softer now. "For your Fetch is not just a copy of you, Sky. You can only control so much."

"Like the berserker in Bjørn?"

"Like the berserker." The fox nodded, such a human movement within the animal. "Even when you go out as an exact physical copy of yourself, with vardogr—like you did at school, like I did in Oslo and many times since—it is often different parts of yourself. Different sides. The Fetch's great gift is that it allows you to be other things. It could be the thief in you that walks, the warrior in you, the rebel, the leader."

"The killer?" Sky felt that shudder pass through him again.

"Perhaps. When necessary."

It was hard, to reach beyond his hawk brain, beyond the needs that were driving him to soar, to swoop, to strike. "But . . . you . . . told me—told Sky!—that one day he *would* be able to control . . . this."

"One day. Perhaps. Would you like that?"

"Yes!" The word came out on a single, sharp call.

"And you will. But remember: Knowledge always demands a sacrifice. Would you give up the instincts of a hawk so soon?"

Silence came then. How could he ever surrender this power? He nearly gave in to it, took off then, pulsing with his desire to fly. Gripping his talons into bark, somehow he held himself on the branch. There was something else he—Sky—had to know.

"Where now?" he asked.

"Toward your destiny. That dictated by your caul, by the secrets you are slowly learning, the ones that whisper in your blood. Can you hear them, Sky?"

"Yes, yes, yes!" Somewhere in the forest nearby, a squirrel chittered fearfully at this hunting cry.

"And you wish to know where next they lead?"

"Tell me," was all he said.

"You must return to the runes. For this transformation is only one half of *Raidho*. The other is—"

He interrupted, impatient. "A journey. We have learned the meanings, Kristin and I."

The fox raised his snout, barked, a long cry. "It is far more than a journey, boy. It is a voyage . . . down!

219

For all who would learn the runes' final secrets must make this journey. They must visit their dead."

"To Bjørn?" Despite the warmth of feather and down on a summer's night, Sky shivered again.

"No, boy." The fox's incisors gleamed in the darkness. "To me."

"You!" Sky's talons slipped on the branch. He righted himself. "Like before?"

"No. For I do not mean in spirit. This time you must come in the flesh. To the place they sent my bones when I died."

This startled Sky. "They did not burn you, Grandfather?"

"They did not. I died on a burning ship, but of smoke, not flame. What remained of me was put in a coffin and sent home." The fox tossed its head. "But do not concern yourself with this. The Vikings may have believed it was better to burn, but it was not necessary to free their spirits. Only berserkers needed the cleansing flames. No one else."

There was something Sky wanted to say, about the drowning of Bjørn, his flesh not burned, his bones bleaching on a seabed. But the hawk had no time.

"Where?" was all he asked.

"Norway. In the high mountains known as the Jotunheim. Where the old gods were born. Where Odin, Allfather of the Gods, hung on an ash tree for nine days, gave an eye . . . for knowledge. For the runes." The fox stood, arched his back, fur raised in a line down his spine. "I was happy there, had a cabin, high up in a valley. You must go there now, to that cabin. Before I died on my last voyage, just as I placed the runestones in the sea chest, I also hid something there. Something that will lead you to nothing less than your destiny." The fox's eyes gleamed. "There is a map in the journal to guide you. Your cousin must come too. You will need her help. For the hardest part of any journey is closest to its end."

The fox placed his front paws on the fallen oak branch. "Go to Norway, Sky, to the mountains of your ancestors. Bring your cousin, the journal . . . and the runestones. Visit your dead!"

With a final howl, that strange, terrible cry like a woman's scream, Sigurd's Fetch ran into the woods, was lost, even to Sky's hawk sight. Free at last, he flew fast between the trees, out toward the sunrise.

221

He soared high, to the limits of breath, to where the cold penetrated even his feathers. Hanging there, nearly motionless, he could look down to his house, see the open window he would fly into. He knew he must return to his body—his other body!—soon. For the moment, he just hovered. The power he had, suspended there! It was like the power he'd felt when he returned from Bjørn that last time. He had experienced death and yet here he was, alive again. So alive!

When he finally squeezed back through the gap between window and sill, when he became just Sky again, it would be to take the last stage of this journey that had begun when the sea chest appeared in his kitchen. He would leave for Norway and find whatever it was that was there—something that would perhaps let him be Hawk forever!

If that wasn't destiny, he thought, tipping a wing, beginning his long fall, he didn't know what was.

CHAPTER NINETEEN

JOURNEY

"Oh, well, what a charming invitation." Her face broadened in a mocking smile. "And what if I don't want to go?"

"You have to! He told me to bring you."

"Oh did he?" Kristin sat in an armchair in the living room. She was obviously in the same mood as the night before. She'd been reading a newspaper when Sky, exhausted from his nocturnal activities, woke up late and sought her out. Now she flicked the pages and carried on reading, replying while she did. "A fox asks a hawk to bring *me* on a journey? So what does that make me, some sort of dog?"

"Hardly. I'm sure they have very strict rabies laws in Norway."

"Ha ha." She glanced at him over the page. "But from what you say, you don't need me to hold your hand. After last night, you can just flap your wings and fly over"—she smiled sweetly—"can't you?" She went back to the page.

God, girls can be annoying! he thought, looking at her, with her crossed legs and her newsprint barrier. Down the hall his mother was singing above the drone of the vacuum cleaner. She was getting near, so he pulled his chair up to his cousin's and said softly, "Kristin, it will be really difficult for a fifteen-year-old to get out of one country by himself and into another."

"Oh, so what you need is a *chaperone?*" The word could not have borne much more sarcasm.

"No," he sighed, "what I really need is a friend."

He had her with that, just for a moment; her eyes when she looked up were not as hostile. So he hurried on. "I can't . . . do it by myself. It's not just the traveling. I don't have a clue what to do when I get there. Lay flowers on his grave? Dig up his bones and burn them? Though he now says that's not so necessary for non-berserkers. Knock on the door of this cabin he used to live in and say to the new owners, 'Excuse me, have you seen my grandfather's Fetch lying around?'"

She gave a snort and, taking it as a suppressed giggle, he went on urgently. "Sigurd told me that he'd hidden something in the hut, something that will guide me to my destiny. But what if I don't like it, this destiny? What if it's more fighting or killing or . . . drowning?" He shook his head. "And you've done all the figuring out from these so far." He pulled Sigurd's journal and *Rune Magic* out from a bag beside him. "I know I've left all this to you, and I *promise,* if you come with me, I'll do my homework on the way. Plus you speak Norwegian and I don't. All I know is 'Thanks for lunch,' and a little prayer my mum taught me when I was three. So all I can do is leave a table politely and appeal to the Deity! Otherwise, I'm bollocksed." He looked straight in her eyes. "Please, Kris? For the Ancient Order of Wall-Walkers?"

She sighed, shaking her head. "I'm promising nothing," she said, laying down the paper. "But I can at least point you in the right direction."

It was a start. He opened Sigurd's journal to the page he'd found earlier. "It's a map," he said helpfully.

"No! Really?" She took the book. "I have been over every page of this, waiting for you. But since the map is just terrain and no words, I didn't have a clue where it was. Where did he say you have to go?"

"The Jotunheim. I've never heard of it, but—"

"I have. Been there, in fact, skiing. It's the area with the highest mountains in Norway. So naturally the Old Norse reckoned that's where their gods came from." She looked up from the journal. "Do you have an atlas?"

"Better than that." Sky moved across to the bookshelves. "Mum has . . . has . . . yeah, here it is." He returned with a map, pulled up a footstool. " 'Norge,' " he read, spreading the map out.

Her finger moved around. "So there's Oslo, Bergen, Trondheim. That's Tromsö near the top."

225

"Where's Hareid?" he asked, craning over it.

"Never heard of it. Where's it near?

"Ålesund," he said, though he had not a clue where that word came from.

"Ålesund . . ." She pored. "There, on the coast. And . . . yes, Hareid's an island just near it."

And between the two, Bjørn's armored bones lie bleached on the seabed. And in his arms . . .

Sky shivered while Kristin's finger kept moving, her voice interrupting his thoughts. "And here," she stabbed down, "is the Jotunheim. That's the tallest mountain in Norway there, Galdhøpiggen. But where this drawing is from, I don't . . ." She was scanning back and forth, between book and map. Now she lifted the journal closer. "Wait, that dot there. It's actually a mountain symbol, isn't it?"

Sky peered. It did have sharp peaks. "Could be."

She went on, "So if Sigurd marked the tallest mountain in the Jotunheim, then that dot there above it, with . . . now I look at it closely . . . with a cross coming out of it is . . ." She put her finger on the map. "Could be the biggest town in the area—Lom. And the cross means a church." She looked up. "It's where we were based for skiing. There's an ancient church there."

"And where there's a church, there'll be a cemetery. Sigurd said he was buried there."

Kristin looked puzzled. "Didn't you say before that he died on a burning ship in Java?"

"Yeah, but something must have survived the fire. And I suppose it was in his will to bury whatever remained of him where he'd been happiest."

Kristin nodded, but she was distracted again by the map. She studied the printed one, then traced her finger along a line in the journal that led to another dot. Three trees were around it. "So this could be his cabin? Southwest here. In a forest."

Sky peered. "You think? It *is* the only other main feature, so . . . probably."

"But how far away is it? This diagram may not be to scale." She chewed at a nail. "We'll only know when we get there, I suppose."

He tried to keep the relief off his face. "So, uh . . . you're coming, then?"

227

She sighed. "You'd only get into trouble without me. Besides, I want to see this cabin." She folded the map, dropped it with the two books into her bag. "Do you have a passport?"

" 'Course."

"Then I suggest you lay your hands on it ASAP. Mine's at home in Derby. So we'll have to go there first."

"How—"

She raised a finger to her lips. The singing had been getting closer, almost drowning out the hum of the vacuum cleaner being pushed along. Both stopped when Sonja thrust her head around the door. "Ah, so Mr. Dozy's up at last."

"Morning, Mum."

"Would you two like a cup of tea?"

"Love one. Oh, Auntie . . ." Kristin waved her cell phone in the air. "I just had a call from my mother."

"I thought she was in America on business."

"She is. But she needs some papers faxed to her from the house. So I have to go back to Derby. And I thought I might stay a couple of days, if that's OK. There's some friends I'd like to see."

They watched her think. "Well, Inge did say you could go back if you needed to." She nodded. "But we'll all miss you. Especially Sky."

"Well, I was thinking . . . maybe he could come too?"

228

Sky looked at Kristin, swallowed, looked at his mother. "Please, Mum. I could use a break—"

"From your old parents?" She smiled. "Well, as long as you stick with your sensible cousin."

"'Course."

"Don't worry. I'll watch him . . . like a hawk." Kristin said the words to Sonja, but her eyes flicked to Sky.

"I'm sure you will, dear. When do you want to go?"

"Today," they both answered, and laughed.

"I think there's a train at two. I'll give you a ride to the station. But let's have that tea first." She went down the corridor toward the kitchen.

"That was brilliant," he said. "You don't waste any time, do you?"

"Nope. And as long as we call in"—she waved the phone at him—"well, they won't know *where* we are calling from, will they?"

He shook his head, admiringly. "You've done this before, haven't you?"

"Once or twice." She smiled. "You can't go to a boarding school and not have escape plans."

Sky frowned. "Uh, there's a very slight problem."

"How slight?"

"I haven't got any money."

"What, none?"

"Almost none. But that doesn't matter."

"Why doesn't it?"

"Because you have lots." He grinned at her.

"So, on top of everything else, I'm supposed to finance your adventures. You cheeky little . . ." She shook her head. "Well, I better have some fun of my own on this trip, let me tell you. And I don't have lots of money, actually. But enough. Enough to get us to Norway, anyhow."

After a night at Kristin's home, they caught a late-morning train north—to Newcastle and the ferry. Though he slept a lot of the four-hour ride—a sleep happily uncomplicated by dreams—Sky woke up with a start when the conductor announced that they were about to pass through York. For though the hedgerowed fields and ordered villages looked nothing like the country he'd marched through with Harald Hardrada, still,

229

this was where Bjørn had fought, killed; where the berserker had been revealed. And because the day was dark, with heavy rain clouds above, the carriage's lighting meant he could see a reflection of himself in the window. A Double looked both back and out upon the land where a Double had walked.

But if that had caused stirrings, it was worse the next morning on the ferry to Norway. The *M/S Wayfarer* sailed the same sea his Viking ancestors had crossed the other way to plunder, raid, invade. It passed nowhere near Hareid; yet Sky knew that trenches furrowed the seabed with currents passing along them that could move objects vast distances. And he spent much too long staring into those iron-gray waters, wondering if the remnants of a mail coat rolled down there with the tides; if, twenty fathoms beneath the keel of the ferry, two skeletons tumbled in its spill, locked together for eternity.

Of course, such thoughts made him think of Black Ulf. And though he had not seen the draug since Ludlow, he had a sense of him still, felt that if he turned around suddenly he'd see him just standing there. He made a point of avoiding any mirrors on board the ship. He didn't think he could take another that reflected nothing back.

After a day and a night, the ship docked the following noon. Kristin had researched everything, and they only waited an hour for the bus that went from Bergen to Trondheim—with a drop-off in Lom.

He had been to Norway a couple of times as a kid to visit his grandmother. But not for years . . . and never in the summer.

"What time is it?"

Kristin groaned. "You asked me five minutes ago. It's ten past nine."

"Just to be clear—that's 21:10, yes?"

"Yes."

Sky chuckled at the bored tone of her voice. "I know you've seen this before. But to me it's just, like, weird."

He turned back to the view—21:10 and bright as midday! He'd heard that, this close to midsummer, the sun barely went down. Just got a little dark around midnight and then got light again fast. It *was* weird. It was also kind of fantastic. Night and darkness were hardly his favorite things.

231

"How do people get to sleep?"

"They don't, if idiots keep jabbering all the time." Kristin had been trying to sleep for most of the ten-hour bus trip. She hadn't had much luck. "Yes, the land of the midnight sun! Yes, the country of our ancestors! It's all very exciting. Now let me get some rest, will you?"

Sky grinned. The bus went over a bridge, an ice-melt river, green as jade, below. A sign read, LOM 3.

"Well, you can try," he said, "in the five minutes you have left."

She groaned, gave up, raised herself from her slouch,

rubbed her eyes. "I feel like death warmed over," she said.

"Do you mind," he replied, mock offended. "When you've died as often as I have—"

"Oh, shut up!" She looked at him. "You're in a good mood."

"I feel great. This is a place where the sun hardly sets. So the creatures of the night can't get me." He said it in the same vampire voice his dad had used a few nights before, when he'd given him the lighter. The thought of Henry made him feel slightly guilty for a moment. He'd called home from the ferry port, claiming they'd gone to a friend of Kristin's at the seaside, where the reception was really bad. Said he'd call again in a few days. He really didn't like lying to his parents. But they'd never have allowed him to go on this trip. And he had to. He felt he was getting closer and closer to something—and he couldn't wait to arrive.

And he didn't have to wait long. "Lom," the driver called back.

"Funny," he said, reaching up for his backpack, "how 'destiny' and 'destination' are, like, the same word."

"So are 'prat' and 'prat,'" she yawned, reaching for hers.

But even Kristin was wide-awake when they disembarked. "So shall we go to the youth hostel? Or find somewhere to pitch the tent?" she asked.

"Neither." he replied. "Let's go find Grandfather."

232

A low wall surrounded both the cemetery and the church, which looked like a wooden island in a sea of headstones. Kristin, who had studied such things, told Sky that it was a medieval stave church. To Sky, used to the stone towers of Shropshire, it was weird, made of slabs of wood, dark with age and weathering; it looked as if several extensions had been added to a main house—which, he supposed, they had. The walls all curved slightly, the wood-tiled roofs ending in points, each of them a dragon's head. Immediately Sky remembered the prow of *Storm-Bringer* and the last time he'd seen it—breaking apart while a slave who hated him fell within his armored embrace.

Suddenly, despite the sun, he felt cold. He pulled at Kristin's arm. "Maybe we should go to the youth hostel. It might close."

233

She'd been staring up at the strange roofs too. Now she turned back. "But we're here now. Don't you want to see him?" She'd nodded toward the graves.

"Not really," he muttered.

"Come on. We've come all this way. . . ." She grabbed his arm, tugged him toward the gate. It was locked, but once they'd taken off their packs, the wall was easy enough to scramble over. When they had, they put their backs to it and stared.

Unlike the graveyards at home, with their irregular-sized monuments scattered higgledy-piggledy across the grass, this cemetery was a little more ordered. The tombstones, though cut from different rock in different colors, were all about the same height, reaching three feet off the ground. They lay in uneven concentric circles, hundreds of them, the church the center of the stone rings. But as in England, most were old, the writing eroded by wind and water on some, green slime or moss obscuring the epitaphs on others. The few more recent headstones reflected the strange late-night light in burnished marble. Flowers flourished on a few, weeds on many.

They stared in silence for a while. Finally Kristin said, "We may have to come back in the morning, when the church is open. They might have, like, a guide to the . . . residents." She waved her hand. "We'll never find Grandfather's grave in this lot."

"We will."

"How?"

Sky's voice had dropped to a whisper. "Because I know where it is."

CHAPTER TWENTY

THE DEAD

He didn't offer an explanation, just pushed himself away from the wall and began walking to his left. He'd known from the moment his feet touched the grave-yard earth. It was as if there were wires running under the ground, sending a pulse up into his body. No, not just one—pul*ses,* two of them. Duh-dum. Duh-dum. Duh-dum. Like a heartbeat.

They walked between the graves, sometimes over them, though both were unhappy doing that. Their footsteps sounded loud, grinding on gravel, squeaking on grass, maybe because there was no other noise save the faintest of breezes stirring in the yew trees that dotted the cemetery.

It was in front of one of these, flush to the encir-cling wall, that Sky stopped, so suddenly that Kristin, who had been scanning for one name on the head-stones, bumped into him quite hard.

"What . . . ?" she said, craning past his shoulder to see what had halted him. "It's just a tree, Sky."

"A yew."

"I know."

"Did you know every part of it is poisonous? That's why they were planted on sacred sites. On tombs. Keeps the livestock off."

"Yes, well, fascinating. But we're not here on a nature ramble—"

He interrupted her. "So it is the tree of the Dead. It leads directly to the Underworld."

"So?"

"So . . ."

He pointed and she looked. Just beside the tree was a headstone. It was half hidden by the lower branches, so they could only see the base of it.

"Is it him?"

No reply.

"Is it him, Sky?"

His voice came as if from away. "It's him."

"How can you know?" Her voice was suddenly angry. "You're just trying to freak me out. It could be anyone, it could be . . ."

She was striding forward as she spoke, bending as she reached the branches, hands stretching to part them. And just as she did, something black burst screeching from the foliage.

"Aaah," she screamed, tumbling back, landing hard on the needles beneath the tree. Sky, who had started

236

to follow her, had to duck as the dark shape shot over his head. He had a glimpse of talons, of a large beak, a reek of something rotten on the breath. Then it was gone.

"What . . . what was that?" Kristin still sat there, hand reaching up to her stunned face, not quite touching it. "It wasn't . . . wasn't a bat, was it?" She began rubbing her clothes as if they were dirty.

Sky knelt. "It was a bird. Like a crow. Maybe a raven."

"A raven? Ravens don't lurk under trees. They might sit on top of one to watch for prey, or circle high up in the air on a thermal, but . . ."

She was speaking quickly, breathlessly, her eyes shifting back and forth. "Who's giving the nature lecture now?" he asked.

He got a slight smile, and her eyes focused on his. "Ready?" he said.

She nodded and they both took a breath. Then, as if by agreement, they both looked.

The light was poor under the tree, everything shadowed. But they could see that the granite tombstone was not as weathered as most they'd seen, hadn't been ground down by rainfall, or lined in moss. And it was newer than many, as the dates carved simply into the granite testified.

"'Sigurd Alfred Solness,'" Sky read quietly, "'8-8-1911 to 14-9-1963.'"

They both stared at it, the silence lengthening. Finally, he said, "Is that it?"

"What did you expect?"

"I'm not sure." He felt . . . disappointed, and he wasn't sure why. "A . . . message of some kind, maybe?"

"There is one." She'd been sitting and now came up onto her knees, crawled forward. "Two, actually."

He joined her nearer to the stone, uncomfortably aware that he was crawling *over* his grandfather's skeleton. It didn't feel . . . right, somehow, to be doing that. But she'd moved even closer, and reluctantly, he followed till he could see past her shoulder to her tracing finger.

" '*Non Omnis Moriar,*' " she read. "Do you know what that means?"

"You're the one who speaks Norwegian," he replied.

She laughed. "What do they teach in that school of yours? It's not Norwegian, dummy. It's Latin. And it means, roughly, 'All of me' . . . uh . . . 'does not die—' "

Suddenly he knew. " 'I will not die entirely.' "

"Yeah," she admitted, "that's probably better."

Now that he was closer, he could see more too. Up in the corner of the stone, something else was cut. This hadn't been done with the precise blows of a chisel. This had been slashed swiftly in four rough strokes. As befitted a rune.

"We know that one, don't we?"

"Yes." Her voice was soft. "*Raidho*. The journey. And . . . transformation."

His voice matched hers. "Does anything on earth transform more than a body in a coffin?"

For a moment they knelt there in silence. Then he

said, loudly, "Let's get out of here," and began to shuffle backward. After a last look, she followed, and soon the two were standing before the tree, the grave hidden again under the yew needles.

"What now?" she said, brushing off her jeans.

"No, I mean, let's get out of *here*!" He gestured around the cemetery and immediately went to the wall, scrambled over, his cousin following. They'd left their backpacks just outside the front gate. Collecting them, they hurried the short distance back to the center of Lom. There was a museum, some offices and shops, a notice board. They dropped their packs again to consider.

"So, what now?" Kristin said. "Shall we find a place to camp?"

"I'd rather have a roof over my head," Sky replied, looking back in the direction of the church. "Didn't you say something about a youth hostel?"

"There must be one, but where?" She was looking around, then said, "Hey," and stepped past him to the notice board. "There's a stroke of luck. A town map."

He joined her. "Hardly luck. We *are* standing in front of the tourist office."

She saw the sign. "Oh yeah. Well anyway . . ." She scanned. "So there is a youth hostel . . . though it seems way out that way . . ." She waved. "And there's a campsite that's . . . over there, and . . . oh!"

"What?" His gaze had kept being drawn to the graveyard, its walls just visible through a gap between buildings. But her exclamation, and her sudden scrambling into her bag, brought his attention back. "What is it?"

"I think . . ." She had the journal out, open, was flipping to a page. "Yes, look." She showed him, pointed to the map in the book, then the one on the board. "If this mountain sign is Galdhøpiggen, and this dot here is Lom"—she held the volume up so he could see— "and this dot is Grandfather's old cabin . . . then . . ." She tapped the map on the notice board. "Then it's up in this valley here, to the southwest."

As she spoke, the bell in the church began to chime the hour. They couldn't help counting. It reminded them of that time in the attic, the first time that Sky had gone to see his grandfather. With the tenth and last *dong* still hanging in the air, he turned back to her. "Let's go," he said.

"Of course. First thing in the morning."

"No, let's go now."

"Are you mad? It's the middle of the night."

"No, it's not. And it feels like day to me, with all this light. I mean, could you sleep now?"

She grinned. "Not a chance."

"Then let's go. We can camp up there if we get tired. How far is it, anyway?"

"There must be a scale here somewhere . . . yes." She studied it, used spread fingers to measure. "Its about ten kilometers."

He frowned. "How many miles is that?"

"Dunno. About five? Five and a half?"

Suddenly he couldn't stand still. He slung on his backpack. "We could do that in two hours. Less."

"Yeah, if we don't get horribly lost. And the sun *does* set, you know. Plus we still don't know how accurate Sigurd's map is, and this one only shows a path. It doesn't show if it's uphill or if it's—"

"Doesn't matter," he interrupted her, walking a few paces away. "Come on."

She sighed, then bent to her own pack. "OK. But let's at least start out in the right direction."

She began to walk the opposite way from the direction he'd headed. After a dozen paces, because she was walking fast, he caught up. They walked down the main street of the town, heading south. The sky was still lit in that same strange glow. The roadway ahead was clear.

"Thanks."

"Never git between a man and his destiny," she said, in her best cowboy accent.

"Non Omnis Moriar," he said.

"I will not die entirely," they said together.

The two-hour walk took five. At first, the road made it easy. But near a crossroads that looked like the one marked in Sigurd's journal, a path was indicated rising up into the forest. The first one they took led within minutes to a little valley filled with huts with boarded-up windows and roofs covered in grass. There were no

241

people, just a herd of cows that ran up and tried to wash them clean with their long tongues. Backtracking to the crossroads, it took them over an hour to find another path. And when they did, it was worrying because it was the barest whisper of clearness upon the ground, sometimes passing between trees that clung so close they had to remove their backpacks. Eventually, though, it began to both widen and steepen, and the lower stands of oak and ash gave way to copses of birch. The higher they climbed, the more silver these became, which was fortunate, as the sunset, such as it was, had come; though it never got to the dark night they were used to, probably because of the cloudless sky, it was still dark enough. They could see the white birch bark, peeling away in strips from the trunks, an avenue of the trees that roughly followed the path. There was no dawn, no sunrise to mark the change. But the light grew from that near darkness to bright and then to brighter. When they emerged from the tree line, the world was clear. Fern and bracken stretched ahead of them, a green and waving sea of it. It flowed around a hill above them.

242

"Take our bearings up there?" Sky pointed.

"After you," Kristin grunted, shifting her pack.

The crest was gained in five minutes. A rock like an inverted steam iron about ten feet across was at the top. "Wow!" said Sky, dropping his pack on it, pulling out his water bottle, which he gave to Kristin. As she gulped, he looked around. In the distance, the opposite direction to the one they'd come from, a snow-covered mountain or glacier shut off the end of the valley, steep slopes rising toward it from where they stood. To their right, the land dropped a little to rise again to another hilltop about half a mile away; to their left, it dropped into another valley. The outcrop they were on was like a stone buckle in a fern belt, the land on every side returning to forest within two hundred yards.

Kristin, revived by water, pointed out the obvious problem. "This must be . . . here on Sigurd's map"—she pointed—"that circle. But the path we want leads off it back that way"—she gestured behind her—"and look."

He did. There were at least four pathways visible, traces of light cutting through the ferns, then disappearing into forest. All led roughly where they wanted to go. Only one would be right.

"Time for sleep, perhaps?" Kristin sat, then lay back on the rock. "Unless you fancy turning into a hawk and asking *him* for directions?"

She closed her eyes and jerked her thumb vaguely in the direction they would need to head. They had heard the cuckoo for the last part of their climb through the wood. Now it was below, hidden somewhere, its strange, two-tone call almost taunting them.

"Very funny." Sky looked down at her, at the rock shelf she lay on, considering. They were both exhausted, sure, and maybe a couple of hours' rest wouldn't hurt. But he just had a sense that what they sought was close. Very close. He wanted to find it . . . now! And

243

why lie on rock when there was a cabin nearby with a wooden floor they could sleep on?

Torn, he undid the waist belt on his pack. And then he looked past her shoulder. There, etched into the shale shelf, with the same simple slashes that had been on the tombstone, was another symbol from the rune-cast. *"Othala,"* he said, "rune of ancestors, rune that summons. By your head."

"Give me a break," she said, but opened her eyes. They widened as she looked where he pointed. She sat up. "Well, well."

There was no doubt. The rune's diamond head was pointing down the central cut through the ferns and bracken. It vanished into a thick clump of birch that went on for about a quarter mile, till the bracken reappeared on the far side and the land began to climb again.

"The map shows that the cabin's in a wood, yeah?" She nodded. "Well, it must be that one." He clicked the belt of his pack. "Come on. We can't be more than ten minutes away."

He was off down the path. He heard her groan, shoulder her pack, follow. He waited for her just where the trail moved under the leaves.

"Those cabins, farther down the valley?" he said.

"Yeah?"

"If they were deserted, then maybe his, even higher up in the mountains, will be too."

"So?"

"So we can rest there for a few days. Whatever it is Sigurd hid before he died, it will be like the secret compartment in the sea chest—hard to find. So we can take our time. Look for clues."

"Well," Kristin sighed, "we have some cans of food, some pasta and stuff. It could last us a few days if we starve slowly. Long as there's water and firewood. Hey, slow down, will you?"

Her agreement pushed him on and he began to move quicker, all tiredness gone. The destination was clear and close. Answers to the questions that had arrived with the sea chest were just up ahead. The waiting was over! And he felt he belonged in these mountains, felt it like he never had in his life. All that moving around England, different houses, different schools? Here, in a remote forest in a strange country, he felt as if he was coming home.

245

"Do you see it?" he shouted, because she was already quite far behind. There was something solid ahead, a structure glimpsed between the tree trunks. "Come on."

He'd always been a fast runner. So he had stood in front of the cabin for a good minute before she puffed up behind him. In that minute he had taken in everything. The turf roof, the grass on it as deep as his lower leg. The log walls, black with the tar that sealed them against all weather. The round stone chimney, thrust through the grass . . .

. . . the smoke rising from it.

Kristin caught up. "Why"—she struggled for air—"why are you standing . . ."

He raised a finger to his lips, then pointed with it. She looked, saw. They stayed like that for a bit, while her breath returned and his heart slowed.

"What do we do?" she whispered.

"I don't know," he answered at the same volume.

"Well, we have to knock at least." When he didn't move, she added, "It might not have been Sigurd's cabin."

"It was. I know it was."

"Well, my mum's always knocking on the doors of places where she used to live, asking to see around. This is similar. People don't mind."

Sky shook his head. "These people might. They don't live in a hut in the middle of a forest because they want visitors. Anyway . . . what *time* is it?"

She reached into a pocket, turned on her phone. "No reception, of course, but . . . it's four-seventeen."

Four-seventeen. The time he'd woken up for three days before the sea chest arrived.

"It's a bit early to be disturbing people, isn't it?" He was already half turned toward the path. "Let's go back to the rock, wait a couple of hours—"

"No," she said, annoyed, pulling him around. "We're lost in the woods, yeah? In the middle of nowhere. They'll understand, give us a cup of tea, maybe let us look around a bit before we go back to town." When he still didn't move, she hissed, "Look, you were the one so keen to get here. And now you're going to back off? It's like with the runes. 'Ooh, I'm *never* going to use them again.'"

Her impression of him was horribly accurate. Another time he might have laughed.

She punched him on the arm, hissed, "Look, will you knock?"

"All right, all right!" he muttered. He took a pace forward, then another. The first step up to the porch was silent, the second creaked, the sound loud as a rifle shot in the stillness of the forest. Have to remember that, he thought. Number two creaks.

He stood before the door. It appeared to have been carved from a single tree trunk. He looked back, to Kristin waving him on. He swallowed. Then he knocked, so softly he barely heard it himself. He knocked again, louder, longer, six good raps, spaced out. Like a cuckoo's call. Like a heartbeat.

Knock-knock. Knock-knock. Knock-knock.

The silence was back and deeper after its violation. He shrugged, began to turn away. Then he heard it. A movement within, the shuffling of feet moving closer, closer. Stopping. There was someone standing just the other side of the wood.

"Hello?" Sky tried to say, but his voice cracked and he couldn't get it back.

There was a rasp of breath. A metal latch scraped up. The door was opened a fraction. Just inside the frame, a glimmer reflected in eyes, the only light in the darkness.

Somehow he found his voice again. "Oh, hello. We're so . . . so sorry to dist . . . at this time of . . ."

A hand emerged, bone white, except where it was threaded through with purple veins. Sky moved quickly back, to the edge of the steps. He'd seen a hand not dissimilar before. It had wrapped around a tree trunk in his garden under a blood-red moon. This one gripped the doorframe, age-thick knuckles whitening even more as the hand pulled the body forward, the face into view.

There was no cloak, no empty gray hood. Sky, poised to run back to Kristin, saw that immediately. But he didn't think he'd ever seen anyone as old as the man before him either. He was so thin, it was like he was made from birch bark, yet not as substantial. Pale eyes stared as if through a mist of skin.

248

Sky cleared his throat. "I'm . . . so sorry if we woke you, we . . ."

"I was not asleep," the man whispered, his voice rusty with disuse, his English accented. "And you are welcome here. So welcome." Something came to the bloodless lips that could have been a smile. "You see, I have been waiting to meet you for a very long time."

It was only then that Sky recognized him. The voice, even though age had made it weak. The blue of the eyes, even if they were behind a veil. Above all, the shadow of hair that ran across the bridge of the nose.

Sky could barely get the word out. "Grandfather?" he whispered.

CHAPTER TWENTY-ONE
SIGURD'S STORY

For the longest moment, Sky just stood there. It was as if his feet had melted, fusing him to the porch. He wanted to turn and run and he couldn't, couldn't do anything but stare into those eyes. For all their milkiness, for all the aged, drooping flesh around them, it was like looking into a mirror.

Then, with an effort that hurt, he turned, stumbled down the two stairs, across the patch of earth, into Kristin. Only the contact with her body, her arms suddenly supporting him, prevented him from running all the way back to town.

"What's the matter with you?" she hissed. "You look like you've seen a ghost!"

"I-I—ha-have . . . ," he stuttered, jerking his head back, pointing with it. His knees gave, and he seemed to have used all his strength just to get down the stairs. A visit in a dream was one thing; a phantom in a doorway was something else entirely.

Then Kristin did a strange thing. She leaned past Sky's shoulder and spoke. "Excuse us!"

Sky jerked away so he could look into her eyes. "You . . . you can see him?"

She frowned, then said very quietly, "The old man? 'Course I can. Stop acting so weird." She called up as she tried to loosen Sky's grip. "Sorry about him. He's a little tired."

Sky couldn't bring himself to look around. But he grasped Kristin's arms even harder, preventing her from moving forward. "It's Grandfather," he hissed.

"Yeah, right." Then she saw his face again, and her gaze returned to the figure on the porch. "That's nonsense!" she said, less certain.

250

"It's him," Sky whispered, his voice hoarse. "And if you can see him too—"

He was interrupted by another voice. "Can you come closer, please? I cannot see or hear you there."

Kristin was trying to move toward the cabin and pull Sky along with her. She hissed at him, "Stop being so rude, Sky." Then called over his shoulder, "Sorry, but . . . my cousin thinks you're his grandfather's ghost."

If he'd had any strength, he'd have punched her! Instead, he just clung to her as he heard the voice say, "I am no ghost. But I *am* his grandfather. And yours, too, my dear Kristin."

Her hands fell away from him. But he could support himself now—his strength returned along with his anger. *This was outrageous!* "You're supposed to be dead," he shouted, turning to face the man. "And if you're not, then you've played a bloody awful joke on us."

Sky had taken a stumbly step toward the house. Kristin passed him, striding to the foot of the steps. "I should have guessed it was all a trick."

"How, my child?"

"Because of the fox." Her voice was part fury, part wonder. "You came as a living creature. But from what I read, the Dead can't take over animal's bodies, they can only appear as ghosts, as fylgyas." She shook her head. "I thought the books were wrong. But no! It was you, lying to us." The fury had taken over. "So . . . was it *all* lies?"

Sky caught up with her. Together, they stared up at the man in the doorway, and he must have sensed the level of their anger because he shuffled a step nearer, his arms spread wide. "No. Please believe me. That was the only lie," he said. "I am so sorry to have deceived you. Both of you. I can only say it was necessary. Vital. And if you will come inside, I . . ." He gestured to the doorway behind him. "Please. You must be hungry, it's a good climb from Lom. And I owe you an explanation; a story. My story. Please."

The cousins stood there silently for a long moment. All they could hear, other than their own accelerated breathing, was that bird calling again from down the valley. *Cuckoo, cuckoo, cuckoo,* it went, as if mocking their stupidity.

251

Then Kristin said, "Well, I for one am starving." She turned and picked up her pack. "The least you owe us is a meal."

Sky went to get his pack. "This had better be good," he said to Kristin.

His mutter was obviously loud enough for Sigurd to hear. "Oh, it will be, Grandson," he said. "Better than you could ever have dreamed."

The cabin was roomier than it looked from the outside, the front door opening straight into a large living area. One wall was taken up by a stone fireplace where a small fire crackled, its glow offering a little light in the dark-paneled room. There were small windows in the front wall and at the back, and curtains hanging over what had to be entrances to other rooms. After the brightness of the Norwegian dawn, both Sky's and Kristin's eyes took a while to adjust to the gloom. When they had, they saw that every available surface— shelves, chairs, a table, the very floor—everywhere was covered in paper. Books both open and in teetering columns, folders stuffed and spilling their contents out, acres of newsprint in a variety of languages, sheets and sheets of writing in the same scrawl that appeared in the journal from the sea chest. The paper seemed to sweep in banks toward the fireplace, rising there like a snowdrift around an old, high-backed leather armchair. It was toward this that Sigurd led them, his bony hands reaching down to clear some space for them in front of it. Papers slid away to reveal a soft, round foot-stool.

"Our breakfast table," Sigurd said, before shuffling off to the curtained doorway at the back of the room, while they squatted down, wedged in by the paper mounds. Despite the slowness of his movements, he returned quickly enough with a tray of food, almost as if he had prepared it before. Kristin rose to take it from him. It was filled with all the horrible things their Norwegian mothers liked to eat for breakfast: cuts of salami and ham, wedges of cheese, bowls of herring, black bread, hard-boiled eggs, a jug of warm milk. At any other time, Sky would have said, "Gross!" But they were halfway up a mountain and he was ravenous. So he tucked in, Kristin overcoming the same initial revulsion to do the same. Sigurd meanwhile had lowered himself slowly into his chair and was looking down at them.

"Shall I wait till you finish or . . ."

Sky's mouth was too full. Kristin spoke for them. "Might as well begin." She waved at the food, at Sky squashing cheese onto a slice of bread. "We may be some time."

To the sound of crunching, Sigurd began to softly speak.

"I know you have questions, many, many of them. The first must be: Why did I pretend to be dead for so many years? The second: Why should I return to life now? Now, when I am so close to my life's true ending?" He coughed slightly. "Well, there were two reasons why I had to disappear. One very practical. One . . . not so." He cleared his throat. "I was a sea captain, going from port to port around the world. It was easy for me to . . . what is the word in English?" He stared above them for a moment. "Smuggle. Yes. *Smuggle* things from one country to another."

Kristin swallowed. "You were a criminal?"

Sigurd nodded. "In a way. I am not proud of it. But a sea captain is not paid well. And I did not want to remain at sea for much longer. Not after my encounter in the shipping company building. There were things I needed to do." His eyes gleamed. "But, of course, the men who paid me to smuggle? They made most of the money, while I took most of the risks. So I thought: If the chance ever came to . . . disappear with my illegal cargo, I should take it." He took a deep breath. "The chance came."

"The shipwreck?"

"Yes, Sky. The matter of that 'death' is easily told. My ship was aflame off the coast of Java, drifting into port. The last of my crew died in my arms. He happened to be the same height and shape as me. So I slipped my wedding ring onto one of his poor, scorched fingers, put my captain's jacket on him. Then lowered myself into the filthy waters before the fire launches came. I watched them finally put out the flames that had consumed nearly everything on board. I waited in Jakarta for the results of the inquest. I witnessed the coffins loaded onto the ship that would bear them back to Norway. I saw one with my name on it returning, as my will dictated, to the mountain town where I'd been happy. And as the ship sailed, I knew that we were free."

"'We'?" Kristin asked, a cracker halfway to her lips. "Who's 'we'?" Then she realized. "Oh, of course. Your Fetch."

"Exactly." Sigurd had stood, leaned over to the mantel above the fireplace. From it he picked up a small teak box, carved with elephants and orchids. Sitting back down, he opened the box, pulled a little velvet bag out. "This is what I took."

At his gesture, Kristin held out her hand and Sigurd tipped the bag onto it.

255

Three small, misshapen stones lay there. "What are these?"

"Diamonds. Uncut diamonds." Sigurd reached down, shaking fingers picking up each stone, slipping them back into their bag, speaking as he did. "There were ten to begin with, and I sold them when I needed to. One paid for this house. Others funded my journeys." When the last diamond had been replaced, he pulled the bag's drawstring tight and held it out to Sky. "I want you to take them, Grandson. I will not have time to spend them now. And I think you will need them . . . as I did." He coughed again. "Keep them safe."

It took Sky only a moment to think of the safest place he knew. Reaching inside his shirt, he opened the leather pouch that contained his caul. Then he took the tiny bag of jewels, folded it, and tucked it inside.

Sigurd dropped another log on the fire. There was a sound like an indrawn breath, a crackle of sparks, the hiss of damp wood heating. Sky shuddered slightly as he remembered sea water pouring onto the shattered planks of a burning longship. Then Sigurd spoke again.

"You can understand why I couldn't go back home. The criminals I cheated would have found out eventually, would have come to kill me, would have killed my family too. And there was another reason I couldn't return." His eyes gleamed. "You know why, Sky, don't you?"

Sky nodded. "The Fetch."

"Yes. The second reason I had to disappear." He smiled, laid a hand for a moment on Sky's shoulder. "We neither of us will forget our first encounter with our Fetch, will we? Mine changed my life, as your encounter changed yours. But there are many who meet them, who walk with their Doubles by their side all their life and ignore them, do nothing with them. That wasn't good enough for me . . . or for you, I suspect."

Kristin shook her head. There was no mistaking her anger. "But the pain you caused them! Our mothers, growing up without you. Your wife! How could anything be worth that?"

"I'd already left them, remember. Letting them think of me as dead was a kindness, in a way."

"I don't believe they thought so."

Sigurd acknowledged Kristin's words with a slight nod of the head. But his gaze came onto Sky. "But there was another reason. A more important one." He nodded again. "Tell her, Grandson. Tell her what you have learned."

"Sacrifice," Sky said. "It's about sacrifice, isn't it?"

"Yes," Sigurd whispered. "The rune *Uruz* speaks of it. Every part of the journey to knowledge demands a sacrifice. For Odin, it was hanging on a tree for nine days, being stabbed with a spear, giving one eye . . . all to gain the runes. For me . . ." He sighed, and his own eyes, already watery, filled with more liquid. "For me it was returning to Norway after ten years, going and watching outside my old house, seeing my wife remarried, seeing your mothers"—his voice caught—"young women by then. I didn't speak to them. What could I say? I just shed my tears, for the life, for the happiness I could have had. Then I walked away."

"Where did you go?" asked Kristin.

"Everywhere! Everywhere people have a tradition of the Fetch, which, if you look hard enough, is everywhere in the world. In Indonesia, where some people believe that even rocks have souls, they knew about the Double that accompanies every man and woman." He waved at the papers that filled the room. "In the forests of Friuli in Italy my Double went out into the fields with the Benandanti, Fetches that battle evil for the health of each year's crop. On the steppes of Siberia I studied with the shamans of the Silver Birch, who use their plants of power to journey beyond their bodies. In the Languedoc in France I met those with their eyebrows joined like ours, Sky"—he pointed to the One-Brow both had—"the sure sign in that land of the werewolf, man in the body of a beast; the opposite of the berserkers of old, beast in the body of a man."

His eyes gleamed and Sky flushed, feeling a surge of energy through his chest. He wanted to get up suddenly, move about. But his grandfather was speaking again.

"Yet it was when I finally returned to Norway, realm of our ancestors and of the old gods, that I made the great discovery: Odin's runes! How they could be used both to move the Fetch, in this world, into the other and"—his voice sank to a whisper—"and how eventually they could be used . . . to *control* the Fetch."

This was what they had talked about, when he'd been Hawk and Sigurd Fox. Sky shuddered, the urge to rise coming even more powerfully. But Sigurd's hand, dropping onto his shoulder again, halted him. "And when I eventually came back, I went for what I thought would be the last time to the old family home. To watch, to mourn for the path not taken." He smiled. "And that's when I saw you, my boy. You were six or so. I saw you and I knew."

"Knew what?"

"That you were the one born to finish what I had started. For even then—eight years ago—I knew my strength was fading and I had not enough years to do what still needed doing. But when I saw you, sliding down a slope of snow, I saw the shape of the caul you'd been born under as plain as the woolen hat on your head, knew you were the one with the destiny foretold. Knew I had to draw you to me." He licked cracked lips. "When I read in a newspaper that my wife had died, I went to Oslo, broke into the house, hid the runes and the journal in the lid of my old sea chest for you to find. The rest you know."

Kristin stirred. "Grandfather," she said, the word still strange in Sky's ear, "Grandfather, I'm not jealous"—she smiled—"well, OK, maybe I am! And maybe I wasn't born under a caul and haven't seen my Fetch. But I do have one . . . or rather two, don't I?"

"Indeed you do, Granddaughter. Your Fetch, which travels in bodies. Your fylgya, the spirit double, which travels in dreams. The caul is useful, one gateway. But it is not the only one. Remember, you also have the blood of my line. It flows in you as it does in Sky."

"So I do have a role in this . . . destiny?"

"Why do you think you are here? Why is it that you have been learning about the runestones while Sky has been occupied with . . . other things." He smiled. "You are both heading in the same direction, working to the same great cause. Sky has begun with the Fetch, you with the runes. Soon the time will come for you to reverse that. But for now, you have both acquired the knowledge you need *now*."

"For what? What is this 'great cause'?" Sky realized

259

he'd been holding a piece of herring in his hand for a minute and he'd lost his appetite. He threw it down, wiped off the juices. These revelations . . . they were interesting, of course. But they didn't give him the answers he sought. He'd run away from home, setting himself up for a lot of trouble when he got back. He'd been . . . lured to Norway. Duped, really. Now he needed to know why. "So tell us, Grandfather. Why have you brought us here?"

Sigurd must have recognized the determination in the tone. He dropped a gnarled hand onto each of his grandchildren's shoulders. "Oh, blood of my blood, flesh of my flesh, wait until you hear what glories await you."

Up to then, all they'd heard beyond Sigurd's gentle voice was the crackle of the fire, the distant call of the cuckoo. Now, in the pause after he gripped them, another sound intruded. One that should not have been there, in a wood, up a mountain.

It was the sound of a motor engine.

Sigurd heard it last. And when he did, his hands jerked on their shoulders, then flew off.

"What's that?" Kristin asked.

Their grandfather's face had gone a little paler, if that was possible. "A man. He comes every week from the village, bringing supplies since I can't get down anymore. He is . . ." Sigurd sighed. "He is not a good man. Wait here and I will try to get rid of him quickly."

He struggled from the chair, Kristin and Sky helping him up. Rooting among some papers, he pulled

out a purse, then made his slow way to the door. The
sound of the engine grew louder as he opened it, went
outside. The door swung shut behind him, barely muf-
fling the roar of the vehicle. A sudden silence came, as
the engine was turned off.

Kristin and Sky looked at each other. "Wow!" was
all he could finally manage.

"You're telling me." She shook her head. "Sigurd's
alive!"

"Not for much longer, by the look of him. I don't
think I've ever seen anyone so old."

"He must be"—she looked above his head,
calculating—"ninety-three? Nearly ninety-four."

"And he's been through a lot too."

Kristin whistled. "I can't wait to tell our mums.   261
What are they going to say?"

"He probably won't let us tell them. I mean, he's
stayed hidden this long. The shock of a reunion might
kill him."

"Do you think he's . . . sane?"

Sky sucked in his lower lip. "Maybe. Probably! I
mean, we both know about the Fetch. We've both
seen . . . things." He shuddered as some memories
came. "But I tell you what . . . sane or not, part of me
is still really pissed off he tricked us to get us here."

"He wanted you to *experience* the runes first, didn't
he?" Kristin had got up, was moving between the stacks
of paper, randomly pulling sheets out, sliding them
back in. "And it seems he wanted me to . . . learn all

about them. But this 'destiny' stuff?" She stopped, turned back to Sky, her hand rising so she could chew at her fingernails. "What's he going to ask us to do?"

As they spoke, they were aware of the voices outside. There was their grandfather's soft near-whisper. But now the visitor's deep voice was getting louder, angrier. Suddenly a stream of what had to be Norwegian curses ended in a shout, followed by the faintest of gurgles.

Sky and Kristin had the door open in a moment, spilled onto the porch, but were brought up short by the shock of what they saw. A very big man had one hand on Sigurd's throat. He had lifted him, so the old man's toes were barely on the ground. And he was shaking him.

"Hey!" Sky was off the porch and moving fast. He jerked the hand away from his grandfather's throat, then shoved. The man staggered back, though it had to be more the shock of Sky's sudden appearance than his strength. He was half the guy's size.

Sky saw Kristin rush to where Sigurd had fallen, kneel, and prop him up against her legs. He was coughing. Sky turned to the man. "What the hell do you think you're doing?"

The man matched him in volume and anger, gesturing at Sigurd. Words poured out.

"I don't speak Norwegian. Why are you attacking our grandfather?"

This stopped the man. His eyes, which were set close

together, anyway, and shadowed in purple as if bruised, narrowed further and blinked repeatedly. The face they were set in was fat, red, very puffy, the jaw stubbled, the nose huge and veined in crimson. Sky thought he looked like a large and angry pig and immediately thought that this was an insult to the animal.

"Grandfather?" The man's voice was a grunt, his English accent thick. "He has no family. So, no . . . grandchildren." He pointed at Sky, then down at Kristin.

"Well, tough, because we are." Sky now turned back to the couple on the ground. "Is he OK?"

Before Kristin could reply, Sigurd said, "I am all right, Sky." But another bout of coughing gave lie to the words.

"What did you think you were doing?" Kristin patted Sigurd's back while shouting up, "He's an old man, for God's sake."

"He not so old," the Norseman said gruffly. "Not so old he try to cheat me."

"*Cheat . . .* you?" Sky took a step forward, his hands clenching and unclenching. He felt a strange stirring at his chest, as if something were scratching at it from the inside. He'd never felt it before . . . as Sky. But Bjørn had felt it . . . and for the first time when he'd seen his father take a spear that was meant for him.

The man watched him come, a smile spreading across his thick lips. "You want something, English boy?"

"Sky!" It was his grandfather, calling loudly, firmly,

263

that halted Sky a moment before he was going to attack the man, twice his size or not. Sigurd was struggling up on Kristin's arm, speaking as he rose. "Do nothing, Sky. He would like it too much. Do not let him provoke you. Please."

"I would . . ." Sky stared into the piggy eyes before him. They were almost begging him on, and he found it hard to resist.

"Please." His grandfather limped forward, helped by Kristin. "I will deal with him."

But it was Kristin who spoke next. "How dare you call my grandfather a cheat?"

The man turned to her. "I bring food." He gestured to the four-wheel motorcycle behind him. There were boxes of groceries strapped to the back. "He does not want to pay."

"I do not want to pay more than we agreed, Olav." Sigurd shook his head. "I already pay you almost double."

The man—Olav—shrugged. "Prices go up."

"Especially for beer, eh?"

Olav didn't deny it, just lifted his hand and rubbed his jaw. Now that Sky was standing still and his anger, while not fading, was at least in check, he could see that this man was either still drunk or very hung over. The smell of the brewery came off him.

"Prices up," he grunted again. "And why shouldn't I make a little more profit, ha? I come up all the way here, early in the morning. I haven't even been to bed yet!" He belched loudly, stroked his stubble again, then laughed. "So more money. Or I take food back. You can walk to town."

"Don't think we won't," Kristin said.

"And when you leave, pretty girl?" A gleam came into his eye as he spoke to her. "Who brings food to Grandfather Sigurd then?"

"I haven't got the money now, Olav. You will have to wait till next time."

The gaze switched back to Sigurd, hardened. "No, wait. Money now or . . ." He looked at Kristin again, this time letting his gaze run up and down her body. "Or maybe there is another way to pay, heh?"

"You . . ." Sky went for him then, his hands reaching to the fat face. But even if the man was still drunk and tired, he was fast enough to react, to grab Sky in his huge arms, squeeze him tight, forcing the air from his body. "Funny boy! You think you as strong as Olav?" He squeezed harder.

"Stop that!" It was Kristin who spoke. "Let him go."

Olav looked at her, smiled, gave a little mock bow of his head, and threw Sky backward. He fell, sprawled on the ground, trying to get some air back into his lungs. He'd need it to attack.

But Kristin stopped him again. Reaching into her pocket, she pulled out her wallet. Bills came out of it. "How much more do you need?"

"Three hundred kroner," he said, licking his lips. "Though I take two if you give me a kiss."

265

"Three hundred," she said, ignoring him, counting out the bills. She thrust them at him. "Now unload the food and go away."

After another mock bow, he swiftly dumped the boxes of groceries, then straddled the bike. "Next week?"

Sky, who'd now got his air back, was about to tell the brute where to go, that they were here now and could get what their grandfather needed, when Sigurd spoke. "In four days, Olav. There is a package coming for me to the post office. They have orders to give it to you. Bring it . . . and more food." He sighed. "My grandchildren will be gone by then."

All three looked at him. But only the brute spoke, "Special delivery, eh?" He laughed. "Costs more. You better have money." Then he added something in Norwegian that made Sigurd shake his head and, blowing both Kristin and Sky a kiss, he kick-started the engine, turned the motorbike, and was soon lost in the trees of the forest. The engine whined into the distance.

"What a . . ." Sky had taken a step toward the trail. "I'd like to kill him."

"Would you, Sky?" Sigurd looked at him for a long moment, then went on. "So would I sometimes. But I need him."

"Because we won't be here in four days?" Kristin had taken Sigurd's arm as he began to edge toward the cabin. "Why won't we?"

"You did not tell your parents that you were

coming here, did you?" They both hesitated, then shook their heads. "I thought so. So you will need to go back soon."

"But I can call them," Kristin said, "now we've . . . found you. You can come with us."

They'd reached the steps and Sigurd paused on the second, creaking one. "I think my traveling days are finished. I have only one more journey to make now. But until then, this man, however horrible he is, he keeps me alive. And I have the money in my bank in town. You can bring me more before you leave."

Sky sat down on the step. He was shaking still, suddenly weak after the surge of anger. "You already talk of us leaving. But you haven't even told us yet why we're here."

Sigurd coughed. "Later, Sky. Right now, I am too tired to discuss . . . destiny. You must be too. We have some time yet. I promise, I will tell you everything. For now I will see to your beds. And then we'll all rest."

"Grandfather . . ."

Sigurd had moved on, shrugging off Kristin's helping hand. Without another word he limped into the cabin, leaving them alone.

Sky looked up at her. "What are we going to do?"

"Nothing we can do. It's up to him."

He shook his head, frustrated. "Well, do you think you *can* sleep? What time is it anyway?" He looked up into a sky that was as bright as midday.

"Five-fifty-seven," she said, looking at her cell phone,

267

"a.m. And still no reception. Maybe there'll be some on top of that rock back there. We'll have to call our mums. Tell 'em we're having a wonderful time by the seaside." She was yawning as she spoke. "Know what? I think I *could* sleep."

She went into the house, and after a moment, Sky stomped after her, certain he'd be awake for hours.

He was asleep in less than five minutes.

CHAPTER TWENTY-TWO

DESTINY

That night—if anything in that near eternal sunshine could be separated into night—they ate a meal made from what Olav had brought. Meatballs, some boiled broccoli, and potatoes; it was pretty dull and they got through it as quickly as possible. It was just fuel, which Sigurd said they'd need. Because tonight they were finally going to learn why he'd brought them there.

Sigurd asked Sky to take the food tray to the small kitchen, then replace it on the footstool with the square of wood, like a large chopping board, which sat on the window sill. He told Sky to place the runestones upon it, though to leave them in their bag. Then he asked Kristin to open the journal to the runecast and lay it down beside the stones. Tasks done, they both sat back on the floor and waited.

For the longest time, Sigurd just sat there, his eyes shut, his mouth mumbling words that neither of them could understand. Then, just when it started to be un-comfortable, when Sky and Kristin caught each other's eyes and were on the point of giggling, their grand-father suddenly leaned forward.

"Tell me what the last rune is, the central rune you have not yet explored."

Sky looked at Kristin, and she nodded at him to speak. "It is called *Pertho.* We think it means a cup to hold dice, to roll them. Kristin read that dice could be used to get answers from spirits too."

Sigurd smiled. "They can. But it is a random way, used by the unskilled for swift and often wrong insight. Yet as a rune, *Pertho* means much more. It is the hid-den secret, revealed. It is a sudden action, like the roll-ing of dice, that gives an answer. And linked as it is with *Othala,* the rune of ancestors, the rune that binds me to you both, that sudden answer is your inheri-tance. What I pass on to you, beyond the secrets of my blood."

He looked at each of them before he continued. "At every stage of the journey there was something hidden in the runecast, which you had to reveal." He closed his eyes, reaching down. "There is something hidden there still."

Sightless, he pressed his hand flat on the book, ob-scuring the page. He began his muttering again, Nor-wegian words tumbling from his mouth. Then, with a sudden yell, he pulled his hand away.

They looked down. There was the runecast as it

had always been, the five runes in their cross pattern. But now they sat within the confines of another, larger rune. It was like a large "H." But the crossbar was slashed diagonally down between the two uprights and ran underneath the five other runes.

Three voices spoke then, two in surprise, one in confirmation. "*Hagalaz.*"

"Yes. *Hagalaz.* Rune of the storm. Of hail, hurling ice from the sky to flatten a crop of wheat and starve a people. Of lightning, a fire spear stabbing a rooftop, turning a town to flame. Destruction . . . transformation! For sometimes it takes destruction for new life to grow." He paused, and they looked up at him, his eyes glowing with more than firelight. "And only in Death can one be born again."

271

"It's the Death card in tarot," murmured Kristin.

"Yes." Sigurd's voice had grown deeper, louder. "But in tarot it can merely mean an ending and thus a new start. But here, in this runecast, Death has always meant just that: Death! Sky-as-Bjørn dealt death to others with his ax. He died as Bjørn later upon a fire-ship. Sky-Hawk killed, because that is what a raptor does. Now Death comes again."

"Yours?" Sky's voice was small in contrast.

"No." He stared at them for a long moment before he answered. "Someone else's.

"Whose?" Filled with dread, they whispered it together.

Instead of answering, Sigurd picked up the bag of

runestones, loosened the drawstring at the neck, tipped them out upon the wooden surface beside the journal. They saw some symbols, but mostly just the shining stone backs. "Close your eyes," Sigurd said, and they did. They heard him invert all the stones, swirl them around. "Now you may look. Use hearts, not eyes, and choose one. Choose and hold the stone in your hand. Do not look at it yet."

The backs of stones glimmered. Nothing distinguished one from another. Kristin almost immediately shot her hand down, snatching one up, clutching it to her chest. Sky waited; not because he didn't know which one to pick. He knew. He just didn't want to touch it yet.

272

The moment he bent slowly forward and lifted the stone from its place, Sigurd rose to stand before the fireplace, beckoning them to follow. They walked together to join him. Above the mantel was a large mirror, its surface smudged with age, stained by corrosion.

"This is where I watched you, Sky. This is where I followed your journeys." Sigurd coughed, and Sky began to turn toward him. A hand on his shoulder turned him back. "Look there, only there. Look beyond yourselves, beyond these Doubles. Within the mirror, through its surface, into its depths."

"What are we—"

"Look, Sky. Then see."

At first there was nothing there except their faces, distorted by the glass's corruption. Both Sky and Kristin saw themselves, each other, Sigurd. Only he stared straight ahead, his milky eyes clear, as if burned clean by the intensity of his regard. So they did as he did, and immediately Sky saw a shifting in the glass, a stirring in its depths, as if smoke was being parted by a breeze or by a body forging through it. Something moved there, insubstantial at first, then starting to hold form and shape, becoming recognizable as an arm, the curve of a jaw, the sudden dazzle of a huge eye looking back. Then everything cleared; the eye, shrunk, fitted into a face, one he recognized just before the man turned away.

"Olav," Sky said softly, hearing the same word from beside or behind him—he wasn't quite sure which because the smoke that had been before him was all around him now and he was in it, blind to any sight other than the man walking down a street ahead of him. Sounds joined sight, the crunch of the boots on the packed snow, music from the pub ahead, louder as they drew closer. It was not as if Olav were on a screen; Sky was just . . . with him. When he went into the pub, Sky went too. When Olav stood at the bar and drank pint after pint, shot after shot, Sky stood beside him watching him do it. When the man beside Olav objected to his shouting, Sky almost dodged the broken bottle, the thrown punch. And when Olav waited in the alley for the man to come, Sky waited, too, waited and watched as the man stepped into shadows he never stepped out of because of the knife lodged in his chest.

273

Sigurd's voice came again, a whisper in the mist. "They suspected Olav, of course. But they could never prove anything. Witnesses suddenly got frightened. A woman swore he had been with her at the time. He got away with it. A murderer goes unpunished."

Then Sky was standing in front of a mirror again, Kristin beside him, both blinking as if suddenly thrust into daylight from the dark. Sigurd had already turned away, was lowering himself slowly into his chair. In the silence of shock, they sat as well, on the floor, and it took a long while for either of them to speak.

"Why . . . ," Sky said finally, "why did you show us this?"

"Why? You can ask why?" Sigurd's voice had dropped so low they had to lean in to hear. "You have seen this man, how he is, what he has done. You can imagine what evil he has yet to do. He is worthless. Yet he is worth something to us. For *Hagalaz,* the lightning bolt, the hailstorm, can change the world in an instant. This murderer, this dog who deserves to be sacrificed, can be *Hagalaz* for us."

Sky couldn't speak. Kristin did, one simple word. "How?"

Sigurd had his eyes closed now as if exhausted. But his voice, if still quiet, was full of purpose. "At the exact moment when the body dies, the Fetch is released. It releases with great energy, like a bomb, an explosion greater in its own way than any weapon on earth. To those who do not know they have a Fetch, they cannot hold it, can only let it go. But to one who *can* see the moment that the spirit departs, who knows how to capture that energy, harness it through the runes, through ancient practices and incantations . . . ones I know"— he paused—"well, that energy can be captured, channeled, sent where I will it to go. Sent into this husk I call a body."

Over their shocked cries, he continued. "Like a blood transfusion, like a heart transplant, his death would let me live. Give me ten years, maybe more. Long enough, perhaps, for me to finish my life's work. Or, if that proves impossible, to teach you, my family, how to finish it for me." He leaned down toward them, and his voice was no longer weak, his eyes no longer dull. "I have given everything, sacrificed everything for this great end: to allow every person on the planet to meet their Fetch. To drag humanity into the sunlight and out of the Kingdom of Shadows."

275

He gazed at their white faces, the terror in their eyes. Sky tried to speak, to force words through his suddenly swollen throat; couldn't. But Kristin somehow did.

"But why, Grandfather?" Her voice was raspy, strained. "Why would most people want that?"

"*You* can ask this? You, who desire to walk with your Fetch more than anything in this world? Well, Kristin, if I live on, with the strength to finish my work, that gift can be yours. And you will see, as Sky has seen, how wonderful it can be." His eyes gleamed.

"Terrible, yes, to find out *all* we have inside of us and then live it. But oh so wonderful!" He turned his gaze onto Sky. "Tell her, Grandson. Am I not right?"

And still, Sky couldn't speak. It wasn't his throat now. There was just too much to say, his mind exploding with the sudden vision of a world of Fetches. But how to sum up all that with . . . words?

His grandfather watched the struggle on the faces raised to him. Then he pointed to their fists. "Show me," he said, his voice calm again. "What are your runes?"

Kristin unclenched her fingers. "I do not know this one," she said. There was a vertical line, a diagonal cut down from the top to the right.

Sigurd leaned forward. *"Laguz."* He nodded. "It is all things liquid, like water, rainfall, the sea. Always changing shape, yet always the same. Part of you goes on as you are, part of you changes with every tide." He closed his hand over hers. "Help me do what must be done, and your life is changed forever."

Silence. Sky's mind was empty, as blank as a mirror turned to a wall. He watched Kristin, the fight on her face, desire, fear. Then, gradually, thoughts came, rising as if from the slime of a seabed, from rusted armor and bones bleached white. I have another life. It has air rifles and school buses, moving vans and new houses. It may not be perfect or exciting. But at least it doesn't involve murder.

He thought of voicing this. It would break the silence. But then Kristin broke it, by getting up, running for the door, wrenching it open. She stumbled down the stairs and ran for the trees, and they could hear her vomiting before she reached them.

The two of them listened to her sounds fading. Then Sigurd turned to Sky.

"And yours?"

Sky stared back. After a moment he said, "You know what it is already, don't you?"

Sigurd tipped his head. "If all I believe to be true is true, then . . . yes."

Sky knew too. The slashed lines were burning themselves into his palm, branding him. He was being marked as what he was.

He opened his hand. Neither of them looked down. "*Thurisaz*," he said, "rune of attack." He swallowed. "The berserkers' rune. Bjørn's rune."

"Your rune, Sky. Yours!" Sigurd rose, began to shuffle toward the curtained-off room where he slept. "We have three days before that man returns. It is much I ask of you, I know. And if you cannot bring yourself to . . . help me . . . well, I will die soon enough." He had one hand on the curtain now, as if it were the only thing holding him up. "I have heard that killing gets easier the more you do it," he said quietly, not looking back. "Tell me. Sky. Bjørn. Hawk. Is that true?"

The days were strangely normal. It was almost as if their parents had sent them on holiday with an elderly relative. The two of them did holiday type things—

they hiked to a waterfall, to an especially stunning mountain view; they swam in a freezing lake. On the day after their grandfather's request, they walked down into the town, to get money for Sigurd, eat pizza and ice cream, and call their parents.

They pretended they were still at a friend's on the English coast, that the cliffs made the phone reception really bad. But something in his tone must have concerned Sonja. She asked him to come home immediately. He pretended that the connection cut out.

"I think we might be on borrowed time," he said, switching the phone off, handing it back to Kristin.

On the walk back up, she tried to talk to Sky about Sigurd's revelation, ask him what he wanted to do; but Sky wouldn't answer.

It's not as hard for her, he thought, pushing ahead of her along the path through the Silver Birch. She isn't marked with the berserkers' rune.

He knew she'd still have to choose to help or not, and it would be a huge decision for her. But she wouldn't have to do the actual killing. Anyway, by the way she spent all possible time at Sigurd's feet, talking runes and Fetches, he knew what she'd want him to do. He left them to it, hiked a lot by himself. He'd already been influenced by Sigurd enough. This was one journey he had to take on his own.

But if the days were eerily normal, the nights were not. When he lay down to sleep, things happened. He could not call it dreaming, just as the lesser brightness that came could not be called night. Things . . . oc-curred. To both of them, if the creakings and moans coming from Kristin's bunk above him were anything to go by. Given his walkings, it had been decided that it was safer if he slept below; but all that meant was that it was easier to escape . . . through the curtain over the bedroom's entrance, out of the cabin, into the forest. For the next two nights he woke under trees. He woke almost calmly, no longer shocked by where his wan-derings had brought him. After what he'd seen with his eyes shut, it was a relief to have them open.

As in most so-called dreams, random images came, like the turns of a kaleidoscope. He'd wander from the Wenlock Edge onto the fells of Hareid; stumble from a classroom onto a longship's deck; sometimes pursu-ing, sometimes pursued; he didn't know by what, by whom. Then, just when it seemed that there would be something forming, a story he could recognize, the kaleidoscope would shatter, colored shards exploding out, each one bearing something different—a father's face as the spear meant for his son was twisted in, a slave on a burning longship clutched in chain-mail arms, a bat spewing blood on an attic floor, the back of a hood, turning, turning . . .

And like any shards, they could cut.

The third night was different. He was running through the forest and he didn't care if he was awake or asleep because it felt so good, as if his limbs had been tied up for ages. And it was darker too—clouds had come, pushed by a strong wind that tried to hold him back and couldn't. It felt like night, smelt like rain. He had to get somewhere, but he would only know where when he arrived.

The summit was no different from when they'd first stood there. He leapt onto the flat rock platform, looked at the mountains of the Jotunheim, where the Norse gods had been born. Beneath these peaks the forces of their world had been recognized, harnessed, then compressed into stones. Released again, the energy held in those runes could change the world.

"Sky-Hawk!" he yelled, willing the transformation, longing for wings now; mostly longing for the instinct of the raptor. He'd killed then, just because he could.

Spreading his arms, he waited for feathers to master the coming storm. But the clouds tumbled over his useless human form, and the wind just tried to hurl him wingless into the valleys below.

He couldn't change. But Sigurd could. He'd come as a fox to the forests of Shropshire. He'd promised to teach Sky how it was done. To be Hawk forever.

How could he do that if he was dead?

His eyes, tearing and stung by the sharp wind, opened; were forced open. Something was there that had not been there before, a shape moving toward him, up the hill, over, not through the ferns, as flat to the land as cloud shadow.

He swayed, his feet held, his arms flailing for balance in the winds that rushed around him. He was trapped, couldn't flee what was approaching, legs prisoner to rock.

The shape slowed but did not stop, a gray cloak creeping across the last two dozen paces, sliding up over the lip of rock, flowing toward him, as flat as water running over stone.

"No!" screamed Sky, just when the top of the hood touched his toe.

His scream raised it, shot it straight up before him, and Sky buried his face in his hands. They were no barrier to the ice that flowed through them and settled around his throat, cutting off his air in an instant.

"Free . . . ee me," came the voice, a whispered shriek. "Free . . . ee . . . ee . . . ee me . . . ee."

The wind rose again, picked up the voiceless words, scattered them, more shards from his shattered kaleidoscope. The ice in his throat broke; he snatched breath just as his feet came free, falling in the same moment.

"How?" he cried into the wind.

No answer came. None was needed. Sky knew that the draug was getting closer to him every time he came. Those icy fingers in his throat? Next time, they might not let him go.

Sigurd had wrenched Black Ulf from the realms of the Dead. Only Sigurd could send him back.

But not if he was dead.

He didn't really care about freeing the Fetch in all humanity. He just knew this: In the end, Sigurd was his blood. And beyond even that, lying on the cold, wet rock, Sky realized two things.

He wanted to live. And he wanted to fly.

When Kristin found him, still splayed on a rock now wet with the first of the downpours the clouds had promised, he told her what he was going to do.

She stared down at him. "What made you decide?"

But he couldn't answer her, could only listen to her sharp breaths. To the crying in the wind.

282

CHAPTER TWENTY-THREE

SACRIFICE

Sigurd showed no surprise when Sky told him that he would help kill Olav.

"It is in your blood," he said, so matter-of-factly that Sky was annoyed.

"Aren't you happy?" he snapped.

Those milky eyes, in the process of turning to Kristin, turned back. "Happy? A man must die so that our great work can live. You have seen how he deserves it, but still"—he shook his head—"the killing of any man is not a cause for happiness. It is only what must be." He looked at Kristin. "And you, Granddaughter? Are you also able to help us?"

Kristin nodded. "Help, yes. I don't know if I could"—she made a vague gesture in the air that could have been a stab—"but I know this man deserves it. Like Sky, I want to save your life, to find out more about your work. Help with it. But"—she bit at a nail—"I have not been a berserker, or died on a long-ship. So, I will help, as I can."

Despite all the emotions he was going through, Sky now looked at Kristin and couldn't help but smile. All that poised exterior! All those chewed fingers! Then the smile went as he remembered what she had just agreed to do. This wasn't walking walls. This was murder. And realizing it, he was suddenly so proud of her. She may not have been a berserker; but she was blood of his blood, all right!

"We would not ask any more of you"—Sigurd laid down the book he'd been reading and rose from his chair—"and it will take the work of three of us to do what must be done. Olav will have picked up the package I had sent to me. He could come anytime. Near dawn tomorrow, with his breath still foul from his night's drinking like last week. Or even later tonight, seeking money for the drinking to come. We must be ready."

He stood and swept his hand over the papers that clung to every surface. "All these must be put away. The books too. This room must be cleared of all clutter and transformed"—his eyes shone—"transformed into a holy space. For make no mistake, what we are about *is* holy, according to the laws of ancient gods."

All day, under his instructions, Sky and Kristin packed books and papers into boxes and carried them to a stone-built hut behind the main cabin, running between the two to try to keep as dry as possible. The

284

clouds had stopped moving for the moment, settled above the valley, releasing rain in slabs of water upon the land.

There was little left with all the paper gone. The few pieces of furniture were cleared into other rooms. By early evening the main room was empty, save for Sigurd's chair. Sky returned from one final trip.

"Where've you been?" asked Kristin. "I thought we were finished."

"Backpacks," he replied, jerking his thumb out toward the hut. "I tucked them away."

It wasn't all he'd done in the hut. Even though Sigurd had said that the runestones weren't necessary for what they had to do that night, Sky still needed to know exactly where they were, to feel that they were still . . . his, their power supporting him in what lay ahead. So he'd taken both stones and journal from Kristin's backpack, along with his caul and the diamonds, and put them into his own. Taking possession of his destiny.

He turned to Sigurd. "Now what?" he asked.

"Now we eat, rest, and wait."

"For Olav?" Kristin could not keep the fear from her voice.

"For midnight, my dear. The time that is no longer today, not yet tomorrow. It is the most powerful moment of day or night. And we need to use that power if we are to succeed." He looked at them each in turn. "I say 'if' to you and mean it. He is a strong and vicious man, and we . . . we are perhaps too old and too young for what we attempt. So we need to get other forces on our side"—he nodded—"and they are best reached at midnight."

The pounding of rain upon the roof slowed to a soft caress; rumbling continued in the distance, lightning stabbed other mountains. The clock's arms slid around slowly when watched, fast whenever Sky dozed. When his grandfather stood, Sky woke up and looked again. Eleven-forty-five, it read.

"It is time," Sigurd said.

"Fifteen minutes yet," said Sky, his voice shriller than he'd expected. Coughing, he lowered it, added, "I was having such a nice dream."

He knew he hadn't fooled either of them. He covered by lifting the chair his grandfather had started to drag and placing it over by the fire. Sigurd went to a long cupboard. "I have something for you, Sky," he said.

The object Sigurd pulled out was wrapped in burlap sacking, narrow and about the length of Sky's leg. His grandfather stretched it toward him, but he was hesitant to take it. "What is it?"

"Something you lost."

Sky reached for it, then had to step up because the weight within the sack pulled his arm down. It was not only weighty but hard. Stripping off the covering, exposing what lay within to the light, Sky gasped.

The shaft was different, new, a beautiful stave of ash, curved slightly to fit the hands. But there was no mistaking the head. Bjørn's carvings glimmered there, beneath an edge Sky could see was brilliant sharp. A bear swallowed by the rune of change, *Uruz*.

Kristin came over, drawn by the shock on his face. "What is it?"

"Death Claw. Bjørn's battle-ax." Stunned, Sky turned to Sigurd. "How . . . how did you get this?"

Sigurd was smiling at his grandson's amazement. "When I returned to Norway after my . . . death, I went to live in Hareid for a while, to feel a little of what our ancestors must have felt. One day I was down on the dockside watching the fishing fleet sail in, and there was excitement around one boat. They'd hauled something other than fish up in their nets. That!"

"Did they sell it to you?"

"They barely knew what it was. It was so encrusted with seashells . . . which is why it survived all those years, why I was able to restore it."

Kristin leaned forward to touch the edge, jerking her hand back with a cry. A little smudge of red was on her finger. "Ow," she said, sucking. "They gave it to you, then?"

"I took it."

"Stole it?"

"The sea waited for me, then returned it. I accepted the gift and left Hareid the next day. But it was never for me. It was waiting for its true owner."

Sky lifted the weapon, then swung it through the air. There was no doubt . . . holding it felt like a reunion.

Sigurd had reached again into the cupboard, pulled out another ax, not wrapped, less beautiful.

"That's not for me, is it?" asked Kristin nervously.

"For me." Sigurd, letting the axhead lower to the ground, leaned on the butt. "I am not sure I can wield it. But I have the blood of axmen in me too." He went close to the back wall of the room, where he began to drag the axhead, the tip of the curved blade scratching a line on the floorboards. When he'd returned to his start point they could see he'd traced a circle, about fifteen feet across and nearly perfect.

He was breathing hard. Lifting the ax so it no longer scraped, he limped over and sank into his chair. "Your . . . turn," he wheezed.

288

Sky was still marveling at the feel of Death Claw in his hand. He looked up as Kristin said, "What are we to do?"

"The runecast. Do you need to look at it again?"

"I know it." Now he had this weapon in his hand, Sky felt impatient.

"Then you can carve it from memory. There, within what I have carved on the floor. Fill the circle with the runes. Make big, bold strokes with your ax."

Sky moved to stand within the circle. He rested the axhead on the floor and leaned the butt against his thigh so that his hands were free. Spitting on them, rubbing them together, he hefted the weapon again. "Shall I begin?"

"Wait! For the cuts alone are not enough. It is the

power behind the cuts, power that is not strength." He turned to Kristin. "You have read about how the runes are carved, have you not?"

"I have . . . read about it. There are incantations, to give each rune power, yes?"

"Yes. So as Sky carves, you will chant a verse."

She took a step toward the door. "I'll get the book . . ."

"You don't *have* to read them. You already know them . . . here and here." Sigurd touched his head and his heart.

"I don't think I—"

"Don't *think* at all, Granddaughter." Sigurd had leaned forward, was staring at her intently. "You asked before why you were here. *This* is why."

Sky looked at the two of them, watched the energy pass between their eyes. For a moment it looked to him as if she might refuse, say she couldn't do it. But then he remembered her better. He watched her eyes narrow, her shoulders drop, her chin rise up.

"Very well," she said, "and, may I say, about bloody time."

She looked back at Sky. He looked at the clock. It was eleven-forty-eight. Twelve minutes to carve five runes . . . six, because Sigurd had added *Hagalaz,* the hailstorm that surrounded all the other ones. He could do that. He'd read how runes were cut into surfaces with blades, that's why they were only straight lines, none that curved. A chisel would be handy. A knife

289

would do. But he knew he had the perfect tool in his grip: Death Claw, the blade exactly the right length for the required cuts.

He stood in the center of the circle, the tip of the ax blade resting on the floor, his hands upon the butt end, like a warrior awaiting the battle. There was no need to ask where to begin. All stories begin at the beginning, and a runecast was a story. Not one he'd read . . . one he'd lived. It had transformed his life, shown him extraordinary sights, brought him from the countryside of England to the realm of the gods in Norway. He knew the rune *Uruz* was not in the cast but he felt like carving it anyway, to mark his passage as Bjørn had marked his on this blade. But that was for another time, another circle. He looked up at Kristin. "Ready?"

"Ready." There was no need to talk about it. She knew the beginning as well as he. She had been with him almost all of the way.

"*Othala,*" she cried, and at the same moment the ax bit down, the first line slashed diagonally from left to right. As he lifted, cut again, right to left to form the cross, she called:

"*rune of ancestors,*
rune that summons . . ."

The ax rose, fell.

"*wisdom of the past . . .*"

The final stroke joined the left to the top, completing all as the last words came:

290

"lost, reclaimed."

Sky lifted the ax, his head, saw Kristin look down and smile at his strokes. As she did, the thunder rolled nearer. The storm was coming back their way. They hadn't seen the lightning yet, but they knew it was there. Something had to account for all the electricity in the air.

He stepped up to the top of the circle, raised his ax, her voice coming as he brought it crashing down.

"Thurisaz,
rune of challenge . . ."
Now, the top of the thorn . . .
"the enemy comes
you strike . . ."
The upward diagonal . . .

"triumph!"
To the right, he could see the imprint of the next rune as if it were already scorched into the dark wood. All he had to do was lay his ax upon the lines.

"Ansuz
a mouth opens
an ancient tongue . . ."
Sky was moving fast now. . . .
"wisdom given . . ."
Slash. Whirl. Slash
"like runes to Odin . . ."
"Yes!" Sigurd had leaned forward, his ax now in one hand. He raised it, banged the haft down upon the floor. It led the next thunderclap by a heartbeat.

Sky swirled again, to the base of the circle. *"Raidho,"* he cried out, just ahead of Kristin, bringing the weapon down in the first of the cuts. It was harder, four strokes required, the blade falling now here, now there, building the rune.

"the journey
within without
flesh and spirit . . ."

He plunged the ax for the last diagonal, just as Kristin finished her chant.

". . . one," they cried together.

Four runes were carved in a circle. Only the center remained to fill. And Sky spun to it, sweeping Death Claw around, leading, being led, he wasn't sure which, Kristin's voice coming as if from far away, as far away as the center of the thunderstorm he knew had reached them, was bursting over them even now.

"Pertho," she shouted as Sky crashed the weapon down, as Sigurd rose from his chair shouting something himself, waving his ax. But Sky couldn't hear, couldn't stop, the ax rising and falling as it had risen and fallen on all who opposed him in battle. Didn't hear anything until he'd finished cutting, until floorboards lay splintered under him and Kristin's voice came to him again, louder than Sigurd's, louder than the thunder.

"Pertho
roll the dice
upside down
cheating and lies."

That wasn't right! Sigurd coming forward mouthing Norwegian at him wasn't right either. He looked down, at the carving beneath his axhead.

Pertho was carved backwards. And he knew, because Kristin had told him often enough, that a reversed rune was bad, all that was good in its promise corrupted, corroded, a distorted reflection in an old mirror.

"That's wrong," yelled Sigurd, in English now. "You've cut it backwards."

Sky staggered slightly. "I don't know why . . . I . . ."

"Never mind! Only one remains. Maybe the most important one. . . ." He lifted his own ax, placed it on the lower right edge of the circle. "Cut that side. Meet me in the middle. Carve *Hagalaz.* Now!"

His shout brought Sky back. Sigurd scratched a line up, Sky passing him with one coming down, Kristin chanting,

"Ice storm
fire bringer
life ended . . ."

As they began the diagonal cut, their eyes met, held as they sliced toward each other.

"life begun."

As they met, blades almost touching, back in the center of the circle, of *Hagalaz* and *Pertho,* the lightning came at last. Seared into their eyeballs because they'd all looked out the window at the same time. Not in anticipation. Drawn by a sound, one buried

293

beneath all the others while they had carved and she had chanted.

An engine was approaching, coming fast. In the moment before the thunder came again, they heard a horn.

"He's here."

The horn, Kristin's whisper, did it. The power was gone, the strangeness of *Pertho* reversed, the exultation of the others. He was standing amid the splinters with an ax in his hand and the man he was supposed to kill shouting from the porch.

Sigurd staggered forward. "You," he whispered at Sky, "wait behind the door. You"—he faced Kristin—"come with me."

294

At first it was hard to hear above the thunder, above the thumping of his heart. His brow was slick with sweat, his hair rising from his head, pulled up by the static electricity in the air as lightning bounced around the valley and the rain still refused to return. Olav must have gone back to his bike; Sky heard his deep, slurred voice telling Sigurd to come get the damn package, the rest of his stuff, that he had arrived early because he needed his money, he had spent his own on these cursed supplies, on the old man's medicines; how he had an appointment in town and he was already late. Heard Sigurd say that the money was inside, wouldn't he come in?

Sky tried to raise the ax. It felt like it was welded into the floor, impossible to lift . . . just as Bjørn had found it near impossible to lift this same weapon on the deck of his burning longship. But the thought of his ancestor stirred him, and finally, with a grunt, he had it up on his shoulder. He had no idea how he was going to get it off.

"Please," said Sigurd, "it's starting to rain. Come inside."

Then Olav decided English was too hard to speak, but Sky could guess what he was saying, the swear-words he was using, telling the stupid old man to get his money and be quick about it, only stopping when another voice interrupted.

"Please come in," Kristin said. "The weather's terrible. All this lightning. It's dangerous out here."

There was a grunt, something muttered. Then Sky heard a heavy foot thump onto the step, the one that creaked, and a huge shape was moving through the doorway, marching to the center of the empty room.

"Huh," Olav said, looking down at the rune circle he was standing in. "You have bad woodworm, yes?"

The door slammed. Sigurd and Sky and Kristin were standing there side by side as Olav turned slowly to them. Sky could almost see the thoughts flick through the piggy eyes, one by one: lust for Kristin, contempt for Sigurd, and . . . puzzlement at Sky, standing there, clutching an ax.

"What's this?" Olav grunted. "What are you doing there, boy?"

"Now!" Sigurd screamed, and tottered a step into

the room. His cry roused Sky, who also stepped forward, pulling his feet as if from thick mud, lifting the dead weight of the weapon from his shoulder, bringing it up, over, down . . . to the point in midair where Olav's raised hand caught the shaft, effortlessly.

They stayed like that for a long moment. Then the Norseman pulled the ax from Sky's hands as easily as he would have plucked a flower. He looked at the weapon, and no one else moved.

"You tried, tried . . ." The voice got louder; with anger, with the need to rise above the thunder rolls coming swifter now. "You tried . . ." Then the anger changed to mocking amusement. "A useless boy! A girl! A sick old man. You thought you could . . ." His laughter came, a nasty sound, instantly cut off. "Well," he said, all humor gone, "what will I do about that?"

He held the ax now in one hand at his side. With the other, he suddenly slapped Sky, back handed, knuckles to face, sent him reeling him into the wall. As he slid down it, Sigurd took a stumbly step toward his chair and the ax that leaned against it. Olav shoved him square in the back. He fell to his knees, his hands grasping the chair arms, his face smothered in the cushioned seat.

"Stop that!" Kristin rushed forward, flailing. Olav caught her easily, one huge hand on her throat. He held Death Claw in the other. "You want some of this, little one?" He laughed, waving the ax, shaking her, only her toe tips on the ground.

Though anger began it, it was blood that brought it on, blood dripping from Sky's mouth, spattering onto the floor. The memory of it, spraying from the wound that Thorkell Grimsson had taken for him . . . for Bjørn, yes, but for him, too, Sky-in-Bjørn, Bjørn-in-Sky. Blood. The blood of family, the family before him now, his grandfather sprawled against his chair, his cousin's neck being crushed in an enemy's grip . . .

There on the floor was the rune, his rune. *Thurisaz.* Only moments before, while he wielded the ax, his cousin had chanted the words.

rune of challenge
the enemy comes
you strike
triumph!

297

This time he recognized the burrowing in his chest. Welcomed it. Someone . . . *something* was forcing its way out.

A roar shook him, a voice no longer all human. Claws ached with the need to rend, tear. Needed to be used.

He was off the ground, rising up fast, kicking off from the wall behind him. The man saw him come. His own hands were full, so he cleared one of them by hurling Kristin across the room.

There was the enemy and there was the weapon, and Sky-Bjørn went for the weapon, both hands on it, two to Olav's one. Pivoting as he grasped wood, he wrenched the ax away. His momentum carried him on, past. Somersaulting, the weapon tucked under him, he was up and standing in one movement.

"You little . . ." Olav stood there, clutching air, staring at his empty hands. Then he looked up, saw Sky, saw the ax. He turned, searching . . . and saw the other ax by Sigurd's chair.

He moved fast, almost as fast as Sky had, knocking the kneeling Sigurd aside, grabbing, spinning around. "Come on then, boy," he yelled, his own ax aloft. "Come!"

Sky came, low to the ground, weapon out wide, luring his enemy to use a downward strike. And Olav fell for the bait, his own ax going high, back, cutting down . . . to where Sky had been, the heavy blade crashing not through flesh but through the floorboard and lodging there, stuck. Frantically pulling at it, he left his whole left side exposed. But Sky had ripped the ax shaft away in a reversed grip. He couldn't strike with the blade. But he could jab and did, driving the butt end hard into Olav's ribs. The big man cried out, fell back, crashing into the door, his movement somehow dislodging the axhead from the floor, the weapon coming with him.

With a yell, Sky spun Death Claw up into the air, caught it the right way around, charged. Olav, with a cry part anger, part agony, pushed himself off the wall. Ax rose to block ax, ash shafts smashing together with a force that nearly knocked the weapons from both their hands. Staggering back, neither hesitated. They came again.

298

Blow given, blow returned, a slash blocked, a cut turned aside. They fought in the very center of the room, within the rune-filled circle. Beyond it, the part of him that was still Sky could hear a chant, the part of him that was Bjørn understanding the Norse words.

"Odin
Allfather
Shape-shifter
Come
Change me
Release me
Blood for blood
Come. . . ."

Sigurd was in the chair now, sat like an ancient king upon a throne, hands gripping the chair's arms, words pouring out, growing in volume to rise above the thunder that rolled nearer, nearer with each verse.

299

"Thor
Thunder God
Bringer of storms
Come
Change me
Unleash me
Blood for blood
Come!"

It was Kristin's shout, her echo of "come!" that did it, pulled Sky out of Bjørn, for just a moment, that one brief, lightning-lit moment. And it was Bjørn who knew how to fight with an ax, not Sky; Bjørn who would have known how to block the blunt head of the weapon that caught Sky hard in the chest, knocked him back, out of the circle, all air driven from him.

Somehow, he did not fall. Somehow, he still held his ax. And as his enemy rushed forward, his own weapon rising high, Sky . . . Bjørn . . . remembered a special cut his father, Thorkell, had taught him. Crouching low, reversing his grip, he swung the ax the other way; from the left, up; as if cutting under a shield.

He drove his blade deep into the man's leg, just below the knee. With a terrible shriek, Olav fell back, the ax slipping from his hands. Then Sky-Bjørn was above him, and Death Claw was rising, rising high, up to where the killing strokes are born. This was battle and he knew what you did. An enemy down, you finished him fast, moved on, found another, finished him, on and on. . . .

Death Claw, at its uttermost height, stopped. Bjørn stopped it, seeking a target on the squirming man, like a hawk just before it stooped. And Sky stopped it, and it was as if his two hands wanted two different things. The left to force the blade down, to cut, to kill. The right to keep it in the air. And in the moment Sky held it up, sounds returned, replacing the battle roar in his ears. The man on the floor crying in agony; Kristin sobbing. Sigurd chanting, urging him to the sacrifice.

"Kill him. Kill him. Kill him."

And as suddenly as it had come, the clawing fled from his chest. The berserker was gone, the hawk gone, then Bjørn was gone, too, and the ax he'd held aloft was now a dead weight in Sky's hands. It slipped from his fingers, crashed to the floor.

"I can't," he said.

From the corner of the room, Kristin whispered, "Thank God! Oh, thank God."

Then Sigurd rose from his chair. "Well," he said, his voice low, "if you can't . . . I can."

There was a moment, a few seconds, no more, of near silence. Then the clock began to strike, shrill in the stillness, and the lightning struck so close to the house, they could feel the charge through their feet, smell the scorched grass.

As if the years had fallen away from him, Sigurd bent, snatched the other ax up, lifting it high, and this time Olav could do nothing to slow the blade's descent. Much of his scream was lost in the thunder crashing closer, closer. Not all of it though.

Sigurd stepped back. The ax he left, held upright in Olav's chest.

"It is done," he cried, arms raised, beckoning. "Odin, Allfather. Thor, Thunder God! Release me now."

Thunder answered, nearly above the house.

"Is . . . is he in you, Grandfather?" Kristin had fallen forward, was staring up at Sigurd, mouth a gash, eyes wide.

"What?" His reply was a different sort of scream, triumphant. "Take from this dumb beast? His brutish strength giving me just ten years? When what I need is another lifetime?"

"Then what?" Sky shouted.

301

Sigurd pointed. Olav's corpse was in the center of the rune circle, and the rune, that slashed "H" that contained all the other runes, smoldered, as if holding back flame. *"Hagalaz,"* he hissed. "Hailstorm. Lightning bolt. Destruction. The sudden remaking of the world." Eyes gleamed. "This dog's sacrifice has freed my Fetch. Yes!" He tipped back his head as if tipping it to rain and laughed. "But it is the lightning that will release me from this used-up shell called Sigurd and let me go . . . into another!"

Suddenly, somewhere deep inside him, Sky knew. "No!" He staggered back, arms raised uselessly before him. "You're coming into me!"

The eyes swiveled onto him. All light within them was gone.

"Oh no, boy," Sigurd said softly, "into her!"

BOOM! The roof exploded, grass and earth tumbling in upon them. Lightning arced into the room, spearing Sigurd where he stood. His back arched but he didn't fall, wispy hair stood straight up, eyes bulged, tongue shot out, already blackening. Kristin shrieked, high-pitched, terrible, slumping to the floor. As Sky leapt for her, clutched her unconscious body to him, Sigurd, flaming with light, staggered backward, fell, collapsing into his chair.

"Kristin! Kristin!"

Her eyes rolled under their lids. Flame had ridden Sigurd to the floor, and every rune was burning now, scorching the wood. Smoke swamped the room in moments. Sky, coughing, thrust his arms under Kristin's shoulders, dragged her to the door, onto the porch, down the steps. Laying her on the ground, he turned. . . .

"Grandfather," he shouted. Though he knew it was too late, he still put a foot on the first step. But the fire was a tower of heat, pushing him back. Breathless, he staggered, fell choking next to the unconscious Kristin.

With a sudden, splintering roar, the walls of the cabin tumbled outward. Grabbing Kristin again under her arms, Sky stumbled backward, just ahead of the logs that sizzled and rolled toward them. Only in the shelter of the trees could Sky finally lay her down, look back.

303

The floor had somehow survived the collapse of the walls. There was Sigurd, blackened, dissolving . . . and still upright in his chair. While at his feet, like a dog sacrificed for a Viking's funeral, lay Olav, the ax sticking straight out from his chest.

CHAPTER TWENTY-FOUR

FROM THE ASHES

A gentle slapping woke him, and a voice kept him awake.

"Sky? Sky!"

His eyes blinked open. Kristin was crouched above him, her face bright with concern. "Oh thank God!" she said. "I thought you'd never wake up."

His head was resting on a root thrusting out from a tree. It ached, inside and out. Pushing himself backward, he leaned against the trunk. "I wasn't asleep, I was unconscious," he muttered. "For how long?"

"I don't know. I only just woke up myself. But we must have been out for a while. Look."

She pointed and he stared past her. At the devastation of the cabin. Everything had collapsed, roof timbers jutting up from the wreckage like spars from a broken ship. All that was not consumed was black. Red patches, lined in white ash, glowed here and there while smoke spiraled up from about four different areas. But the fire was essentially out. Only the front doorframe still stood somehow. Through it, they could see the trees and mountains beyond, sun dappled. It looked like a holiday poster.

"Is he . . . ?" Sky gestured to the destruction.

"I haven't . . . I couldn't . . ." She shrugged. "I thought I'd wait for you."

He nodded, forced himself to stand, swayed when he did. Every part of him felt weak. "Let's take a look."

Somehow the porch, though singed, had not caught, which explained why the doorframe was still up. "Maybe it was too soaked from the rain before and wouldn't burn," he said.

"Or maybe the rain later put it out. Aren't you soaked? I am."

He felt his shirt. Sodden! He shivered. He hadn't noticed till then how cold he was. "So their bodies might . . . might still . . ." He waved his hand up the steps.

"We better be careful," she said, putting a foot on the first one. "It may not have burned, but it will still be weak."

Somehow they found they were holding hands as they carefully climbed. Both steps, the singed planking, it was all creaks now. When they'd shuffled to the door, he took a deep breath, said, "Ready?" She nodded and they both looked in.

Down. The floor beyond the door had collapsed into the cellar below, filling it with soot and ashes, trails of smoke rising from it. A breeze stirred it, making it ripple like a gray-black sea.

"Stone walls"—he pointed at the charred foundations—"must have acted like a sort of oven in a . . . a . . ."

"A crematorium?" He nodded, and she continued. "Then there'll be nothing left down there."

But he'd seen something. "Almost nothing." Before she could stop him, he'd stepped through the frame, onto the smoke-black stones.

"Sky! Come back! It's too dangerous!"

"Just a second."

He lowered himself to sit on the wall of the cellar, then let himself slide down it. His feet sank through soft ash. Still hot, it burned his ankles, but he pushed through it to the center of the room, to what he'd seen, the faintest glimmer of light in the blackness. Taking off his damp sweater, he wrapped his hand in it, reached down.

"What is it?" she called.

"This." He lifted the blackened axhead into the light. "Death Claw," he said, feeling hot metal even through the sweater.

"Come out of there, Sky." Kristin was beckoning him frantically from the doorframe. "This might all still fall in."

He moved back, set the axhead onto the stonework, hoisted himself up. As he tottered back toward her, they both could hear the creaking in the wood.

"Quickly," she hissed, "quickly!"

He reached her, grabbed her hand. Together they leapt over the steps, just as they fell apart, just as the porch sagged and the doorframe tumbled into the cellar. From the safe distance of the forest's edge, they watched as ash, smoke, and soot shot up, sparks rising like angry bees.

"Gone," she said. "He's gone."

"Yes," he replied softly. "He was gone last night. When I couldn't save him."

"You saved me." She turned to him fiercely. "And he didn't want to be saved. He wanted to die like"— she waved at the ruin—"like . . ."

"Like a Viking with an ax in his hand." He shook his head. "But what he *really* wanted was to live on . . . in you! That was his master plan, and everything—the visits, the séances, the runes, the time travel—that's what it was all leading up to." He looked hard into her eyes. "So?"

She stared back for a long moment, till a smile briefly edged onto her face. "What? You reckon I'm . . . *possessed?*" She said it in a zombie voice, her eyes crossing as she did. Then seriousness, sadness, returned to them. "No. I'm afraid our grandfather was just . . . just mad, I suppose."

"But the lightning, your chanting, the rune carving, all of it. Didn't you feel . . . weird?"

"Totally. But who wouldn't? This is even beyond anything we'd get up to in the dorms." That faint smile

307

came again, was chased away. "I think we got . . . caught up in the whole thing. I mean, he did have some amazing powers, didn't he? He came to you in your dreams, in the forest. Or rather, his Fetch did. He sent yours back in time, through the runes." She shook her head. "So it was easy to believe he could cheat death as well. He believed he'd found a way to do it. But obviously"—she shrugged—"he didn't."

"I suppose." Sky looked down into his hands, feeling the heat from the axhead wrapped in his sweater. Its warmth made the rest of him feel really cold. "We helped kill a man, Kristin. What the hell are we going to do now?"

"Think of a really, really good story." She started gnawing at her fingernails. "Because, believe me, when our parents find out about even half of this . . . we are in deep, deep trouble."

The police inspector in Lom bought their story—that they were runaways from England and had been camping up in the mountains when they'd seen the flames. They had their tent, stove, and some supplies—retrieved from the stone hut behind the house—that had been singed but not burnt. The books they left in it, but all Sigurd's papers they stuffed into a large metal trunk and buried in the forest near a recognizable tree.

The policeman made them accompany him and a younger colleague back up the mountain on four-wheel motorbikes to view the ruin. "Poor old man," he said. "We only saw him occasionally in town and not recently at all. I was thinking of looking in on him." He tapped Olav's bike. "We knew this fellow brought him supplies. Where is he now, I wonder?" He stared into the ash-filled cellar. "I think we may have to get forensics up here."

Their parents were another matter. After the police phone call, both mothers came to get them, Kristin's having already flown back from America when Sonja reported them missing after her last conversation with Sky. The initial joy that they were safe swiftly moved through anger to deep concern. It wasn't stated, but both mothers obviously felt that the cousins were in love, that that's why they'd run away. So the only possible action was to separate them immediately. Kristin was taken with her mother back to America on the interrupted business trip. Sky returned to Shropshire and the longest grounding of his life. He only left the house twice in the first two weeks, both times to visit a shrink. His mother was once again convinced that "all this acting out" was because of the new house, new school problems. His old "night terrors" were dug up again; yet, strangely, Sky was sleeping better than he had since moving to Shropshire. There was no walking, no waking anywhere but his bed. If he had any dreams, all traces of them fled by the time he opened his eyes.

After two weeks, his father's pleading on his behalf

worked—the limits of his grounding were extended so he could walk on the Wenlock Edge. Yet no talking fox followed him up there. He was half hoping one would, he had so many questions to ask.

There was no draug either. It was Sigurd who'd dragged Black Ulf back from the dead, using the power of the runestones. The draug had only begun to follow Sky when he'd received those stones . . . and then only when Sigurd's Fetch was around, controlling everything. So now that Sigurd was dead, his Fetch released by the burning of his bones, the draug was released too. It was perhaps the one good thing to have come from that terrible night in the mountains—the berserker had found his rest again. No shadow ever lurked in the corner of Sky's vision now, no ice choked his throat. They were both free.

And yet . . . he wasn't. He couldn't be. Not after the amazing adventures he'd had. There had to be a way to have them again. Not the killing; he'd managed to stop himself—Bjørn-in-himself—from murdering Olav, believed he could stop himself again. But if Sigurd had lied about many things, he hadn't about the most important one: that he had somehow learned not only to send the Fetch out at will but to control it as well. Sky couldn't . . . not yet! So though he spent every spare moment walking in the forest, sitting in trees, reading everything he could find, on runes, on Fetches, he didn't try to travel. He didn't know if he'd be able to get back. Especially since there was no longer someone there to watch over him.

And then there was. The Edge had started to slip from its summer greens to a hint of autumn red and still all remained quiet under the canopy. A week before school began he came back from a walk and his mother met him in the kitchen, a slightly strained smile on her face. "You have a visitor, Sky," she said. "Uh, leave the door open up there, will you?"

He took the stairs three at a time. But no one waited for him in his bedroom. Climbing the next flight, he saw that the ladder was down. Though he had mostly avoided the attic since he'd been back, he took the steps eagerly now.

"Hallo, Kristin."

"Sky!" His cousin, half buried in the sea chest, turned to him. "Oh, Sky!"

They hugged, something he couldn't remember ever doing with her. Then they sat cross-legged on the floor facing each other. Her face was in shadow, the skylight behind her.

"I wanted to . . ."

"I tried to . . ."

They spoke together, broke off with a laugh. "Me first?" she said.

"OK."

"I wanted to call you so badly."

"Me, too. But my mother . . ."

". . . wouldn't let you? Double ditto. Mine took

away my cell phone. Can you believe it?" She put the back of her hand to her forehead, struck a pose. "It was like losing an arm!"

Sky laughed. She gripped his hands and he felt a slight pain. Looking down, he noticed that her nails had grown long, were painted a deep red. "Oh Sky, there's so much I need to say to you. Have you . . . have you thought much about what happened?"

He shrugged. "Nah, not really. Been too busy playing football." He laughed at her shock. "Idiot! I've thought of nothing else."

"Me neither." She giggled, then looked serious again. "And I've been doing lots of reading. You too?" He nodded. "So we should, you know, pool our knowledge, eh? Help each other figure it out."

"Figure what out?"

"Everything!" She shook his hands. "From what I've read, Sigurd was really onto something. This Double— should be Doubles, really, because the Fetch is just one, right?—they were so much part of our ancestors' culture for so long. Centuries and centuries. So even though he died, his . . . mission lives on, doesn't it?" She let go, stood, began to pace the little space between the sloping roofs of the attic.

"Which was . . . what exactly?" He thought he knew. But he wanted her to say it.

"What he talked about. Making people— everyone!—recognize that they have a Fetch. Bringing it out of the Kingdom of Shadows and into the light."

"Yeah, but why?" Sky bit his lower lip. "Why would that be so great? Your Fetch is not . . . controllable. Well, not until you've learned to master it, like Sigurd must have done. For everyone else, it just does the things *it* wants to do."

"Exactly! You can do things as your Fetch you wouldn't ever normally do. It's like . . . you get to live all of yourself, *all* your desires, not just the bits people think of as normal or . . . healthy." She gave a little mocking laugh. "How cool is that?"

"But some of those things you don't want to live, believe me!" He suddenly saw an ax blade falling, talons reaching for pink flesh, and he shuddered. "And if everyone was doing it . . . just doing all these things they secretly desire . . . wouldn't it be total chaos?"

"More like total freedom." She raised her face to the broken window pane, sniffed the air. "Its like your parents telling you what to read, what games to play, who to hang out with . . . when only you know what's right for you." She'd paused in her pacing, to smile down at him. "We must have these Doubles for a reason, right? Be a waste not to use them."

Sky shifted. He'd thought about this endlessly; wanting to soar again as the hawk; to be back aboard a longship racing for the shore, ax in hand. It was so tempting. . . .

Kristin studied him. "And didn't he say that exploring the runes would show us how to do that? Have you tried to use them since?" Before he could reply, she

313

continued, "I hadn't thought of them, what with the police and our parents and all the fuss. I just assumed they were still in my pack. So it was a shock when I got home and found they weren't. Then I realized: you must have taken them." She smiled. "Why'd you do that, Sky? Don't you trust me?"

"'Course," said Sky hastily. "It was just before we were going to . . . you know . . . Olav." He shook his head. "I just needed them in *my* possession. Like they would support me in what I was going to do."

She was still smiling. "Makes total sense." She nodded, turned, and gestured to the sea chest. "I was looking for them. Where are they?"

"Safe," he said. "Look, sit down, will you? You're giving me neck ache."

314

"Can't. Too excited."

She paced away, turned back to speak again, but he got in first. "I've been thinking a lot about the runes too. Especially the ones we carved into the floor, remember?"

"How could I forget?" She halted, stretched her arms out, chanted.

"Thurisaz
rune of challenge
the enemy comes
you strike
triumph!"

She laughed and would have gone on, but he interrupted. "But what about that other rune. *Pertho?"*

"The dice cup?" She stopped pacing. "What about it?"

"It was reversed. I carved it backward." He hugged his knees. "Why? Why'd I do that? Or maybe I didn't. Maybe my Fetch was trying to warn me. Warn us."

After a long moment, she said, "So? What does it matter now?"

"What does it matter? It *matters* because that reversed rune corrupted all the others. All that was good in the cast—the adventures, the learning—all became . . . rotten, somehow." He leaned forward, tried to see her face more clearly. "You do remember the verse, right?"

"Not really."

He stared. "How can you not remember? It's burnt onto my brain, like . . . like the runes were burnt onto that floor." He cleared his throat.

"Pertho
roll the dice
upside down
cheating and lies."

He shook his head. "Sigurd made me believe I was leading the way, exploring the world of the Fetch. But I was the one being led."

"No, he—"

"Yes!" Sky came up onto his knees. It was something else he'd thought hard about over the summer; but it was only now, explaining it to Kristin, that real understanding . . . and real anger . . . came. "I think

315

it was *all* lies. Sigurd used us, and wanted to keep on using us. He let you learn most about the runes, because he thought he was going to possess you in the end and would need you to have rune lore. He used me, trained me to be his . . . hit man. 'Go back in time, learn to kill. Come to Norway and kill again. Oh . . . and bring your cousin.'" The laugh that came was bitter.

She began pulling at a piece of insulation on the roof. "What does it matter? It was just Sigurd . . ." She sighed. "I mean, he lied to us to get us there, yes. But compared to what he wanted to achieve? What's one little lie?"

"One little lie?" he said incredulously. "He lied so we'd help him *kill* someone." He shuddered. "We watched him kill someone."

"Oh, that." She shrugged.

"Yes . . . *that!*" He stared up at her. There was a long silence. "Kristin, I need to ask you something."

"Ask away."

"Your nails."

Puzzled, she lifted her left hand, holding the perfect red ovals up to the skylight. "Don't you like them?"

"I think they're lovely. It's just . . . you used to bite them all the time."

She rolled her neck. "It was a disgusting habit. So I cured myself. Some people give up smoking, I . . . ta-da! . . . stopped biting! Big deal. Anyway, it's not important. But shall I tell you what is?"

"Please." Sky stood up, and she moved away from him, waving those manicured fingers in the air, putting herself deeper into the shadows under the eaves.

"I don't know about you, but I'm fed up with reading. I want to be *doing*. For that, I need the runestones." She turned back. "*We* need them. We've done his cast, yes? So now we start casting our own. With no lies in them, eh?" She laughed. "What a team we'll make! The Ancient Order of Wall-Walkers reunited." She began to move toward him. He could see a glint of teeth, a smile on her lips. "So . . . where are they? Oh, and his journal too? Where's that?"

He watched her come. "I buried them," he said softly.

"Then you'll dig them up for me, won't you, dear Sky?"

She stopped, leaned in. It was the first time she was directly under the skylight, and for the first time he could see her eyes. See the ghost of a line that ran between her two eyebrows.

He managed to keep his voice steady. "You have to tell one thing. Then I'll go get them."

"Anything!" Delighted at his promise, she reached down and took his hands again in each of hers.

It took a while to form the words, and then they came in a whisper. "Have you seen the draug lately?"

She couldn't hide the shock from him—they were too close for that. And she couldn't hide the fact that he was right. The fear flashing in her eyes, her hands pulling away from his, told him that.

"What?" She stepped away, returning to shadow. "What are you talking about?"

He let his empty hands fall. Of course! He'd got it wrong before. The draug hadn't been freed. It was still a soul ripped from wherever it had been, drawn to the man who had ripped it. And now that man . . . existed in another form. That was why Sky had not seen a walking corpse all summer. It had been following Sigurd's Fetch. Yet the draug was also drawn to the tools used to jerk it from its rest: the runestones. And since Fetch and stones were now both in Shropshire . . . These realizations came in a flash, vanished as fast, swept away by a terrible sadness. Suddenly he felt . . . bereft. At the beginning of the summer, Kristin—the old Kristin—had come back. Now she was gone again. No, he thought angrily, not "gone." She'd been taken away.

She'd retreated again to the shadows. There was another long silence. "You know what," he said quietly, eventually, "I think I'll just have to leave the runestones where they are."

She spun toward him. "They are as much mine as yours, boy. They belong to our grandfather. Blood of our blood—" She broke off at the phrase, then shouted, "Give them to me!"

"No."

A voice called up from the landing below. His mother's, anxious. "Is everything all right up there?"

Immediately Kristin moved past him, knocking his

shoulder with hers. When she was halfway down the ladder, when only her head was visible, she looked at him again. "You'll be hearing from me," she said.

"Which one of you?" he murmured to the space where she'd just been.

CHAPTER TWENTY-FIVE

ILLUMINATION

When he finally got to his bedroom that night, Sky had no need to look out of the window. He knew what was down there, among the apple trees. It frightened him; and yet, in a strange way, reassured too. Because he'd finally learned what drew the draug—Sigurd's Fetch, now returned. And the runestones. Not buried, as he'd told Kristin. Safe, though. Safe, for now.

Something else was back, as well—an end to quiet sleep. His eyes closed fast enough, but as soon as they did, images came, a jumble of memory and fear. Twice he was up, woke once near the window, his hand on the curtains his father had only just got round to putting up; once by the door, reaching for the handle. When his feet touched the floorboards the third time, he gave up. It was better to keep his eyes open and just lie there. Safer, anyway.

He didn't want to switch his lamp on. The room

was quite bright, what with the full moon and the thin curtains. The only other light came from the glowing numbers on his clock radio, which changed so slowly. Watching them flick, he suddenly wanted some other comfort. Food? Go downstairs, make himself a sandwich, watch TV? No. His mum would be down in a moment. She had tried to question him over dinner about Kristin's visit, her sudden departure. Probably why he hadn't eaten much. She'd try again.

He got up. Surely there was something edible in his dresser?

He started at the bottom, though it didn't much matter—there was no order to the contents. Sonja would get him to reorganize every few months—socks in the top drawer, T-shirts in the next, etc. Within a week, everything was everywhere. So the bottom one was just as likely to contain the half-eaten chocolate bar he thought he'd dropped in there . . . a few days before. He wasn't sure, so he searched carefully. He'd thrust fingers into some interesting science experiments over the years!

Nothing! Not in that drawer or in the next two up. Opening the top one, he shoved a book aside—the Dickens, his summer assignment, totally unread—and there it was. Not edible at all. But actually what he was looking for.

He picked the lighter up, holding it carefully by its sides; because now he saw it, he remembered what had happened when his father first gave it to him, how he'd let his thumb slide into his grandfather's thumbprint on the brass front and he'd had those strange flashes— the bald woman singing the sad lament, the wolf, the dying wildcat. He also remembered why he hadn't touched it since—he'd had enough going on with his one grandfather, Sigurd. He couldn't have dealt with another!

He lifted it, liked the way the moonlight lit the brass. He'd watched smokers at school, lurking behind the gymnasium with their Zippo lighters, doing their tricks—opening the lid with a downward strike on their trousers, then spinning the wheel and lighting it with a swift strike up. He'd envied them their cool; not the cigarettes, he didn't smoke. But he'd always liked a good flame.

322

"Burning longships a specialty," he said, and chuckled.

He was still holding the lighter gingerly so he needn't touch that worn thumbprint. But then he realized he could get it lit without that. With a one-handed technique, just like his classmates with their Zippos.

He pressed one side into the pads of his fingers, then used his thumb to flick up the brass arm that covered the wick. It clicked into place. He used the thumb again, on the flywheel. Whoosh! Sparked and caught first time, with the heady scent of lighter fluid and a blue-yellow flame.

He used his forefinger to push the arm down, dowsing the flame. Cool, he thought. But cooler if I do it quicker.

He pushed the arm up, spun the wheel. Flame came, and he extinguished it again with another flick.

How many times would it light in a row?

He flicked. It sparked, flamed. As it did, a breeze came from the window, pushing the blue-yellow cone to the side, changing its shape. Two peaks formed like . . . like ears on a head. Like a wolf, raising its snout to howl.

Close. Out. Again.

Flick. Spark. Flame.

The *sound* of burning, on a note, a sung note, the note changing, rising and falling. He could hear the sadness in it, a lament for a lost soul. . . .

Kristin!

Sound cut off with a brass arm, falling. Rising immediately.

Flick. Spark. Flame.

No breath stirred it now. The fuel burned with its own sound while Sky stared at the fire, into the fire, through the yellow and on, down into the blue. It was like looking into a tiny glass . . . or a mirror hung on a cabin wall that showed what was, is, could be. Within it, a wildcat stirred, stunning, beautiful . . . dying. Then hands reached for it, scarred hands . . .

. . . Sky's hands!

Flick. The brass arm came down, cutting off sight, snuffing out flame. Sky laid the lighter down, then lay down himself on his bed. He wasn't hungry now. And he still wasn't tired.

He was waiting.

He didn't know how he was there, climbing over the barbed-wire fence at the edge of the field, slipping into the forest. He didn't even know if it was him walking under the trees, or his Fetch. Since it was two in the morning, it could have been either. Somehow it didn't matter. Something was drawing him in. Someone.

He knew the way well, along this faintest of tracks. He probably could have found the rendezvous in the dark; but the full moon's light was penetrating the autumn-thinned canopy. The clearing was even brighter, the moon directly above. Ivy now swirled up the ash he'd climbed at the beginning of the summer; other than that, all was as it had been. The same oak branch lay there, a little more decomposed from maggot and rain. He found the same handholds and toe grips beneath the ivy's leaves. Resting his back against the trunk, he waited to find out what had called him here.

He heard it first in the alarmed chittering of a squirrel, glimpsed something moving between the trees. In another moment, a creature had jumped onto the fallen branch and begun to lick between its long, dagger-like claws.

He watched it for a while. He had seen it twice before, of course; most recently only a little earlier that night, held within blue flame. But now he had time to study it, he recalled its name: lynx, a beast long since hunted to extinction in these woods. He'd seen pictures, recognized the tawny coat, the bobbed tail, the tufts of hair at the ends of its ears. He'd heard there were still some in Spain, so this one had come a long way. Been *brought* a long way.

The wildcat arched its back, stretched its neck till its head was pointing almost up at him. When it opened its eyes, it sat back swiftly as if startled, and the two stared at each other for a long moment.

"You're already here," the animal said, at last.

"I am."

Sky slid down the tree trunk, walked slowly to the fallen branch.

"No fox?"

"That was Sigurd's Fetch. This"—a tongue came out to flick at a long incisor—"is Kristin's."

Sky tried to keep the revulsion from his voice. "You've taken it over?"

The lynx purred. "Borrowed it. Kristin sleeps, so—"

"But you told us that the Fetch does not survive the burning of the bones."

It was weird to see an animal smile. "My Fetch had already moved on. I could find another. I will, when Kristin and I . . . hunt together. But why seek one now when Kristin's is so . . . magnificent?"

There was no attempt to form words with the mouth; the lips did not move, nor the tongue. The jaw just opened, sounds emerged. And it was Sigurd making the sounds.

Sky was struggling now with his anger. But anger

325

wouldn't get him what he wanted. Quelling it, he said, "So you did survive, Grandfather."

"As you see." Before Sky could go on, could begin to ask the first of a thousand questions, the lynx continued. "And I have come for you, Grandson. We need you."

"We? You're 'we' now?"

"In one way. In another, we are still separate. She sleeps. I . . . walk. But it is 'we' who need you."

"You don't need me, you need the runestones, your journal. To carry on doing . . . whatever it is you plan to do."

"It's true I'd like them back. I spent one lifetime pouring energy into those stones, learning to unleash it again so I could experience . . . amazing things. We could again, Sky. All of us." The cat nodded its head at him. "They retain great power, and without them . . . well, my work will not be impossible; but it will be so much harder." The cat gave what sounded like a sigh. "Yet know this: Without *you* it will be harder still."

"Me?" Sky frowned. "Why me?"

"Because, my boy, in so many ways you are the most powerful of us all. Unformed, yes. Needing guidance, of course. But that's why I am still here. Isn't that what you most want, Sky? To learn how to reach your Fetch, at will?"

Sky tried to keep the desire from his face, his voice. "Go on," he said.

The lynx stretched forward. "Think, Sky. At fifteen . . . oh, the things you have already experienced!

I knew nothing of the Fetch at that age except in dreams. By the time I discovered mine, I was already almost too old to really use him to go back. It is . . . draining, as you know." Sky could hear the smile in the voice before the cat continued. "Yet here you are. You've journeyed, fought for a cause, for your family. Felt the power of your ancestors within you. Lived as them. Died as them."

"*Killed* as them." Sky's anger overcame his yearning. "You . . . manipulated us, Kristin and me. Lured us to Norway to help you kill an innocent man . . ."

"He was hardly innocent. You saw—"

"I don't *care* what he'd done. It was not for us to be his executioners."

The lynx lowered its head. "You are right, Sky. I regret it in some ways, though if ever a man deserved to die . . . well. But in helping to kill him, you saved me. His sacrifice helped me to live on. To continue with my work, my mission."

"One that uses lies, murder, the stealing of souls."

"Only rarely. And only when absolutely necessary." Sigurd's voice was still a gentle contrast. "And trust me—all the suffering will be worthwhile in the end."

Sky shook his head. " 'The ends justify the means.' Isn't that what tyrants always say?"

" 'Tyrants?' " The lynx bent its head in that puzzled way again. "Sky! Sky! Think about what I am asking you to do. To allow people to explore the world of the Fetch. To know that there is life beyond death, not in

327

some future, but here . . . now!" The animal stood, as if it could not contain its excitement. "Come, a little suffering at the beginning so that humanity can live forever."

"Live forever?" Sky could no longer keep the disgust from his voice. "Why do you think everyone wants to do that? Do you think Black Ulf does, walking the nights as a headless corpse?"

The lynx shot its claws forward, scratching four lines on the damp wood. "And who will protect you from him, Grandson, if I do not?" He looked up, head tipped to the side. "I raised him, yes; but he's drawn most to you, for some reason I do not understand. Maybe it's because you are the possessor of the runestones now. They brought him here. They are needed to send him back. *I* can send him back." The claws slowly traced the lines they had made in the soft, rotting wood. "Another good reason to hand them over, eh? And to join us. Take pity on one of the Walking Dead. Together we'll return the draug to his rest."

It was so tempting. It was part of what he'd realized on that rock in Norway, why he'd decided to help his grandfather kill—to free the draug. And the other part was now being offered to him. Sigurd was promising to teach him how to control his Fetch.

So tempting! Yet there was one thing he still could not accept. "Tell me. Does Kristin know?"

The scratching stopped. "Know what?"

"That you . . . possess her."

"Share her, Sky. Share her." The lynx looked up. "No. She does not know. You could tell her, but she will never believe you. No one will."

"So you've hijacked her life?"

"No. She will carry on as she was. School, university. She has . . . more of a purpose now, that's all."

"'All'? It's *your* purpose, though, isn't it?" The cat's eyes narrowed. There was no denial in them, and it finally made Sky shout, "What about her 'purposes'? Her will, her destiny?"

"This *is* her destiny." If a lynx could indeed smile, it did then. "The way you thrust your chin out when angry? I bet your father does it just like that. The way you hold an ax? So like Bjørn. And did your mother not tell you that your first cry was like her own father's laugh? Oh yes, Kristin told me that." The laugh came, and it did indeed shake the wildcat's whole body as it had shaken Sigurd's in the mountains. "We are all made up of everyone who has gone before. It is encoded in our cells. So I was already in Kristin anyway. I am just a little more . . . influential now."

Sky thought for a moment, spoke again, his voice calmer. "If you have always been in her, and always will be, why do you need to remain in her now? And if you say I am potentially the most powerful . . . well, you've told us what we have to do. Taught us many things. Together, Kristin and I will master the runes. We'll pursue this mission you've given us. You'll still be there, within us, all the way." He stared intently into

329

the lynx's oval eyes. "But I'll only do that if you leave her free to choose."

The lynx stared back. For the longest moment there was silence between them. "No, I cannot," Sigurd said at last. "I do her no harm. I just want to help her fulfill what she already desires to do."

Sky shook his head. He had the answer at last. "No. What *you* want is to live forever."

The ears went back, there was a ruffling of fur along the spine. It was all so clear now. Sky went on. "And your great work? Freeing humanity's Fetch? That's about followers, isn't it? Or should I say 'worshippers'?"

The lynx stayed silent. Sky knew he was right. About everything. There was just one last thing he needed to know.

"Olav. The man we helped you kill?"

"What about him?"

"What you showed us in the mirror . . . it wasn't true, was it? He may have been a nasty piece of work. But he wasn't a murderer, was he?" The lynx just stared. "Was he?"

A shrug. Nothing more. No denial. Yet instead of fury, Sky felt his anger fade, replaced by something else—a calmness. Here was an end of lies. And for some reason—perhaps because he was remembering that night in the cabin and that last time he'd felt Bjørn within him—a memory of the Viking came now. Not from battle, or when the berserker was born or died. It was of that moment when Bjørn had used his father's given name for the first time; used it to show he was now a man, worthy to go into battle. He couldn't use the term "grandfather" anymore. Not when that grandfather had betrayed him. Not when he'd stolen someone Sky loved.

"Well, Sigurd," he said, softly now, "I won't let you use Kristin for your crusade."

The lynx's eyes narrowed. "You won't?"

Sky shook his head. "Years ago, my cousin and I used to walk the walls of my old neighborhood at night. There was only one rule: If either of us fell off and was caught, the other always came back." He took a step closer, holding the cat's gaze. "I'll be coming back for Kristin."

"What will you do?" For the first time in the clearing, the soft tones Sigurd had used took on a harsher color. "*Fight* me for her? *You?*" The word was heavy with contempt. "I said you had some potential, boy. But how could *you* hope to fight *me?*"

"I'll learn how. I'll use the runes. Go back again and again until I have mastered the meaning of each one. Each ancestor will teach me as Bjørn did."

Sigurd's voice came out on a cat's hiss. "I have explored many of our ancestors' lives. It would take you years to learn all I know from them. Decades! And any weapon you could take from them, I would already know how to turn aside."

Suddenly Sky saw it. Saw it within the flame of a

331

lighter that had traveled as far as any runestone. "I have other ancestors. Through my father's line."

The lynx sat back and tipped its head, gave what could only be a laugh. "Most peoples have long forgotten the Fetch. It is only because you are of Norse blood that you remember yours. What is your father's *line* anyway?" There was no mistaking the mockery.

"He's English." Sky was looking straight into the animal's eyes. "But he wasn't born here."

The bored tone continued. "Oh yes? And where *was* he born?"

"Corsica."

"Corsica?"

If Sky hadn't started to get used to the lynx's expressions, he might have missed it. But the fur on the back of the spine rose again at the echoed word, the whiskers flattened to the side of the head. The cat was agitated. Emboldened, Sky continued. "I'll travel to Corsica. I bet my ancestors there know some tricks you don't."

The flash of concern had left the animal's face and body. The voice was gently mocking again. "Oh, I am sure they do." It rose on four paws, arched its back, walked down the decaying trunk to Sky, halted just a foot away. "Go, then. Follow your destiny, and we— Kristin and I—will follow ours. You will find that they are twin paths—three paths, perhaps—all leading to the same destination. For all you will discover in Corsica is that your destiny lies with us, and to us you will return . . . and return stronger for your ordeals." The cat was purring under the words, leaning into Sky. It felt vaguely disgusting, and Sky put his palm into the fur to shove the cat away just as it spoke again. "For believe me, boy, ordeals there will be."

With a sudden snarl, the lynx struck, razor claws ripping down the back of the hand that had pushed. Then, in a flash of teeth, it was gone.

"Good," said Sky, despite the pain, sucking the blood that seeped from the four slashes. He knew they would scar. He even knew how they would look. Because he'd already seen those same scars before within a lighter's flame, as his hands reached to a dying lynx. "These will remind me. I will not rest till you are free, Kristin."

333

From somewhere nearby came a shriek, the cry of a hunting bird. Was it the same hawk whose body Sky had entered that night? He couldn't know. All he did know was that he had to fly like that again.

"One day," he said, taking the first step along the path. "One day."

Above him the hawk cried again, soaring up through the branches, rising into the moonlight.

CHAPTER TWENTY-SIX
THE EXORCISM

It had been a glorious day, summer's final fling of heat. A day to celebrate—even if it was the last day of the holidays and school was starting tomorrow. Because it was also Sky's birthday.

Sonja had let her vegetarian principles slip. A son didn't turn sixteen every year, and he had the right to choose his supper. Gnawed rib bones lay heaped on the table, huge mounds before his and his dad's places, a few delicately nibbled before his mum's. A pewter beer tankard—Henry's gift—sat before Sky, the foam from the latest batch of home brew curling around the top. His father had insisted he have a pint.

"Sixteen now. You're a man!"

It was, Sky thought as he studied the debris, a scene of which a Viking would thoroughly approve. Though he doubted there'd been many lemon meringue pies consumed in Valhalla.

"Have another slice, lad," his father said, when he saw where Sky was looking.

"Oh, I couldn't . . . well, all right." Sonja happily shoveled the last huge slice onto his plate, and Sky set to. As he ate, he looked at his parents looking at him.

They'll be OK, he thought, once they get over the shock. They'll be fine.

The thought of what he was going to do made his stomach contract. He concealed it with a grunt, throwing down his fork beside the half-eaten piece. "I can't!" He held up his hands in mock surrender. "I'm beaten."

"You sure? Absolutely sure?" Henry said.

"Certain."

"Well," said Henry, leaning over, snagging the plate, dragging it before him. "Be a shame to waste it."

335

Sonja began to clear. He got up to help. "Uh, Mum, I think I'm going to walk to school tomorrow."

"All that way on your first day?" She put the forks in the sink, used the back of her hand to push aside a straying hair. "I thought I might drive you. You know, see you settled in."

He saw the concern in her eyes. The last term hadn't ended well, with all that sleepwalking. And then there'd been the Norway business. But since he'd come back, they'd not had to come into his room once for nightmares. And they'd been amazed, then thrilled by how often he went to the library. He'd told them it was to do his course work for school, but he'd been there for . . . other studies. They'd even relented over the grounding and let him go, by himself, to London last week. He said he needed to visit a museum to finish his summer project; but where he really needed to go was Hatton Garden, the center of the country's jewelry trade. There, six different jewelers made six different offers for the smallest of Sigurd's uncut diamonds. Only one was outrageously low, the rest about the same. He took the highest, naturally. In cash. It had been strange and scary carrying so much money around. Strangely wonderful too.

He looked back at Sonja now, at the concern on her face. "Nothing to settle, Mum. I'm fine. Looking forward to it." He smiled. "First football match on Friday."

336   "How will you play with your hand like that?" Henry pointed to the bandages.

Sky had told them he'd done it climbing over a barbed-wire fence. "I'm a center forward, not a goal-keeper."

"But," his mother said as she fetched more plates, "this walk. It'll take over an hour. What time will you have to leave?"

"Oh, I want to have a little time in the woods, so . . . about five-thirty, I guess?"

"Then I'll get up too."

"No, Mum, really . . ." He kept his voice even. "Just fancied a walk on the Edge. I've had my last supper"— he nodded to the piled-up bones—"now how about the condemned man's last request?" He mimed his hands being shackled, being dragged forward. His father laughed.

"The lad's sixteen, love. Doesn't want his mother dropping him off at school."

She reached up, touched between his eyes, where the One-Brow had grown thick over the summer. "Hardly seems possible. Sixteen years ago. What a night that was! It was as hot as today, wasn't it, dear?"

"Hotter," his father said, in one of his funny voices. "They had proper summers in them days."

"And the stars . . ."

Sky sat. "So you weren't, uh, cold in that birthing pool, Mum?"

"Cold? No, no." Sonja had rejoined them at the table, sat. "They'd heated it, you see, with hot rocks from the fireplace and . . ."

337

Sky made no protests about hearing the story again. His mum enjoyed the telling. And he enjoyed watching her tell it.

He had everything ready by three, his backpack checked, checked again. Then it was just a matter of waiting. There was no point leaving too early; the first commuter train out of Stretton left at six-twenty-eight, and it was about an hour's walk to the station. But he'd decided to leave at four-seventeen. It had become his special hour, the same time that he had woken up those mornings when this whole business had begun, the same time he'd arrived at Sigurd's cabin; and though he'd obviously not had a watch then, he was pretty sure it was the exact same time that Bjørn had drowned in sea water and blood, a dying slave in his arms.

He went to the window. The darkness was deep, brushed through with a faint mist that hovered over the ground. No moon to light it, dawn a while away yet; but since there were no clouds, starlight filled the garden with shadows. And there, beneath the laden boughs of an apple tree, was the deepest shadow of all.

Sky stepped back, just as the shadow shifted. Every night since his . . . *visitors* the week before, he had looked down, every night a hood had raised to him. He never saw the draug anywhere else, though sometimes he thought he felt it nearby, an icy finger within a warm wind, an almost physical sense of sadness, of despair nearby.

He hadn't been ready before. Now he thought he was. Hoped he was. Because if he wasn't . . .

He stood with his back to the wall beside the window and pulled the lighter from his pocket. His thumb was in the print, but no flashes came. He didn't need them repeated, they were embedded in his memory. And, anyway, he knew they were questions now, not answers.

He flicked. Nothing stirred in the flame's depths, and he wasn't looking for anything anyway; just trying to beat his record of forty-three consecutive strikes. But he refilled the lighter twice and he still didn't make it. The red numbers on his clock shifted slowly. At four-ten, he dropped the lighter into a trouser pocket and put on his sneakers. At four-fifteen, he shrugged into his ski jacket. A few seconds left and he picked up the long object wrapped in sacking.

The clock flicked to four-seventeen. His fingers were over the radio alarm. He'd set it just in case he fell asleep. A soft voice spoke one word before he could press the button down.

The word was "ghost."

Sky gasped. Then, a little smile came. One of the many books he'd read over the summer said there was no such thing as coincidence. Checking that the letter to his parents was tucked in the sheets—they'd find it, but not straightaway—he hefted the backpack, left the room. The stairs that creaked, he stepped over. The front door gave the faintest of groans.

To the left of the garden gate was an old holm oak. Just within his reach, some creature had carved out a home, long since abandoned, a hollow about the width and height of his spread hands. He reached, pulled the cookie tin out. Inside it was a bag and a book and a debit card for an account that held ten thousand pounds. He tucked them all into his backpack.

He didn't look back. Not at the house, not at the orchard. Didn't need to, knew what was behind him. At the road, he looked east. There was no light yet, only the hope of it.

Putting his back to that hope, he began to walk west, toward the graveyard.

The little church lay shrouded in night, a dark center to the darkness that surrounded it. The tombstones spread around it like teeth in an uneven mouth; some new, bright, and thrust straight up; others old, chipped, leaning at odd angles. He could tell the more recent additions from the fresh flowers placed in urns upon them. Bending to one, he could just make out the carvings, dates in this new century. The old ones, the ones that leaned, most of them would be unreadable even in the brightest daylight.

The one he finally stopped by was one of those. It lay just to the right of the main path, halfway between the boundary wall and the church, close to its front door; closer, Sky supposed, to salvation . . . or so the rich man or woman who paid for it must have thought. Now all their efforts to be remembered had been thwarted by Time, their name unreadable, their dates obliterated, the inspiring poem carved on the tombstone reduced to the single word that Sky could just make out, more by the touch of his fingers than his eyes.

Before.

Six yew trees made a semicircle around it, a cave of branch and needles. He remembered telling Kristin, back in that other cemetery in Lom, that for the Norse, the yew was the tree that led to the Underworld.

Kristin! The thought of his cousin, of that last time he'd seen her, her anger, that shade of a One-Brow between her eyes . . . he shivered. Well, he was here for her, in a way. The first stage in a journey on her behalf. At least, that's what he kept telling himself.

He dropped his pack, leaned the wrapped object against the tombstone, straightened. He could feel his heart, beating fast, feel the weight of his caul in its leather pouch dragging from his neck. He even fancied he could feel the tiny weight of the two remaining diamonds within it. He realized he hadn't been breathing for a while; knew he'd need breath for what he was about to try. He took a deep one, another. When he was finally ready, he spoke.

"Are you there?"

There was no answer, none expected. He knew he was there. He had heard the churchyard gate open and close behind him just as he had opened and closed it. It had almost made him laugh. Why would a draug use a gate at all? Did it make him feel more . . . alive?

All humor went with the breath that moved across his neck, as cold as water flowing under ice.

He didn't turn. "I know who you are," he whispered. "I know what was done . . . the wrong that was done to you."

He heard movement, a stirring. He hurried on, tried to make his voice firmer, stronger. "I want to help you—"

He never finished. The words were choked off, his neck gripped, clamped in ice and bone. Skeletal fingers, pushing through flesh and sinew, were crushing his windpipe. He was being shaken as if he were a doll thrown about by a child. There was no air, none to clear the red that flooded his eyes. He felt like Bjørn had felt, sinking in his armor to the seabed. And then he remembered what that was like, reaching that point where pain faded, struggles ended, peace came. There was nothing he could do now; that time was gone. Better to sink, sink faster . . .

He fell forward, onto his pack. Thrusting a hand into its depths, he reached what he needed and snatched it out, dropping it on the ground beside him. Instantly, the iced grip left him. He lay there, choking and coughing, on top of the grave.

It took him a long while. When he could breathe again, he lifted what he'd dropped, heaved himself up, put his back to the tombstone. Holding the bag with Sigurd's runestones out before him, he was ready to look up.

He had never seen the draug so clearly, even with so little light in the sky.

"He used these to drag you back, didn't he?"

A hood needed a head within it to nod. And yet, Sky knew, if he could, he would have.

"And the death you seek? The one you spoke about at the castle?" Sky swallowed. "It's not mine, is it?"

It was like it had been at the street market, when no image had appeared in the mirror. They were outside Time again. If he had been wearing a watch, it would have stopped. If there had been people nearby, they would have frozen. Here, in the still of a graveyard, he could only tell because the wind no longer ruffled the branches of the yews, and the bird that had begun to sing stopped.

Silence. Time suspended. He waited for an answer. When none came, he whispered again, "Is it?"

If someone without a head could shake it . . . there was an almost imperceptible shifting in the gray. Side to side.

Sky hadn't been sure before. Now he was. "It's your own. Isn't it?" He whistled softly. "Of course it is. You want your death back."

As he leaned forward, the runes clinked inside the bag, and at the sound the draug drew back, shrinking into gray as if cringing from a whip.

"It's all right," said Sky, "I don't want them any more than you do."

343

From his pack he pulled a short folding shovel. He pushed between the yews, reaching out with the metal blade till he struck stone. Not a gravestone this time. The boundary wall of the graveyard ran close to the path. It wasn't perfect, but it would have to do; he couldn't risk carrying these runestones around any longer. They were his grandfather's possessions, in-fused with his power, attuned to his desires. Well, his and Kristin's now. That's why they were both so eager to get hold of them. He suspected they would act like some sort of tracking device every time he used them. And the last thing he needed was for Sigurd to know exactly where he was.

He emerged, shaking the mud of the shallow grave he'd dug from his hands. The draug was where he'd left him, motionless.

One weight was lifted from him, the weight he'd carried ever since he'd found the runestones. He had never used them. They had used him. Sigurd had used him.

Another burden stood before him. He could feel the draug's hopelessness, his yearning. And he had just buried the runes that had first dragged him from his rest. Could they have been used to send him back? Somehow, Sky didn't think so. The answer had to lie elsewhere.

But where?

344   The bird began to sing again. Time had returned. A breeze riffled through the yews.

Yews, he thought. Gateway to the Underworld.

He stepped up to the trees. He could now see that one of the six was dying. Its bark was sheering away in patches. Its needles were red, the red of rust, red of dried blood. *Blood?* He had blood on his hands. Digging the runestones' grave had opened the cuts inflicted by Sigurd's—by Kristin's—Fetch.

"You will learn to hear the secrets that whisper in your blood," his grandfather had told him.

He listened now, took his knife from a pocket. "Forgive me," he said, stretching through the foliage, grasping a small branch, cutting, though it did not truly need the extreme sharpness of his knife. The branch snapped away easily, so dry from the long, hot summer. The dead tree was like tinder, only awaiting a spark to be consumed.

He sensed the presence behind him shift slightly. Out of the corner of his eye he could see the forest beyond the church more distinctly. The sky had grown a little lighter. Laying the yew branch on top of the tombstone, a scant inch of its end thrust over its edge, he whispered, "For Odin," and slashed down. Once, twice, again, pushing the branch forward each time.

Three disks lay at his feet. Picking them up, he saw they were the size of his finger and thumb circled. Almost the size of a runestone. He laid them out, looked at them, closed his eyes, saw them still. There were shapes already within them, forms waiting to be born. They needed the right words to bring them out. The right . . .

345

Raising his knife high, as once he had raised an ax in a cabin in the mountains of the gods, he cried out,

"Algiz
stag and doe
sacrifices
to feed the tribe
berserker
sacrifices
to save the tribe . . ."

He didn't know where the words had come from. He didn't know what language they were in. He only knew that as he spoke them, his blade slashed a line straight down, two more coming in from an angle to join just below the top. He knew it meant "deer." He knew that was just a word. For this was another rune of sacrifice, like *Uruz*, which Bjørn had carved onto his axhead. But this wasn't the giving up of childhood. This was the giving up of a life. Meat to feed the tribe. Death for life.

Behind him he heard a sound, like a ragged, indrawn breath. He couldn't look. There wasn't time to look. He raised the knife, slashed shapes onto the second disk, the words coming stronger, louder.

"Tiwaz
eldest god
of war
of victory
a spearhead forged
when it strikes
justice . . ."

A spear had burst onto the wooden disk, born of wood and steel. Behind him, there was more than just breath now. A voice came on it, echoing the word he'd just cried out.

"Justice!"

The . . . spirit had been terribly wronged. Sigurd had ripped it from its rest, brought it back to walk in a world where it could no longer live, where it could only see and suffer. Justice was what it needed now. Freedom was what it craved.

Something else was needed. The last blank disk,

the third . . . there was knowledge within it. But knowledge demanded sacrifice, the sacrifice that the first rune, *Algiz,* had told of.

Hadn't Odin been gouged with a spear, given one eye to receive the runes?

Hadn't Thorkell Grimsson given his life—again to a spear—so that his son could live?

What could Sky give? With another spear cut into wood before him, what could he give?

Then he remembered what Bjørn had given when he'd cut the first ash stave that had ever held Death Claw. And remembering, he struck. His actions were no different—the raising of his knife, the slash down— yet this time, before he cut wood, he cut through flesh. The blade was as keen as his ancestors had always kept theirs, and it lopped off the very tip of his thumb as easily as an ax had ever split an enemy's helm. And because of that sharpness, that swift strike, there was a moment before the pain came, a moment to slash three strokes in the last disk, three strokes for his blood, and all its secrets, to pool in. An "S" carved in straight lines.

"Sowilo
the sun rises
night banished
lies vanquished
shining truth
rune to return
the lost soul!"

Now the pain came. But he had no time to think

347

about it, only time to stagger back from the eruption of light before him. The sun shattered the darkness, the first beam of it pouring down onto the ring of yews. It lit up the one he'd cut, the one that had given an arm as he had given his blood. And it told him what he had to do.

The lighter was in his pocket. He fumbled it out, flicked it, but his blood-slick fingers slipped on the wheel. No fire came, but he smelled gas in the air. Wiping his hand on his trousers, he flicked again, saw the spark . . .

The yew exploded into flame.

Now there was plenty of light to see by. He turned, saw the hooded figure bend toward the ground as if shying from the sudden conflagration. Slowly, so slowly, it began to rise.

The hood was no longer empty. A head was there. A face.

Sky had seen it before, of course, in dreams, in nightmares. But the very first time he had seen it, it had been reflected in the iron boss of a shield.

"Bjørn," he cried.

The face was old, the face of the man who had hauled himself onto his longship for that final voyage. Yet even as Sky watched, the face began to slip, back and back, loose flesh tautening, wrinkles fleeing, gray hair turning fair, the One-Brow shading from wisp to full in moments.

A young man stood there, draug no more. A ghost,

Bjørn's spirit double, insubstantial in the gray cloak that was turning transparent. That man looked back at Sky and, for a long moment, longer than they'd ever had in their other encounters, they just stared. Then, with the briefest of smiles, Bjørn moved swiftly, with a young man's stride, toward the flames he'd craved for a thousand years. The yew was an inferno, sparks flying up, branches running crimson and yellow. Then, at the very threshold of his desire, Bjørn hesitated, drew back.

Sky knew what was missing. A Viking can never hope to come to Valhalla without a weapon in his hand. He'd have felt just the same.

The cloth came off the ax in a heartbeat; in another, Death Claw had been shoved forward, the shaft Sky had cut and carved during late summer bright beneath the gleaming axhead. For a moment, both of them held it and neither did. For a moment, there was a last meeting of eyes.

349

Then, bearing his weapon, Bjørn stepped into the fire. Flames turned blue and surged around him, swallowed him, burnt him clean. In a matter of seconds, all form was gone, even the ax that had served them both. Only light remained.

Dogs had begun to bark in the nearest house. It was time to go. Wrapping a handkerchief around his one hand, grunting with the effort of lifting his pack, Sky walked swiftly away.

"Six-twenty-eight to Crewe," he muttered through

clenched teeth. "Seven-thirty-four to London Euston. Eleven-oh-three London Victoria to Dover . . ."

A spasm shook him and he sped up, muttering train times and connections to distract himself. It would take him two days to reach his destination. Once there, he had not a clue where he would go, what he would do. Except try to catch the whisper of other secrets in his blood. He had to learn them if he was going to come back and fight Sigurd for Kristin's soul.

Soon, despite the throbbing in his hand, he began to whistle. He'd be all right, he decided. Pain faded, wounds healed. Whatever ordeals he had yet to go through, he knew he had an interesting future. That was something he didn't need to read in the runes.

350   A car was coming up behind him. Without hesitation, he stuck out a thumb—bloody, he noticed with a pained grin.

The car stopped. A young man wound down the window. "Where you going?"

"Corsica," Sky said. And smiled.

To Kate Jones

A GUIDE TO THE RUNES

rune: a mark of mysterious or magical significance
(The Oxford English Dictionary)

Runa: secret, whisper (*Old German*)

❦❦❦

Just as the word *alphabet* is taken from the first two letters of the ancient Greek alphabet *(alpha, beta)*, so the Elder Futhark is named after the first six letters of the Old German alphabet: *F(ehu) U(ruz) Th(urisaz) A(nsuz) R(aidho) K(enaz)*.

There are variations on each rune name, depending on whether it is from the Germanic, Old English, or Scandinavian Futharks. I use the Germanic (though even this has some variations)—the oldest, with the most runes, twenty-four. The order of the runes is consistent in this Futhark, except for the last two, *Othala* and *Dagaz*, which are often switched.

Runes have both literal and symbolic meanings. The symbolic meanings of each rune can change depending on the other runes in a particular cast—how they work together, for weal or woe.

❦❦❦

Rune	Some Literal Meanings	Some Symbolic Meanings
Fehu	Cattle	Prosperity/Fertility
Uruz	Wild ox	Risky gain/Transition
Thurisaz	Thorn/Ice demon	Test/Berserker's rune
Ansuz	Mouth/Questions	Seeking advice/Answers
Raidho	Journey	Travel/Visiting one's dead
Kenaz	Torch	Initiation/Purification
Gebo	Gift	Sacrificing/Receiving
Wunjo	Glory/Joy	Untapped power/Thrust to destiny
Hagalaz	Hailstorm	Random, uncontrolled events
Naudhiz	Need/Necessity	Sudden power/Success
Isa	Ice/Spear/Staff	Freezing action/Challenge
Jera	Harvest	Rewarded effort

Eihwaz		Yew tree	Solutions/ Strengthening the will
Pertho		Dice cup	Chance
Algiz		Elk	Defense/Protection
Sowilo		Sun	Returning life/ Salvation
Tiwaz		Spear	Victory/Justice
Berkana		Birch tree	Purging/Atoning
Ehwaz		Horse	Fetch/Out-of-body travel
Mannaz		Man/Humanity	Perfected being/ Reason/Intuition
Laguz		All liquids	Essential life
Ingwaz		The people	Fascination/ Stored power
Othala		Inheritance	Blood secrets/ Summoning ancestors
Dagaz		Return of day	Moment of blinding truth/Banished dark

AUTHOR'S NOTE

Though there is probably a part of me on every page I write—some observation I may have made years before, some person's quirk or characteristic noted down, some escapade I was involved in, all translated into my fiction—*The Fetch* is certainly my most personal novel so far . . . even allowing for the Walking Dead, time travel, and metamorphosis! Mainly because I share so much with my protagonist, Sky.

I am a sleepwalker and talker. (I was going to write "*was* a sleepwalker," but last week my wife found me kneeling by her side of the bed at two a.m., looking for . . . leaves? Snakes? Who knows?) I don't end up outside the house anymore, but my subconscious still forces me up and about sometimes while I try to distinguish between dream and reality.

My mother is Norwegian—born with a caul over her face, under a full moon, on the shortest day of the year. And in my first cry, she *did* hear her father's laugh. My grandfather *was* psychic. He did walk into a building in Oslo and terrify the elevator operator, who swore he'd taken him up five minutes before—his first experience of *vardogr*. He also picked up a pointed rock once and immediately fell to the ground as he flashed on the rock being used, many years before, to kill someone . . . hence Sky's experience with his grandfather's lighter.

I am very drawn to my Norwegian side and believe it explains a lot of my character and actions. Though I am a peaceable fellow, I am attracted to all forms of bladed weaponry. I was a fencing champion at my school, wore a silver ax around my neck for twenty years, have choreographed stage fights for a living. I *know* my ancestors were Viking warriors. So writing this novel was truly a case of "listening for the secrets that whisper in my blood." Sometimes, scarily, it was almost like taking dictation!

I have also been a student of the runes. Though no expert, I learned their meanings, meditated on their symbols, slept with them under my pillow, and, when I realized I was going to be a writer, had one tattooed on my right shoulder. *Uruz,* rune of change, of transition, of artistic creativity.

When I first considered writing this novel, I remembered what I'd read in my teens—historical fiction, preferably with plenty of battles, self-sacrifice, bloodshed; and horror, the scarier the better. And I have always been interested in what makes us do things, our motivations (as an actor for twenty-five years, I need to know why the characters I play do what they do). Is our behavior dictated by our genes, inherited from all our ancestors stretching back through time? Is it how we were raised? A combination perhaps—but in what proportion? What can we control and what can't we help? And if we do have a berserker somewhere inside us—or an artist, a saint, a thief—how will that manifest itself in our daily lives? When someone says, "Oh, that's not like you!" which "you" are they talking about?

This all came together for me in the concept of the Fetch, this "other" that so many cultures in the world recognize. It keeps appearing in literature, in film—from Mr. Hyde to Neo in *The Matrix,* from Lyra's Pantalaimon in Pullman's His Dark Materials to *The Sixth Sense,* where the dead converse only with those gifted—or cursed—to hear. Deep down, don't we all suspect that there is something essential locked behind a door in our heads . . . if only we could find the key?

In Norse culture, someone born with a caul is born to "walk," to do things the person still asleep in their bed can't do—become a night wanderer, human, animal or bird; fly, fight . . . kill. In Friuli, northern Italy, the Caul Bearers, called *Benandanti,* go into the fields at sowing and at reaping, to fight the evil spirits for the health of the harvest. In Corsica, the *Mazzeri* go night-hunting. When they kill an animal, they turn the dying animal's face toward them, and if they see someone they know, that person will be dead inside the year!

These are just a few examples. The Double, under a number of names, appears from Africa to Siberia, North America to Australia. I wondered what would happen if someone like me was to discover his Fetch. What adventures would I be led into? What terrible things would I do?

This novel is the result of that speculation and a lot of reading that further stimulated my imagination.

359

Witches, Werewolves, and Fairies by Claude Lecouteux explores the world of the Fetch brilliantly. *Using the Runes* by D. Jason Cooper and *The Runic Workbook* (my old textbook!) by Tony Willis got me back into those explosions of energy cut into stone. *The Viking World,* edited by James Graham-Campbell, reminded me of their beliefs and habits, not to mention their longships, their way with weapons, and their draugs.

There were also several people who helped develop and shape my vision and to whom I owe much thanks. My mother—the Caul Bearer herself—who told me all the family stories. The Shropshire Lads—the Wright Family, especially Badger, who let me go to their inspiring cottage and write; Paul Evans, folklorist, botanist, and journalist, who generously shared the secrets of the Wenlock Edge; and Robert Petty, who let me come to William Brooks School, Much Wenlock, and get a feel for the classroom again. Karim and Naomi Jadwat, at whose riverside cottage I watched a hawk and finished the first draft. My wife, Aletha, who gets ideas bounced off her all the time. My superb agent, Kate Jones, at ICM, London, who suggested I should think about this kind of book. My New York agents at ICM, Richard Abate and Liz Farrell, for their skill and insight. And I must thank all at Knopf for being so supportive, most particularly my wonderful editor, Nancy Siscoe, whose penetrating queries, relentless enthusiasm, and fantastic laugh have gently guided me in my rune quest.

Finally, a last dedication—to those who have discovered that one's shadow is more than just darkness on the ground, one's reflection not just an image in a mirror. This book is for those who, in the darkest part of the night, realize that something else is there . . . and then walk to find it.

Chris Humphreys
July 2006

THIS IS A BORZOI BOOK PUBLISHED BY ALFRED A. KNOPF

Published in the United States by Alfred A. Knopf, an imprint of Random House Children's Books, a division of Random House, Inc., New York.

KNOPF, BORZOI BOOKS, and the colophon are registered trademarks of Random House, Inc.

www.randomhouse.com/teens

Educators and librarians, for a variety of teaching tools, visit us at
www.randomhouse.com/teachers

Library of Congress Cataloging-in-Publication Data
Humphreys, Chris.
The fetch / Chris Humphreys.
p.   cm. — (The runestone saga ; bk. 1)
SUMMARY: After exploring a sea chest full of runes and a journal belonging to his deceased grandfather, fifteen-year-old Sky summons the old man's ghost, who teaches him how to travel through time and space.
ISBN 978-0-375-83292-5 (trade) — ISBN 978-0-375-93292-2 (lib. bdg.) —
ISBN 978-0-553-49475-4 (trade pbk.)
[1. Time travel—Fiction. 2. Adventure and adventurers—Fiction.] I. Title.
II. Series: Humphreys, Chris. Runestone saga ; bk. 1.
PZ7.H89737Fe 2006
[Fic]—dc22
2005033349

Printed in the United States of America
10 9 8 7 6 5 4 3
First Knopf trade paperback edition May 2007

Here is a special preview of

THE RUNESTONE SAGA
BOOK 2

VENDETTA

Available August 2007

CHAPTER TWO

OLD ENEMIES

The shadows hid him, and perhaps the man's eyesight wasn't so good. Because Lucien Bellagi didn't react to Sky being there, just turned and shouted back into the house, up the stairs. And Sky, fully awake now, understood the French words.

"Cease your weeping, woman. I told you there'd be no one there."

As he spoke, the flickering, black-clad women, whose cries had turned again to whispers as soon as the door was opened, now redoubled their shrieking. Sky reeled back, both hands again over his ears. But the man did not hear. With a glance up and down the street, he shrugged and turned back into his house. The door closed, bolts were thrown, a key turned.

The shrieking stopped in an instant. For a moment the black shapes solidified, all facing the door, their backs to Sky, the coffin in their midst. And then, as one, the shrouds turned. Within each was the bone-white face of a woman with eyes that were pools of total blackness—and entirely focused on Sky.

"Oh, crap!" he muttered. He'd been able to move before, had found this place against the wall. Why couldn't he move now?

They began to flicker again, in and out of his vision. And the whisperings returned, high-pitched, unintelligible. Then, as one, the shapes began to move toward him. As one, hands as white as the faces emerged from the dark sleeves, reaching for him.

His shoulder was gripped . . . but not from the front, from the side. He jerked it away, turned from the approaching nightmare . . . to another! There was an alcove beside him, an old bricked-up doorway; in it stood two people. The first thing he saw was that, even if they didn't flicker, these two women were also dressed entirely in black. The second was that each woman held a knife in her mouth.

He would have run, if his legs were not frozen; would have screamed, if his throat worked. As it was, he let out a grunt of terror. Then one of the women, the younger one, raised another knife, and held it, handle first, toward him. With her other hand she removed her own dagger just long enough to say, *"Faites comme ça."*

Perhaps it was the calm way she said it. Perhaps it was because, without turning back to look, he could sense the shrouded horde within a foot of him now, could feel their phantom hands reaching. So he did as the young woman said, took the knife and held it in his mouth, his teeth gripping the wooden handle, its cutting edge facing outward.

Whisper became shriek became wail. He half turned now, enough to see the phantoms withdrawing their hands as if burned. Then, on a rising shriek, the horde bent, picked up the coffin, and ran down the alley. They vanished before they turned the corner.

In the sudden silence, Sky could clearly hear his heart, thumping against his rib cage. He became aware that he could move again, and he staggered away, just as far as the light under the lawyer's door. His feet hit the front step, his legs crumpled, and he was sitting, staring up at the two dark figures opposite, still half hidden in the shadows.

Each woman reached up now and took the knife from her mouth. Something was whispered; the younger one stepped toward Sky. She spoke and he did not have a clue what she said.

"Ungh," he replied before realizing that he still had a weapon in his mouth. Removing it, he said, "Are you . . . one . . . of them?"

"How could I be?" The voice was low, heavily accented. But to his great relief, the words were English. "For they are dead. And I—" Her hands lifted the veil down from her head, "I am alive."

A girl stood before him, around his own age, maybe a little younger. She was . . . *petite,* the word came to him, perhaps a foot shorter than him, yet the right shape for her height, not too thin; the dark dress was tight on her. Her hair formed a second veil, shadowing her face in two black waves that fell to the shoulders. But the darkest thing about her were the eyes.

She studied him as closely as he did her, unblinking. The silence held for a moment and then was broken by a shuffling and a cough. The girl reached back to the alcove. A hand emerged, as old as the girl's was young, with skin that looked like stained parchment, blue veins a map of rivers upon it. It gripped, like talons, and Sky saw the girl wince, forced to bend and take the weight as she led the second figure from the shadows.

He saw immediately that they were related, even though the old woman was so thin, the dark dress hanging off her, while the hair beneath her veil was white and bound in a severe knot. But the similarity showed in their faces, despite the age difference. The old woman's white skin was drawn tight against prominent bones, her lips a shocking gash of red, the makeup emphasizing her pallor. But the eyes were also twin pools of infinite dark, even if hers were filmed over, like the surface of a pond too long without rain.

After a moment, Sky reversed the knife, held the handle out toward the girl. "Thank you. I don't know what it did but . . ."

Slipping her hand from the older woman's, she

took the weapon. "I always carry two when I stalk the Dead. They do not like an open blade."

Sky took another deep breath. His heart was just beginning to slow. "The Dead?"

"You see them, here, before this door. We watch you see them, these ghosts. Il Squadra d'Arrozza."

"The . . . what?"

"*Squadra* is . . . like in army."

"Squad? Squadron?"

"So. And *Arrozza* is our name for . . ." She frowned. " 'Erodda? The king who kills the babies. Looking for Jesus?"

"Oh . . . Herod!"

" 'Erodda. Yes!"

Sky shuddered. To anyone else, he supposed this conversation would be absurd. But he had already had dealings with the Dead. "What were they doing here?"

"What is the word? 'Gathering'? Perhaps, yes? Gathering their own." The girl turned to her grand-mother, spoke rapidly. After a moment, the grand-mother nodded. The girl turned back. "But what do *you* do here?"

"Here?" It was a multiple-choice question for which he really didn't have a good answer. So he just said, "I was looking for the youth hostel."

"Youth hostel? It is closed."

"Yeah, I know. But . . ." He shrugged. "Maybe I'll wait till dawn."

Another whisper from the older woman. The girl turned. "We have a room you could stay."

He was shocked again—and delighted. "Well," he said, suddenly very English, "if it's not too much trouble . . ."

"No trouble. You come!" She held an arm out again to the old lady, who latched on; then they began to walk, quite rapidly, back toward the main town—away, Sky noted thankfully, from the direction the phantoms had taken.

He caught up. "This . . . Squadron of the Dead?"

"Yes?"

There were a million questions he could ask. He chose one. "Well, I . . . I was there—by chance but . . ."

The dark eyes shot up, searching his. "Chance? You think so?"

"Well . . ."

She shook her head. "We were not there by chance. My grandmother knew the Squadra would gather tonight."

"There? At that house?"

"Certainly. Only there. Because . . . how do I say this?" She stopped, looked straight into Sky's eyes. "Because it was my grandmother who killed Lucien Bellagi."

They had reached the main street. Sky spotted the bench he now wished he'd stayed on. "Killed? What do you mean? He's not dead. I saw him in his doorway."

Instead of answering, she walked on, to the entrance of an alley opposite. "Come," she called back.

Reluctantly, he crossed to her. "Do you mean she's . . . cursed him?"

"No curse . . . ," the girl began, but was then distracted by the old woman talking rapidly. She listened, looked up. "Grandmother is right. We do not know your name. How can we welcome you into our house?"

They'd stopped again, before a large oaken door. The old woman was reaching beneath folds of cloth. A key emerged. Sky was a little bemused by the sudden switch of conversation, but he replied, "Uh, my name's Sky. Sky March."

"Sky? It is strange. Like the . . ." She pointed up.

"Exactly. And you?"

"Jacqueline Farcese." She offered her hand, Sky took it, and she gave him a brief, formal shake. Turning, she said, "And this is my grandmother, Madame Farcese. *Grandmaman, je te présente Monsieur March.*"

The old woman pulled up her veil, stepped forward, and the hand that he'd seen fasten on Jacqueline's now descended on his, not taking it in a handshake but resting on top. As bony as it looked, the grip was fierce. He found it hard to look into her eyes. But when he finally did, he gasped. "She's . . . blind, isn't she?"

"Yes. You did not notice this before?"

"No." Now he was looking so closely into the old woman's eyes, he could see that what he'd mistaken for light was actually its reflection. They were more mirror than lens, and the darkness behind them was lifeless. She asked a question.

"I am afraid my French isn't good enough to . . ."

"She does not speak French but the older tongue of our island, Corsican," Jacqueline said. "She asks if she can touch your face."

"My face?" Sky swallowed. "Um, why?"

"To see you."

At last he nodded, bent so she could reach him. Jacqueline said something, and the claw-hand left his, rose up. He flinched when it first touched him, again when the other joined it. But the journey they took was light, skimming the contours of nose, cheekbones, mouth, tracing the line of the two eyebrows he'd let grow into one. The only discomfort came when the hands sank from his brow. He felt the slight pressure of finger pads on each closed eye, and it made him think of the body in the coffin, silver coins weighing down the lids. The hands pressed there a moment, then both dropped away, one hand taking his once more.

She was talking again, and the girl translated. "She see how you see the Squadra. She says you have the sight, the gift. Gift that can also be a curse. So she is happy for you . . . and sad for you also. She says she knows your sight has brought you pain."

Perhaps it was the recent pressure on them, but his eyes began to smart. It had been a night of such strangeness at the end of a long journey from even more. And here was a woman who touched upon all he'd been through—and whose pretty granddaughter had offered him a place to sleep! But before he could put any of his gratitude into stumbling words, the old woman spoke again, gripping him harder as Jacqueline translated.

"But she wonders how it is that you have this sight. Few do, even in Corsica. And she has heard of none from outside our land who can see the Squadra."

Sky wanted to remove his hand, so fiercely was it now being squeezed; he'd have liked to look away, so intense was the old woman's sightless regard. But he found he could do neither. He had to answer her . . . and he didn't know how to begin. He looked down to his own hand, saw, beneath her skeletal fingers, the four purple, puckered scars—still healing, still scabbed— and they reminded him of all that had brought him there. How could he even begin to explain it, to two strangers, in a strange town, in the middle of the night?

But the dull black orbs demanded an answer. And looking directly into them, he found the beginnings of one. "I have talked to my own dead," he said softly. "I know where they can be found."

He said it in English, and the old woman didn't even seem to speak French; but she cut off her grand-daughter when she began to translate, and Sky knew she'd understood well enough. She released him, reached again for Jacqueline, who guided her to the door. When she opened it, a wave of warmth, a scent of baking emerged, making Sky realize just how hungry and tired he was. Then, as the women beckoned him in, he remembered the other reason he could have been attuned to this land. It was definitely something he could share.

"I'm also half Corsican," he said, stepping forward, then halting because they'd halted, though they did not turn.

A whisper came from one mouth, words from the other. "From where?"

"From? Near here, I think. I'm not sure."

Another whisper, quieter, yet harsher too. "Your name?"

"I told you, March."

"Your Corsican name?"

"Oh." He had to think a moment. He'd only learned it himself a few months before. "It's Marcaggi," he said. "That was my grandfather's name." Both women turned now to face him. He coughed. "I'm probably not pronouncing it right, am I? Mar*caggi*?"

"Mar . . ." It was the old woman who spoke, said just half the name. Only half because the rest was lost in the shriek she gave. Suddenly she was rushing at him, throwing herself off the step with a speed Sky could not believe she possessed. It was only because he moved back fast that her hands, their sharp nails leading, missed his eyes. She slashed at his face again, and he was forced to grab her wrists. She twisted and struggled in his grip, and he didn't know what to do except push her back toward her granddaughter. It was only a little shove, but she tottered and the girl caught her, sank with her onto the step.

For a moment the only sound was the fast breathing of all three of them. "What . . . ," Sky blurted at last. "What was *that* about?"

The old woman was weeping now, a low moan like a growl building in her throat. Jacqueline had pulled her close, was rocking her in her arms. "Go," she said fiercely. "Go away."

"But what have I . . . I've done nothing."

The grandmother's sobs grew louder, taking on a note at once sad, lost, and furious.

"You have said your name," the girl hissed. "It is enough. Now . . . go!"

Sky backed away, staring, disbelieving. Then he turned and ran back toward the main street, toward light, away from the voice now wailing his father's family name like a curse into the night.

"Marcaggi!"